A Puhaka Books Selection

puhakabooks.com

A Jack Wesley Novel

Shaking Off Futility

W.B. Martin

Also by W. B. Martin

The Jack Wesley Series

Trouble Leaves Too Slow
Shoving Back the Shadows
Only Pretty Lies
Chasing the Blackbird
Just Empty Every Pocket
Pleasure Smiles
Be Prepared to Bleed

Other Novels

German Golfers Who Changed the World
Sweetness in the Dark
Endangered Species
Cubo Zoan
Vincent van Gogh Likes Cats

Shaking Off Futility

#7 in the Jack Wesley Thriller Series

Printed by permission of
Puhaka Publishing

Printed in the United States of America

Edited by Jessica Schmidt

Cover Layout by Morwenna Rakestraw

Version 1.1.2

Print ISBN 978-1-940554-21-1
eBook ISBN 978-1-940554-20-4

First Edition Septmeber 1, 2018

To Alanis Orlando
Always and forever

Chapter 1

Stanley, Idaho

Winter had started early in the Stanley Basin. But winter always arrived sooner in this part of Idaho. Located at 6,253', the small community of Stanley could have frost year-round. But this winter had begun extra early according to the locals.

Located beneath the majestic Sawtooth Mountain Range, summer in Stanley was to be savored. For the local businesses, summer was the height of tourist season. Money earned during the short three months of tourists had to keep things going the rest of the year.

The rafting companies that plied the local whitewater rapids with screaming passengers paddling their hearts out kept the resorts full. Horseback riding and hiking the nearby U.S. Forest Service trails added to the influx of people. While the Sawtooths were almost as stunning as the Teton Range on the east side of the state, lacking a national park kept the hordes away.

And the locals liked it like that. Eastern Idaho with Yellowstone National Park and Grand Teton National Park were all together much to busy for people from the Gem State. Idahoans liked their outdoor time less crowded and commercialized.

But winter was a different animal in the Stanley Basin. All the rich, beautiful people stopped south of Stanley in Sun Valley. Long a haunt for the rich and famous, Sun Valley, with its downhill ski area was considered more like California than Idaho. Established as the first destination resort in 1936 by the Union Pacific Railroad, Sun Valley had seen its share of well-heeled residents for decades now.

But Stanley was the poor cousin to Sun Valley. Over more recent times, the local ranches had succumbed to the recreational demands of the entire area and had changed. Winter was still a sleepy time, however. Only a few hardy cross-country skiers ventured out from their warm cabins. And snowmobilers. They arrived in the winter to use their allotted area of the public lands. The Forest Service personnel were busy keeping the two divergent groups from recreating close to each other.

But one other type of person came to the Stanley Basin in the winter. With the Sawtooth Mountains close by, winter mountaineers tested their mettle on the jagged peaks. It was such a group that now emerged from Stanley Lodge and surveyed their mission.

"I thought you could see the Sawtooths from here," Jack said.

"If it wasn't snowing Dad, you could," Carl offered.

It had been snowing ever since the group had left Missoula, Montana yesterday at noon. Jack Wesley had driven to Missoula from his Jackson, Wyoming home to join his son on this adventure. Now, as they loaded up into Jack's crew cab pick-up truck, he wasn't sure of his decision.

"I know you told me that the current snowfall won't affect the climb. But doesn't snow increase the avalanche danger?" Jack asked. He had lived in Jackson long enough to grasp that snow falling meant avalanches. Having spent his first fifty-two years in Eugene, Oregon hadn't educated him about the Rocky Mountains' greatest threat.

The Cascade Mountains also got snow in large amounts but was often referred to as 'Cascade Concrete'. Not the stuff pictured on the news racing down the mountains clearing all in its path. He assumed that the Cascade Mountains had their avalanche danger, but nothing like the Rocky Mountains.

"Dad, snowing is good because there is a cloud cover. A cloud cover means cloudy nights," Carl explained, a certain exasperation in his voice.

"If the snow stops, the nights will be clear. We don't want to be out in the mountains if it clears. We have to deal with avalanches no matter what. We don't want to deal with cold on top of that."

Jack had been in the outdoors enough to understand his son's reasoning. But he had brought warm clothes and after the last four winters spent in Wyoming, he certainly knew cold weather.

"OK son, you're the expert at this, not me. I'm just along for the bachelor party fun. The dancing girls will be meeting us at base camp, right?"

Carl shook his head and climbed into the front seat of the truck. Two friends climbed into the back seat. A second vehicle loaded up with four more climbers. Jack shifted the truck into gear and pulled out onto Idaho State Highway 75 headed south.

As the two vehicles paralleled the Sawtooth Range, the snow falling was gentle and light. It was almost as if the snow was the air itself. Jack kept the defroster turned off the windshield. Cold glass caused the light snow flakes to just blow on past. If he had cranked up the heat, the snow would stick, melt, and become a frozen mess as he attempted to clear his view with the windshield wipers.

Everyone in the truck was bundled up and didn't mind the cool interior. The passengers were intent on locating their intended objective. A rider in the back seat had a ma in his hands to keep track of where they needed to park.

The snow banks limited parking and obscured signs. What was normally visible in summer now lay under six feet of snow. And where the state highway plows had cleared the highway, the snow on the edge of the road was even higher.

"Slow down, I think we're close," a voice from the back seat said.

Jack slowed gently on the hard snow packed road surface. He had invested in a set of studded snow tires upon moving to Jackson and they did their job.

"This might be it," the voice added.

Jack signaled his stop and the second vehicle slowed with them. Pulling over in a wide spot that had been plowed off the right-of-way, Jack stopped. A sign post protruding from the snow announced Fourth of July Creek Trail Head. An arrow pointed off to a road that lay beneath the snow. A quick conference by the three others all confirmed that they had reached their destination.

"Dad, we need to turn the truck around and park the other way,' Carl said.

Not wanting to question his son, Jack did as he was told. The second car copied the maneuver before pulling in a few feet behind the pick-up.

"Time to load up," a voice said from the back. The rear door opening announced itself with a cold swirl of snow laden air.

All eight men began the task of donning ski gear and soon moved to their backpacks. Jack adjusted his ski as he stepped into his three ring bindings. Years ago, he and his brother had taken up ski mountaineering. They didn't climb mountains in winter, but they enjoyed the high country for is open vistas, at least when it wasn't snowing. While similar to regular cross-country gear, ski mountaineering gear was more heavy duty. His skis had metal edges, good for the often icy conditions in the Cascades. His three pin bindings were extra heavy to match his winter boots.

"Dad, I hope those boots do the job for you. They might have been fine in Oregon conditions, but if we get a cold snap, I'm afraid . . ."

"It's OK. I'm used to them. I didn't want to do this in new boots," Jack said.

He and his son had gone around and around on this subject. Jack looked at his seven fellow adventurers and saw that they all had double boots. With a felt liner inside a leather boot, their boots were designed for the cold that the Rocky Mountains could throw at someone. Carl had offered to buy a pair for his dad, but the price almost knocked Jack over. He knew that he wouldn't use them much and that his son didn't have that kind of extra money, not with him getting married in a week.

"So, tell me again, how is this a bachelor party?" Jack asked. "The ones I remember from my police department days were a little raunchier than what I'm expecting up here on the side of a mountain."

"Dad, it's the 21st Century," Carl explained. "This is Montana we're talking about. And I remember your friends on the force, every get together pushed the raunchy scale."

Carl is right about that, Jack thought. When cops get together to blow off steam, it can get plenty exciting. Jack tried to recall taking his son to any of the more boisterous affairs but couldn't remember that he had done that.

"Come on Dad," Carl said, breaking Jack's reminisce of thirty years on Eugene, Oregon's police force.

The other six climbers were already climbing the road side snow bank and heading west toward Snowyside Peak. At 10,650' elevation, the fifth tallest in the range, it was the intended target.

Jack made sure his pick-up was locked and followed Carl up and over the snow bank, side stepping. A broken trail in the snow lay ahead and the two skied to catch up with the others. As the last in line, Jack had an easy packed trail to follow.

He shifted his six-foot frame to settle the pack on his back. With close to fifty pounds in it, the pack contained everything he would need for the next four days. As Carl had explained, two days of skiing up Snowyside Creek to a base camp below Mt. Snowyside. That would be a gain of about 2,000' elevation.

Then a day to climb the mountain and its remaining 3,000' to the top. The last day they would ski out to their vehicles if their packed trail was still fresh. If they had to break trail the entire distance out, it might take them two days to ski back out.

Jack was jolted to reality as he passed one team member standing by the trail. He noticed for the first time, the man didn't have a pack. Glancing back, he saw him kick a turn and head back to the road. That was when Jack noticed the stray pack lying in the snow. As he turned, he skied past another pack lying in the snow.

In another two hundred feet, the process was repeated. A man standing by the trail followed by a lone pack in the snow. Soon, Jack was in the middle of the group as the people that had broken trail moved to the rear to gather their pack.

"OK son, I get it now. You tried to explain it to me. It's like riding in a peloton on bicycles. The first one breaks the wind for a time and then falls back to the end to draft."

"Just the same," Carl offered. "But as you will experience, this is somewhat more taxing."

Jack thought about his son's statement as he passed another skier waiting on the side of the trail. Now Carl was second in line and Jack felt the difference. His son struggled breaking a trail with snow up to his knees. Jack followed along packing the trail. *More work than at the end of the line*, he thought.

Soon, Carl dropped his pack as the front man stepped aside. The former lead man leaned on his ski poles as he breathed hard. Jack saw him pulling his top off before skiing back for his pack.

Now Jack struggled with breaking a trail. Right in front of him, he saw why. Carl was wallowing in powder snow that reached his armpits. Without a pack, it took all his strength to lift up his ski tips and push the snow down. Then he moved ahead and repeated the motion.

Jack's body temperature rose as he continued along behind Carl compacting the snow. Soon Carl stepped aside so Jack could take the lead.

With heavy breaths Carl said, "Ok Dad, you're lead. You don't have to take a full turn."

That's what he thinks, Jack thought. *If I'm on this trip, I'll pull my own weight.* Dropping his pack into the snow, he began his wallow stretch. And there's was no other way to describe it. With powder snow to his armpits Jack fought to bring his ski tips up close to the surface to then plunge down on them. He dragged his ski poles and planted them for the next plunge.

Being used to Cascade concrete, he tried to balance on his ski pole, but fell over. Where Oregon snow was thick and would support a pole plant, Idaho fluff just gave way. Jack learned the the poles were more like balancing sticks than poles.

Struggling to right himself, the man behind him offered relief. "It's OK, Mr. Wesley, I can take over now."

Mr. Wesley, that's my old man, Jack thought. *I might be 56, but I can still do my job.* Jack regained his balance and moved out stronger. At the two-hundred-foot mark, he stepped aside and the thirty something drove past him, pack landing nearby in the snow. Jack leaned onto his ski poles and sucked in the fresh mountain air. He was still bent over when Carl passed by on the end of the seven-man train.

Good, he didn't say anything, Jack thought. Flipping one ski into the air, he twisted it one hundred and eighty degrees and placed it next to his second ski. Then lifting the second ski, Jack swung it into place heading back down the trail.

Skiing quickly the short distance to his pack felt like heaven, with no pack and a well-groomed trail that ended too soon. After turning around once again, he pulled his pack out of the snow and swung it onto his back. Grabbing his ski poles, he worked hard to catch up to the advancing train. Just as he caught the end, a lone skier waited to return to his pack.

The morning continued as each took their turn at the front. Jack soon realized that unlike cycling, the last man worked almost as hard as the first. The whole motion of returning to the pack and catching the group expended as much energy as breaking trail. The next to the last position was the relaxing spot. That was where each skier could catch their breath.

Lunch was soon called and packs were dropped in the snow. A warm top and hat were added to keep the sweat from getting cold while the group ate. Pre-made English muffins with peanut butter and jam brought the energy level back up. As Jack drank from his water bottle the others all discussed the morning's progress.

One turned to Jack and asked, "Is this what you expected, Mr. Wesley?"

"First, let's dispense with the Mr. Wesley," Jack said. "My name is Jack. I think we're close enough by now to be on a first name basis." The group all nodded in agreement. "And yes, it's similar to what I've done in the past. But Oregon snow sure doesn't compare."

"You mean Oregon ice," Carl offered. "Growing up and skiing in the Cascades, all I remember is that falling down hurt. Too much ice to really enjoy skiing there."

"I have to agree. Falling down here you have to worry more about suffocating," Jack said.

The group finished eating and stood up from sitting on their packs. Most shed their hats but kept their tops on. A few turns breaking trail would warm everyone back up. Everyone would add top removal to their pack retrieval time as they took up the last spot in the group. The train breaking trail would continue on unabated.

The group luckily found the bridge to cross the Salmon River and continued skiing west. The ground began to rise, adding to the work load of breaking trail. In spots, the leader had to traverse the steeper sections in order to maintain a steady route. Too steep a trail would bog them down, too shallow a route got them no closer to their goal.

A quick check of a watch told them the day was ending. Having skied an estimated five miles and gained about one thousand feet, the team called it a day. Soon, everyone was stomping out flat areas in which to pitch tents. Carl was teamed up with his dad as a tent mate and they worked together getting their spot ready.

Once the snow was packed packed, the tent was spread out and a snow stake was clipped into each corner. Snow stakes are normally used during climbing for protection. A long t-shaped extrusion of aluminum, a stake driven into the snow with a climbing rope attached by a carabiner offered protection from falling. But a snow stake was useful only in hard packed snow, which Idaho didn't have in abundance.

They were carried on the off chance that high on the mountain, wind packed snow allowed their use. Until then, they worked as tent stakes.

Spreading out their sleeping pads and bags, the two climbed into the tent. The other six climbers shared two other tents and also disappeared inside. After a short time, each tent sprouted one person and a stove.

"What's your choice for dinner tonight?" Carl asked.

"What are the options, steak or lobster?" Jack asked.

"Close, beef stroganoff or shrimp creole."

They settled on beef as Carl got the stove going. Placing the pot on after filling it with snow. The snow sizzled slightly as it began melting. Carl poured a shot from his water bottle in to get the melting started.

"You and your friends seem at ease doing this," Jack said. "I've seen some of your pictures but how often do you get out?"

"We try for once per month in the winter. And remember, the winter in Montana is a lot longer. So, I guess we get out three times each year."

"You don't come down here, though do you?" Jack asked as he considered the half day drive from Missoula.

"We're usually up in the Bitterroots. We can do a peak on the three-day weekend," Carl said. "Most of us have flexibility in our jobs that we can get one day a month to run out. Montana businesses are more understanding that way."

"I'm sure in hunting season its practically a ghost town."

Carl added more snow as the liquid level rose in the pot. With the light fluffy snow, Carl added snow often to get the required water. They would only run the stove in the morning and the evening when water for drinking as well as for eating would be melted.

The water was soon steaming as the daylight faded. Jack looked out but only saw snow continuing to fall. It hadn't slowed all day and it appeared that it would carry on through the night. He unwrapped two Mountain House freeze dried packets and opened the interior pooch. With hot water ready he got his cup set to make tea.

Passing each dinner to Carl, hot water was dipped out of the pot and poured over the food. Handing the packet back to Jack, the wrapper was closed up as the water reconstituted the beef stroganoff. More hot water was poured into Jack's cup and he threw in a tea bag.

Adding sugar and powered milk, Jack stirred his drink. Carl added more snow as his job melting snow continued. He turned down the stove to a lower flame before retreating inside the tent to eat. The two opened their wrapped dinners and let the aroma take over. After a day of hard skiing, they didn't linger long before devouring their meal.

Dried fruit provided dessert as the two drank their tea and soon a second cup added to their liquid intake. Between the sweaty exercise all day and the cold dry air, everyone worked to keep hydrated.

"Dad, I'm glad you're here," Carl said. His head lamp shot a beam across the tent as he turned, the moisture cloud of his breath visible in the light.

"I'm just happy you felt like you could invite me. It's not every Dad that gets invited to his son's bachelor party, you know."

"Well, it's just that you and Stacey go way back."

There, it had been said, finally, Jack thought. Four years Carl and Stacey have been together, and this is the first time the subject's been brought up. And now with there about to be a wedding, Carl broached the issue.

"Is there a reason your bringing it up now, son?" Jack asked. "Don't you think it's a little late, like I have some issue that could matter."

"It's just that we've never talked about the time you and Stacey rode together."

And I'm damn sure not talking about it now, Jack thought. Four years earlier Jack and Stacey had hooked up while riding the Trans Am cross country bicycle trail. They had spent time together crossing Oregon and Idaho before Stacey got back with her former boyfriend.

Soon after, Jack teamed up riding with Carl. By Missouri, Stacey had reentered the picture without the old boyfriend. Carl then had hooked up riding with Stacey as Jack headed back to Wyoming. And the two of them had been together ever since.

Carl and Stacey had continued their bicycle trip to Virginia and then decided to continue riding. Picking up the Atlantic Coast Bicycle Route, they had hit Florida as the cold weather set in. They found temporary jobs near Pensacola before joining up with the Southern Tier Bicycle Route in the spring. The Southern Tier Route took them to San Diego where their money ran out.

Short on money, they found out that Stacey was pregnant. Missoula had been the answer to settling down when Carl got a job offer. Jack was excited to see his son settle moderately close. The idea of becoming a grandfather was another deal entirely.

Jack had adjusted nicely over the last two years. Now with Stacey pregnant again, the parents finally decided to do the right thing and get married. *I think it's the right thing, and long over due,* Jack thought. *But nobody asked me, and I'll keep my thoughts to myself.*

The long stretch of silence added a bit to the suspense of Carl's question. Jack decided to choose his words carefully.

"That was a long time ago," Jack started. "You and Stacey have made a wonderful life for yourselves in Montana. I couldn't be happier for you both. And now to add another grandbaby to the Wesley clan. That's great."

"But . . ?" Carl asked.

"But nothing. I couldn't ask for a better daughter-in-law. Stacey seems to make you happy and she's great with kids. What more is there to say?" Jack hoped that was as far as he needed to go. His son didn't need to hear any details of his and Stacey's time together. *This isn't the Dr. Phil Show, or whatever show where they have father's who sleep with their son's girlfriend spilling all*, Jack thought.

"OK. We just never talked about those times and . . ."

"And nothing. Move on in life. You have another mouth to feed coming into the world in six months. Focus on the real things in life. Not the what ifs."

The two lay in their sleeping bags thinking about what had been said, the headlight beam illuminating their breaths. Jack had almost nodded off when Carl broached another subject.

"Dad, I've been waiting to tell you something."

Shaking himself awake, Jack turned to see his son staring at the ceiling of their tent.

"What is it?" Jack asked.

"Kotone will be at the wedding," Carl said.

Chapter 2

Vluchteling, Dutch Antilles (Two months previous)

The twin engine prop plane circled around the small island to line up for landing. Karla Schmidt looked out the window at the tiny airstrip close to the ocean. As the plane continued to circle around, she wasn't convinced that the plane could make a safe landing in such a short distance.

Assuming that the plane's track record of landing safely three times each week would continue, she sat back. From all that she had heard about the island, the flight was worth the risk. Moving her gaze up as the airport disappeared toward the front of the plane, Karla scanned the hilly, heavily wooded landscape.

Nestled on the north side of the island was the only town. With only one thousand permanent residents on Vluchteling, it was one of the less visited islands in the Caribbean. Similar in size and population to the island of Saba, Vluchteling was about five square miles. And now she could see why it was not well traveled.

Only low two-story buildings lined the waterfront where a promenade and a seawall separated the buildings from the sea. The harbor was a large crescent with rocky headlands on both ends.

Karla estimated that it might be an hour walk from one end to the other. The brochure explained the limited accommodations on the island. There were no modern hotels built and that had been the draw for Karla.

As a young German woman traveling the world to see the natural sights, this trip was unexpected. She had heard from a fellow world traveler about Vluchteling. As the plane prepared to land, Karla studied the hills above the town. Tomorrow she would head up there to see the island's main attraction.

As she contemplated her stay, the plane streaked in over the beach, barely clearing the stone breakwater. Karla noticed the few people on the beach didn't even flinch with a plane so close.

Then the thump of the wheels hitting the runway and the brakes halting the plane. Her body pushed into the seatbelt as the pilot quickly brought the plane to a stop. Looking out the window, Karla saw the plane pivot at the end of the runway and taxi back toward the terminal as there were no taxiways alongside the main runway.

Karla looked back to see the end of the runway where it abruptly stopped at the base of a hill. *Not much room for error*, she thought. The plane soon reached the small terminal and a set of steps were wheeled into position.

Grabbing her carry-on, Karla joined the fifteen other passengers as they exited the plane. The three steps down onto the tarmac brought her into the warm Caribbean breeze. The trade winds were blowing as usual and the temperature hovered near eighty.

Perfect weather for enjoying myself, she thought. Two days ago she had been in New York City dealing with snow and ice. Visiting a friend from Germany, Karla had spent a month experiencing the Big Apple.

Now she was beginning a year long stretch traveling through South America. But first a stop in the islands for some sun. And monkeys. Vluchteling was the only spot outside South America to see New World monkeys.

"Are you here to see the monkeys?" A male passenger asked.

Karla had noticed the man on the flight from St. Vincent, where she had spent the night after her flight from New York.

"Yes, and you?" She asked.

"What else? There isn't much else on this island to do," he said. "Have you booked a room yet? I heard they're difficult to get."

"No, I don't have a room yet," Karla said. "And the internet hasn't reached here yet. At least none of the hotels were listed."

"Do you know the history of Vluchteling?"

Karla got nervous that she had attracted a talker. Traveling the world, she had learned to spot the obnoxious ones early and to avoid them. People who talked non-stop about everything, and usually themselves. She hesitated because she didn't want to encourage him. *But he is about my age and good looking. And the airlines aren't appearing very prompt with our bags, so I guess there'll be a wait,* Karla thought.

"A little," she finally offered.

"Well, the island has only been open for a little over a year to tourists," the man offered. "Before that, you couldn't get a visa to visit. Only wildlife researchers were allowed on the island. Unless you knew someone. Locals could get a visa for relatives to visit, but only from the island officials."

"But Vluchteling is part of the Netherlands Antilles. Couldn't the Dutch government provide visas?"

"Actually, the Netherlands Antilles was dissolved in 2010," the man said.

Karla was suddenly nervous that she was about to get an earful. *Where are my bags?* she wondered. She glanced from side to side looking for the ground crew, but nothing was moving.

The man continued unphased, "And Vluchteling was never part of them anyway. This island is the personal property of the Grand Ducat of Luxembourg. It goes way back."

Karla now regretted her decision to be friendly. But as he talked, other waiting passengers gathered around to listen to his history lesson.

The islands of Bonaire, Sint Eustatius, Saba, Curacao and Sint Marten were all part of the Dutch territory known as the Netherlands Antilles. Over recent years, all had become formal Dutch municipalities, just like Amsterdam, the man explained

"The island of Vluchteling is unique in that it was never considered part of the other Dutch islands," he said. "Its history went back to the Golden Age of the Netherlands which lasted from 1581 through 1795. It was during the fourth Dutch-Anglo War from 1780-1784 that the Netherlands lost possession of Vluchteling to the Grand Duchy of Luxembourg. The daughter of a rich merchant had married Charles, Prince of Nassua-Weilburg, who received ownership of the island for her father's support to the crown. Under the Treaty of Loosdrecht, the family became perpetual heirs to the island.

Karla's eyes were beginning to glaze over as the man droned on. *Where were those damn baggage handlers?* she wondered. *Surely they must have the plane unloaded by now.*

"So, do you know how the monkeys got here?" he asked.

Karla was afraid to answer. She certainly didn't want to encourage him. Someone else in his little listening group responded instead.

"I'll tell you," the man started. "It was the late 18th century and Vluchteling was a rather disreputable spot in the Caribbean. Like many small islands with almost no government, privateers, some call them pirates, would settle here for water and food. I hear there were other delights to be had here also." The man grinned and looked at Karla.

Oh, great, God help me if those bags don't come soon, she thought. *And if he asks to share a taxi to a hotel, he can forget it. I'd rather walk.*

The man carried on, "Its assumed that one of those privateers arrived with a couple of monkeys as pets. That was common in those days on sailing ships. The monkeys must have escaped onto the island, and lacking any predators, they flourished over the years. That's why this is the only place outside the Amazon jungle that you can find Black Tufted Marmosets. For those of you here to see them, and who isn't," the man laughed at his own joke, "look just under the tree canopies. They aren't a ground monkey."

The shed door opened and the first bags slid down the stainless-steel chute. Too small for running baggage belts, each of the fifteen passengers stepped forward and grabbed their bags. Karla spotted her black duffle and moved past the still talking man.

She hefted the bag onto her shoulder and headed toward the sign that said Customs. She hurried so she wouldn't be stuck near the talker and hit the short line with just one person in front of her.

"Next," an official said.

Karla stepped over to one of the two inspectors working. She placed her bag onto the table and waited for instructions. Traveling the world, she knew to follow instructions and never assume.

"Is this bag yours?" The inspector asked in English.

"Yes," she answered.

"Please open it for inspection."

Karla followed the man's instructions and unzipped the bag's long zipper. Her personal belongings spilled out the top. *That's unusual, she thought. I know I packed those things in their own plastic bag.* While she contemplated how her more personal items had come to be on top and not in a plastic bag, the man spoke again.

He had reached into the bag and was bent over judiciously studying the contents. His hand dug deeper into the bag. The search stopped as the man looked up at Karla. He slowly removed his hand, a small plastic baggie in his palm. Inside the bag was white powder.

Karla's heart raced as he held up the baggie. *What the hell is that?* she thought. Unfortunately, she was all to familiar with what was likely in the bag. She had seen white powder like that many times, but never in her travel bag.

"What's this?" the Custom's official asked.

Panic welled up in Karla as she stared at the bag. She had no idea how it had come from her bag. She tried to speak.

The official spoke first. "Bringing illegal drugs into Vluchteling is a very serious offense. We take these matters very seriously here. This isn't Amsterdam where such things are tolerated."

Karla knew she wasn't in Amsterdam. She looked around. The other passengers were noticing her predicament and moving away. Even the talkative man was silent as they all witnessed the German woman about to be arrested.

The Customs official waved over two nearby police officers. Their demeanor changed as they walked up to Karla. Holding the baggie, the official opened it and took a small sample. Rubbing it on his gum, he motioned to the police.

Karla's arms were pulled back and handcuffs placed on her wrists. Now in a state of panic, she looked quickly around at the other passengers. She had traveled the world and knew time was critical.

"Please, someone call the German Consulate in St. Vincent and tell them Karla Schmidt has been arrested. Please help me," she pleaded as she was led away.

The passengers looked away so as not to involve themselves in an obvious drug arrest. The monkeys were waiting and they had their hotels to find.

* * *

Nearby, a man watched intently. He had the bearing of a European aristocrat and looked the part. Tall, well-tanned, impeccably dressed with just the right style sunglasses on, he stood and waited. He studied the rest of the passengers as they quickly moved through Customs. When the room was empty, the inspector that had discovered Karla's drug stash came up to him.

"Good work inspector," the European man said. "She will do nicely. And from her plead for help, it would appear that she is quite alone. No one will miss her anytime soon."

"Unless one of her fellow passengers feels a duty to call St. Vincent," the inspector said.

"And you know how unreliable the phones are on our island. I'll make sure that the line to St. Vincent is out of service for a couple of days like normal. By then, these people will either be gone or will have given up in frustration."

"Yes, your excellency," the inspector said. "Smooth as silk. Just like the other times."

"Yes, it's so easy. They all just fly right into our little nest. Come to see our monkeys, receive a prize instead," the man said to no one in particular. Certainly not the lowly bureaucrat before him. But he did have to humor them. "And the usual in your next pay."

"Thank you, your excellency. Till next time."

"Yes, you may withdraw now," the man said. He adjusted his sunglasses as the inspector bowed slightly and backed away.

Now to the jail to see that our new prisoner gets settled properly, he thought. *I'm just glad that my staff is trained right. They will prepare the woman properly. Yes, they were becoming quite good at the preparation.*

He stepped outside into the hot sun, a black Suburban with a driver waited. It would take the European aristocrat to the castle on the point.

Chapter 3

Stanley, Idaho

Jack lifted his ski and plowed ahead into the snow. Swimming through snow was a more apt term to use. This was the third day of breaking trail. At least the team was on the side of Mt. Snowyside climbing toward the top.

Finishing his two-hundred-foot spell, Jack stepped upslope. He had to lean his shoulder into the deep snow just to get out of the others way. But with only day packs at this point, at least he didn't have to retrieve his pack.

As the last skier passed, Jack stepped back onto the trail and easily glided forward. The joy of being the last man struck home. Just as his time on a bicycle riding in a group, the relative ease of the journey was short lived.

Soon he was back on lead dog duty. And like for Husky dogs everywhere, at least the view improved. He scanned the terrain ahead and plotted his route forward. Halfway through his stint at the front he felt something as he lifted one ski. Stopping, the seven followers stood waiting. With him not stepping out of the way, Jack knew he was holding things up. But something in his lower back suddenly didn't feel right.

He stepped up hill out of the way as he bent over, attempting to stretch out whatever it was that had just announced itself. Carl skied up and stepped aside as the others skied on.

"What's up Dad?"

"My back just did itself."

"How bad?" Carl asked.

"It's there son. Not bad, but something popped."

The other six members continued their climb as the two talked. Time was moving on and Jack realized he had to make a decision.

"I still have to ski out tomorrow. I think I'd better call it a day and head back down to base camp. I'll wait for you there."

"Your call," Carl said. "You've got your transponder on. Just stick to our track so you know where you're going. We'll watch on our way back to make sure you got down OK."

"Have fun and take some pictures for me. And be safe please."

Carl gave his dad a hug and sprinted up the trail to catch the group. Jack watched as they disappeared around the ridge. Looking around, he realized that he was very alone now and very high on the mountain.

The group had risen early to get a jump on climbing and Jack estimated that they had been climbing for about three hours now. Leaving base camp nestled in the trees, they had climbed up to a frozen lake and had skied across the lake to gain the first ridge. Above the lake, open alpine conditions allowed views below the cloud cover.

The group had traversed back and forth up the ridge in the open ground, always with snow up to their armpits. The depth of the snow combined with its lightness amazed Jack. Looking around, the lower portions of the neighboring peaks were visible. Snow continued to fall, making visibility limited.

But Jack could see the compacted trail where they had crossed the lake far below. Making the decision that he could shorten his trip back by heading straight down, Jack muscled his skis through the snow till they were aimed downhill. He angled them slightly to the fall line so as to not get out of control with to much speed.

Zipping up his jacket, Jack pulled his snow goggles out of his pack. Pulling them down onto his face, he picked a line down and pushed on his poles. He didn't move. He shoved again and nothing, the snow holding him in place.

Shifting his skis so they were aimed directly downhill, he pushed again. This time he moved. But considering how steep the hill was, he wasn't moving very fast. But he learned quickly that the trick to deep powder was to lean back and let the ski tips float up.

With snow flowing over his shoulders, Jack skied off the mountain. As he descended, he became more comfortable with the deep snow. Stopping at the top of an extra steep drop off, he looked down. The slope disappeared from view only to emerge about fifty feet below him. In Oregon, he would never contemplate even trying such a slope.

He carefully pushed with his poles as he practically fell off a cliff. At least his heart felt as if he had just fallen off one. The snow floated over his head as he tried to keep his ski tips up. It felt as if he was falling through a cloud. With a sudden stop at the bottom, he disappeared under the snow.

Fighting to find the surface, Jack worked his legs and then his arms to stand up. Sweat ran down his back from the struggle when he finally broke free. He turned and looked back up the way he'd come and was startled at the steepness of the slope he had just come down. Suddenly, the thoughts of avalanches struck him as he got moving.

Reaching the frozen lake, he joined the trail the group broke earlier as he skied across to the other side. Now following the trail with short diversions where he could cut a switchback, Jack was soon back in camp.

His backache was still noticeable as he stood his skis and poles up in the snow and climbed into the tent. Warm in his sleeping bag, he dozed. He was awakened by seven people screaming his name. Startled, he stuck his head out the tent door.

"What's up? Why the commotion?" He asked.

"Oh Dad, you're alive," Carl said. "We weren't sure you made it."

"Why not? I followed the trail back."

"Dad, the trail's gone. Even the lake's gone."

"What happened?"

As the others listened in, Carl explained what they think happened. Once they were high on the open ridge, they left their skis and roped up for protection. While they were traversing a narrow portion of the ridge, one of them fell through the cornice. Carl described the snow overhang as exceptionally large. But with the climbing rope attached, no harm happened, and the climber scrambled back up onto the ridge.

When they were descending, they discovered that the fall through the cornice had set off an avalanche. As they skied lower, they discovered that the lake had been the target. The avalanche had hit the frozen lake with such force that all the ice was pushed out the far side of the lake. Trees had been knocked over by the ice and all the water was gone.

"When we got to where we had crossed the lake, our tracks disappeared," Carl said. "We had to ski around where the lake had been looking for where the track emerged. We finally located your trail below the huge ice blocks and knew you'd made it that far."

"Well, that's good," Jack offered. He could see the concern in the seven climber's faces.

"But when the lake got displaced, all the water rushed down the creek. Your tracks disappeared again until just outside camp."

Jack climbed out of the tent with his down booties on. He walked over to his son and gave him a hug. The other six men all gave Jack a high five for surviving.

"I guess it wouldn't do to have the father of the groom get killed just before the wedding," Jack joked. He had retired as a police detective after thirty years on the job. Three decades of close calls. And he knew people that hadn't avoided the close calls. His black humor at times of danger took over as it had served him well over the years. "But at least I delivered your present already. You wouldn't have missed that."

"Oh Dad," Carl offered. He pushed his dad and Jack stumbled on the snow in his slick nylon booties.

"Oh, my back," Jack yelled in jest.

"Just keep it up or we'll leave you here."

That night after dinner of shrimp creole out of a pouch, the two Wesley men snuggled in their warm sleeping bags and talked. Jack wasn't sold on the winter camping aspect of their adventure.

Since it was mid-December, the daylight disappeared around four o'clock. Dinner and drinks took up at most two hours. Each night they tried to stay awake talking, but the day's activities would soon catch up with them and both would fall asleep about eight. No matter how much he held out, Jack's age would force a midnight run to relieve himself. Back asleep after a cool bathroom break, Jack found himself sleeping until about four in the morning. That was about the time when his required eight hours of sleep would end. That left the coldest part of the night until daylight arrived about seven. Three hours of huddling awake in his sleeping bag, trying to stay warm.

Added to the cold and awake span till dawn was the added joy of sleeping with various friends. Inside his sleeping bag, Jack slept with his two water bottles. If left out, they would freeze solid and be useless in the morning. Also accompanying him inside his sleeping bag were his boots in a plastic bag. The plastic bag kept the sticky snow seal on the boots from getting all over everything. The boots were there like the water bottles, to help them dry out and to keep them from freezing.

Jack had noticed the pain when putting on cold boots even after a night inside his sleeping bag. It had taken a good twenty minutes of skiing each morning before he could really say he could feel his feet. But this, their last night in the mountains, dawned bright and sunny.

"Rise and shine everyone. We need to be out of here today. We don't want another night out if it's clearing," This was spoken by one of the team as he got his stove lit.

Carl quickly had hot water for oatmeal ready. Jack stirred his hot breakfast and chowed down. Finishing with a quick tea, he added more hot water to clean his cup, drinking the residue.

They packed quickly and were soon headed toward the road. With the sun shining, the trip took on an Alice in Wonderland feel. The snow reflected the bright sunlight, and without sunglasses it would have been painful on the eyes.

It soon became almost a race out as all eight skiers maneuvered down the trail wearing packs. Whenever they arrived at a steeper section, the trail was forgotten as each skier took a more direct path down. Jack worked hard to keep up with the younger members and felt good when he pulled ahead in the race.

Stopping to admire his accomplishment and to give his younger compatriots a hard time, he stood on the trail they had packed on the way in next to a large fir tree. As the first member skied past, the snow gave way and Jack found himself falling into a tree well.

Tree wells form when snow falls, and the limbs shed the snow out. The resulting hole under the limbs can be substantial, and Jack found himself falling into an eight-foot-deep pit. He knew the depth precisely since his skis caught on the upper boughs and his body fell in head first. Jack's six-foot frame hung inverted, his head just inches from the bottom.

He heard the laughs as he hung in the tree unable to move. His pack had ridden up over his head, pinning his arms down in front of him. As Carl skied up, Jack was struggling out of his pack. Carl kicked snow on his dad and skied off.

With his arms now free, Jack reached up and released one binding. The ski fell down into the well. He struggled to reach the second ski and dropped unceremoniously into the well once he undid it. Now he was eight feet down in the snow well with a fir tree blocking his way out.

He threw his pack up onto the trail, then each ski. His poles were next as he swam his way uphill to freedom. Collapsing on the trail, he glanced at a smiling Carl not far away.

"Thanks for all the help," Jack yelled.

"I wouldn't have skied off too far. Just wanted you to enjoy a good Idaho tree well,' Carl said.

Carl was right in that Oregon tree wells could kill, Jack thought. Often just as deep as the one he had just climbed out of; Oregon tree wells were often covered in ice. One slip and you could find yourself rapidly heading straight into a large tree. *People had been killed by head injuries sustained by such encounters,* Jack thought. *There was that case of a University of Oregon student that was killed that way.*

The cold was increasing in spite of the sun and everyone knew a cold snap was moving in. To spend another night out would be dangerous. They skied hard to reach the road while the daylight continued.

Reaching his truck, Jack found out why Carl had him park the opposite way. The road crew had been plowing the past four days and now the team got out the shovels to clear an exit. Carl pointed out that with the rear of the truck facing the incoming snow of the plows, he had seen people's rear windows get smashed in from the weight of the snow hitting them. He pointed to Jack's truck canopy window as he spoke.

Both rigs were started and while they warmed up, a half hour of brisk shoveling freed the two vehicles. The eight adventurers loaded up and headed north as the last of the daylight disappeared.

"I think we need to stay in Stanley tonight," Carl said. "We're all tired and a night's drive over Lost Trail Pass is too risky."

"No argument from me son," Jack offered. He was bone tired from their endurance ski out of the Sawtooths. The added joy of rescuing himself from the tree well only added to the feeling of exhaustion he felt.

"You do have a block heater?"

"Installed one the first winter in Wyoming,' Jack said. *Certainly never necessary in Western Oregon,* Jack thought. A block heater was an electric pump/heater that circulated warm water through the truck's engine block. Most cold weather vehicles had them and only required an electrical plug in to park for the night.

"I think I saw receptacles at the place we stayed on the way down," Carl said.

Later that night, showered and fed, Carl and Jack lay in their double beds in the room they were sharing. The parking lot lights reflecting off the snow drifted into the room. They had walked across the street for dinner and already the biting cold had announced itself.

"It's going to be a cold one when we wake up tomorrow," Carl offered.

"Real cold," Jack replied. A spell of silence filled the room.

Carl broke it first. "Dad, we never did talk about Kotone being at the wedding. Can we talk now?"

Another poignant pause of silence passed. Jack stared out the window without responding.

"Dad is it going to be a problem?"

"Son, Kotone and I are both adults and know how to behave," Jack answered. "I think I'd be more worried about your Mom being there. Was her boyfriend invited?"

"We couldn't ask her and not include him. You know that."

"I know," Jack said. He continued his stare across the dark room. The window view offered an escape from the real topic.

"Dad, if it's not going to be a problem, I'd like to ask you to be my best man," Carl said.

"You don't have some buddy that you want? Having your father is a little unusual."

"I have my buddies, most of which you've been with for the past week. But I don't want to single one out. It sort of implies best buddy standing. Since Stacey and I are having a small wedding, we don't have any groomsman or bridesmaids."

"I see. Well, I'd be proud to stand up with you. You know you and your sister are the most important people in my life," Jack said.

"At the time you and Mom divorced I would have never thought that I'd be asking you. But we've grown closer since then," Carl said.

Yes, we have, Jack thought. Jack thought back to the time of his divorce. Of his ex-wife leaving town before the ink was dry on the final papers with her new boyfriend in tow. That hurt, but Jack could live with it. He had made mistakes in their marriage. Every cop did. Too much overtime, too much stress and too much schooling trying to move up in rank.

Making detective after ten years on the force had taken a supreme effort on his part. Coming out of the Marine Corp after four years and being hired as a rookie cop, Jack soon realized that to get ahead he would need a college degree. Earning a B.S. in Psychology at the University of Oregon while attending part time combined with his full-time job took its toll.

While he focused on being a good provider, missed family time wasn't supplanted with money. But the wake-up call was when his daughter chose to go with the mom as they headed to Colorado Springs and a new life.

Jack had thrown himself into repairing his relationship with his son. It had taken time and effort but being asked to stand up at his wedding seemed to announce that Jack's effort had paid off.

"Besides, Stacey asked me to ask you," Carl said.

Jack's feelings of closeness with his son vanished. *So, it had been Stacey's idea, not Carl's,* he thought.

"Look, if Stacey's asking, then I'll bow out. This doesn't need to be complicated. It's your special day. Do it the way you want."

A noticeable pause ensued as both men thought through the issue. Jack wasn't about to start his son's married life on the wrong foot. There was already enough history where Jack and Stacey were concerned and more didn't need to be added to the pile.

Again, Carl spoke first. "Dad, I'm sorry I mentioned it. Stacey did suggest it. But I'd like you there beside me."

Jack let that linger before answering. "OK, it's your call."

"Thanks."

The Wesley men lay in the dark for some time. Jack was tired, but the talk of family affairs had his mind working. He didn't want to be blamed for his son's wedding having any glitches. There were two grandkids involved now.

J.J., as his grandson was called, needed both parents in his life. Now two years old, and with a sibling due in six months, he needed those parents married. *Too many unmarried parents running around,* Jack thought. *I don't like the trend of today's young people playing at being married.*

Jack was old fashioned and certainly from a different generation. A generation where words meant things and bastard had a meaning all its own. *I never want someone calling my grandson any such thing,* he thought.

Carl broke Jack's thoughts. "There's one more thing."

Jesus, what now? Jack thought. He kept his attitude in check and asked, "What is it?"

"Stacey has asked Kotone to be her maid-of-honor ," Carl said.

"Oh," Jack answered. Silence returned as the news settled.

"They've become quite close," Carl offered. "Ever since they rode across Missouri together. And then when Kotone and her sister moved to Missoula last year, she and Stacey ran into each other. I think you had a hand in that."

Oh sure, blame me, Jack thought. Yes, he and Kotone had passed briefly through Missoula when they were together. And yes, last year he had told her to take her sister to a small place away from Los Angles. But, now his son was accusing him of creating the situation.

"Look, I'm happy to stand up with you," Jack said. His voice had a bit of anger in it from his son's comment. "I'll perform my duties as need be, which includes being pleasant to the bride's choice for her support. It's only a day, and then I can drive back to Jackson." Jack rolled over on his side away from his son, announcing the discussion was over.

Chapter 4

Darby, Montana

The Bitterroot Mountain Range lie just the west of Darby, a small town which was a ninety-minute drive south of Missoula. Selway Lodge sat in a scenic spot overlooking the mountains as the Bitterroot River flowed by just outside its expansive windows.

Carl and Stacey had completed their wedding vows and the presiding minister had just given Carl permission to kiss the bride. A round of applause from the forty invited guests filled the great room of the lodge. Lodge guests standing outside the privacy ropes joined in the celebration with their own applause.

Jack stood in the black suit he had purchased for the event and smiled while he joined his hands in applause. As the newly married couple turned and walked down the aisle headed to the reception, Jack's smile wavered slightly.

Kotone stepped forward and offered her arm. Jack placed his arm through hers as they followed. He kept his smile going the best he could while the woman he was paired with walked beside him. Inside, thoughts swirled as he walked. Some were of pleasant of times he and Kotone had spent together. But mixed in were the disappointments.

Times when Kotone had suddenly left him only to discover she really needed him. Their relationship had been torrid at times and frustrating at other times. Jack had strong feelings for her but was crushed each time things seemed to be getting serious. And now he had her in his arms again, or at least one arm.

And then it happened. Kotone swung her free hand over and gripped his arm. With her one arm in his grip and her other hand on top, she pulled him close as they walked. Her free hand slowly rubbed his arm. The sensations flowed through Jack; warm, caring, sensuous feelings.

She pulled him tighter and he felt her breast against his side. A breast that he had held and touched and caressed so many times. Only to have it stolen away again and again. His heart raced as he thought of the times they had lain together exploring each other.

Then it stopped. Kotone released her companion as they walked into the lodge's dining hall. She quickly walked over to Stacey to congratulate the bride. Carl walked over to his dad and hugged him.

"Everything OK Dad?"

Jack took a second to recover from his thoughts. "Oh, yes son. Just fine."

"Just making sure. When Kotone couldn't make the rehearsal dinner last night I knew you two meeting at the wedding might be a problem."

"No problem," Jack answered.

The guests began to arrive in the dining hall as Carl grabbed his dad for photographs. The wedding party returned to the now deserted main room and took up their positions. The photographer snapped shots of the two couples and then asked Jack and Kotone to step aside. As he went to work recording the married couple, Jack and Kotone stepped quietly into a far corner.

"Jack, it's so good to see you," Kotone said. "Sorry I couldn't make the dinner last night. Last day before Christmas break at the university. The Bursar's Office has a ton of work to get done."

"Yes, Carl told me you and your sister both have jobs at the university," Jack said.

Kotone explained how lucky they had been getting jobs so quickly when they landed in Missoula. Her sister was an instructor in the Computer Science Department. *That makes sense considering she has two degrees in the subject from Berkley,* Jack thought.

"And you, counting money again, I see."

"Yes, my New York City banking experience actually paid off I think. But you're looking good. How's the book coming?"

Kotone asked about the novel Jack had been writing since retirement. She had seen him working on it during the winter they had been together in Jackson.

"Can you believe it? Four years later, I finally have a publisher that's looking at it. I self-published it last fall and by chance went to a writer's conference. They had pitch sessions, and I gave it my best sales job. The agent took an interest and they've got an editor working on it right now. There's even talk of translating it into German and Dutch."

"So it's the same story. What was it again?" Kotone asked.

"The Zweip-Widerkehr murders. Same one," Jack said. "It's changed quite a bit since you read it three years ago."

"It wasn't finished when I read it. But that's great news. How soon before its available?"

"They said this spring at the earliest. The self-published version has sold well in Germany and the Netherlands even though it's in English."

"I can see why. It made the headlines for months in Europe. Even in the news reports here, it's surprising the way its lingered on," Kotone said.

The Zweip-Widerkehr murders had caught the world's attention when they happened six years ago. Jack was the lead detective on the crime, his most famous case. Mary Zweip was a Dutch exchange student attending the University of Oregon. Marie Widerkehr was a fellow exchange student from Germany.

Along the way, they both had connected with an American attending the University of Oregon named Robert van Patten. He had been raised in a family with a Dutch speaking father. A common language had brought the three together. German, being closely related to Dutch, made Marie fit into the trio.

The relationship had moved past friendship and into a love relationship. Jack had discovered that the three were very passionate together and that had led to things getting out of hand. The end result was an aggressive German taking out the Dutch woman in a jealous rage. The American man tried to defend his first lover, only to end up killing his second.

With two dead women, van Patten had been charged with both murders. The controversy started when his defense attorney claimed his client had only acted in self-defense. At the trial, all the titillating details of their bedroom romps came out as the attorney laid out a pattern of aggressive lovemaking.

And it wasn't just confined to the bedroom. The three had ventured far and wide to find locales for their trysts. Each detail was closely examined by the media in nightly reports on the more risque entertainment channels.

But it was all good for Jack's book. After retirement, he had the time to put his investigation notes together from his perspective. Another author had produced a quickie book on the incident to capture the lurid interest the news account had generated. But Jack knew the writer had left out much of the story, only focusing on the sexual aspects. Jack was determined to set the record straight, the sex remaining, as he knew what sold books.

"I'll send you a copy when it comes out," Jack offered.

"Thanks, I'd appreciate that," Kotone said. Her gaze caught Jack by surprise. There was more in her loaded words than an expression of gratitude for a free book. The arm squeeze along with the breast feel and now that look. *Was there something more there?* he thought. *Did all those misstarts and past failures mean nothing? Was she trying to express something special to me in spite of our history?* Jack never got to ask the next question.

"Hey you two, you're on duty in the dining room. The bride and groom just walked in," Jack's daughter, Inez, said.

Kotone turned at the admonition and headed to the reception. Jack gave a hug to his daughter and said, "A beautiful wedding, don't you think?"

"Yes, and you have responsibilities today. Stop hitting on your old girlfriend and man up."

Jack took his daughter by the arm and escorted her toward the dining room. "And who made you so self-righteous? Your Mother?"

"Watch it, Jack Wesley. There'll be no fighting at my brother's wedding," Inez said. "I'm just making sure you measure up today. Then I know you're housebroken and I can have you at my wedding."

"What, are you announcing something?"

"No, not yet. But things are serious," Inez said. "He passed on being here. Said too much family at once might be bad. You men are all the same. But if it happens, I do want you to walk me down the aisle."

"Not what's his name?" Jack asked. His tone towards his ex-wife's boyfriend evident.

"Be nice. You know his name. And no, he doesn't get to walk me down the aisle. I have a father and that's his role."

"Thank you. I couldn't imagine a more beautiful bride to walk with," Jack said. "Besides, I have a new suit. So, you better make it snappy before it goes out of style."

Inez gave her dad the eye roll and released her grip. She gently shoved him toward the head table where Kotone sat next to Stacey. Jack walked around to join his son.

The formalities were attended to: the toasts, the dinner, the cake, the dance. It was during the dance taht Jack caught up with his new daughter-in-law. As Carl danced with Stacey's mother, Jack took a turn with Stacey.

"So Jack, who would have ever thought this would happen way back there in that campground in Oregon," Stacey said. She smiled.

Jack's stomach tightened as he remembered the two of them riding bicycles cross country together. It had started slowly at first, but when the dam broke, the two of them had become quite an item. And now dancing with a slight baby bump hitting him in the stomach, Jack pushed those memories back.

"Who would have thought?" he said.

"Well, it led to me finding your son. So, I have nothing but good thoughts about the whole time."

Good, then keep them as thoughts and stop bringing them up in conversation, Jack thought. Stacey seemed to notice Jack's hesitations and changed the subject.

"I bet it was a surprise to see Kotone here. But I'm sure Carl warned you."

"It's a guy thing. We don't like too many surprises when ex-girlfriends are involved."

Stacey smiled at the reference to both she and Kotone. "No, I bet not," she replied.

The music stopped, and Jack was happy to turn Stacey over to Carl. His son motioned that it was time for the parents to dance with the couple. Jack noticed Stacey's parents standing together waiting. *Great,* Jack thought. *Play nice.*

He looked around and spotted his ex-wife. She was ensconced with her boyfriend. Inez was sitting at the table with them.

Jack walked over and said, "Duty time. It's the parent's dance with the happy couple." He held out his hand. He glanced over and got daggers back from the boyfriend.

"We haven't been this close in ages," Jack started as they swung around the floor. He noticed that Stacey's parents were smiling as they enjoyed the time together.

"Too close," his ex-wife said as she pulled back from Jack's embrace. "We can keep a good Catholic school fist between us, thank you."

"Afraid I might squeeze those tits too tight?" Jack asked. "You used to enjoy it when I held you tight and squeezed them."

"I used to enjoy a lot of things, but then I grew up," she said. A pause in the conversation ensued as they glided past the other two couples.

"But I see there are other tits here that you've squeezed before."

Does she know? Jack thought. *She would certainly know about Kotone, the two had met once in Colorado. And Kotone and I hadn't hidden that we were living together. But Stacey, does she know about that?*

Jack changed the subject before things got out of hand. "Well, we sure produced a great son together. And a great daughter. No one can deny that."

Jack was happy that his statement shut down the attack mode. The rest of the dance was done in silence as he thought he saw his ex-wife get a little teary. But as soon as the music ended, she was gone like a shot, back to the safety of her table.

Now he had one last dance to perform, the two attendants with the married couple. As Jack scanned the hall, Kotone swept from behind him into his arms. The music started.

There would be no Catholic school dance safety zone between them as Kotone purposely pulled herself tight to Jack. Her breasts flattened against his chest as she moved around the dance floor. Jack's feelings surfaced again as he smelled and felt her hair close to his face. He relaxed and went with it, the difference from his last dance notable.

"So, do I compare?" Kotone finally asked. She moved her face away from his shoulder, so they could look into each other's eyes. Jack noticed that the change hadn't affected her breast plant.

Compared to what?" Jack asked.

"Your last dance. I noticed the slight pull back. She gained the correct school girl separation on you, I see."

"No comparison. You should know that," Jack offered. *This might not be the place, but I have to say it*, he thought. "Kotone, we've certainly had our hard times. But through it all, my feelings for you have always stayed the same. It's just the off again, on again pattern we seem to experience that is hard on me."

Kotone settled her head back on Jack's shoulder without saying a word. The music carried on as the two quietly enjoyed the dance. Jack noticed his son looking over at them and smiling. *What was that all about?* Jack thought.

Done with his official duties, Jack retired to the head table and sipped his wine. Things were getting too much too fast for him. He had planned on attending a simple wedding and things were turning out much different. The music continued, and the floor was now open for all the guests.

Carl came over after dancing with some of the women guests and sat down next to his dad.

Stacey swirled around the floor with one of the climbing friends that had made the ski trip. Jack looked over and J. J. continued to be happy in his grandmother's arms. Stacey's mom had a way with little kids and his grandson hadn't ventured far all day.

"Having a good time Dad?" Carl asked.

"Hanging in there, son," Jack said. "Lots of memories," Jack almost kicked himself after he spoke. Then added for clarification, "Your Mom and me. We were so happy on our big day. And when you and your sister arrived, we couldn't have been happier. And then . . ."

"I know Dad. But Stacey and I will be different, trust me," Carl said.

If you only knew, Jack thought. Every couple starts the same way. Full of hopes and dreams, only to be run over by the big truck of reality. But Jack kept those thoughts to himself.

"I know you will son. Stacey is a wonderful person. J.J. is a great kid. The baby will just add to it all. I'm very happy for you," Jack said.

"Did I hear something about Stacey being a wonderful person?" Stacey asked as she walked up and joined the men.

"Relatively, that is," Jack added. "For an older woman." Jack smiled as he said it, as Stacey was five years older than Carl.

"Oh, the truth comes out. You calling me a cougar?" she asked.

"I'm not here to start any arguments, but if the truth hurts, who am I to judge," Jack said.

"Oh, Jack Wesley, you're impossible." Stacey grabbed Carl and headed toward the dance floor where she announced that it was time for the garter and flower toss, all single men and women needed to step forward.

With a drum roll, Carl slid Stacey's dress up her leg, revealing her garter. As the drums took on a more seductive beat, he slid it down over her foot.

Jack was content to let the young singles have their fun when Carl motioned Jack to join the group. With the crowd chanting in unison, Jack finally relented. But as he walked around the table, he drifted over to J. J. and grabbed his grandson.

"If age isn't a restriction, I want all the single men out here," Jack said.

He wrapped his arms around J.J. as the two took their place with the other bachelors. A look of disappointment crossed Carl's face as he turned his back to ready his toss. Another drum roll followed by a cymbal crash and the garter flew out of Carl's hand. Its trajectory was straight at his dad.

Jack dutifully held up J. J., who went for the target only to be beat out by a young twenty something lunging in from the right. J. J. started to cry for his lost prize and Jack carried him back to his grandmother. Now settled down and the excitement forgotten, Jack walked over to his son. Stacey was lining up the single women for the bouquet toss.

"You were supposed to catch that," Carl said, admonishing his dad.

"Hey, blame your son," Jack said. "I held him in the perfect position. He was no match for the other guy, who sure seemed overly anxious to catch it, by the way."

"Long story," Carl offered. "Here goes Stacey."

Another drum roll and crash and the flowers flew over the bride's head. It was a perfect throw as they landed right in Kotone's midsection. Kotone quickly wrapped them up before the grasping hands of ten females could snatch it away.

"So, was that the plan? Me with the garter, Kotone with the flowers?' Jack asked.

"No comment," Carl said as he walked off and joined his wife.

The wedding wrapped up as the happy couple headed off to Missoula airport for a late flight to Denver. There they would catch a flight to

Orlando and a week at a resort there. Stacey's parents were here for that time to care for little J. J..

Jack finally loosened his tie as he said good bye to his daughter. As he turned to head to his truck for the ride back to his hotel in Missoula, Kotone interrupted him.

"If you're headed to Missoula, I could use a lift. The people I arrived with are staying the night," Kotone said.

"Sure thing, let me help you with your coat."

They chatted about what a nice wedding it had been as the motored north. As they drove along the snow lined road, Kotone finally asked a pointed question.

"So, Jack, how long are you in town?"

"Don't know. My grandson seems mesmerized by his grandmother so don't think I'll get much time with him this trip. Inez is with her mom and the only two people I know in town just left," Jack said. He let the statement lie for a bit.

"Not everyone you know has left," Kotone said.

"The six guys I spent a week with climbing didn't offer to buy beers for me, if that's what you're asking," Jack teased.

"You know that's not what I'm asking,"

"Kotone, if you have something on your mind, speak up. You know I'm flexible."

"I just thought maybe we could do something together. Maybe go skiing"

"Sounds fun. Tomorrow? Day trip to Lolo Pass?" Jack asked.

"Yes, I'd like that."

Chapter 5

Vluchteling Island, the Caribbean

It had been two months since Karla Schmidt had been unceremoniously hauled off to prison on a charge of drug smuggling. The confusion now worn off, her life turned into a nightmare as a trial was quickly held the next week.

With no word from her German Consulate on St. Vincent in the Grenadines, she knew she was all alone. Her court appointed attorney practically rolled over and played dead as the prosecution ran through the evidence. The selected jury members sat stone faced as her case was presented, brief though it was. But it was a video tape of the Customs official asking her if the bag in front of her was hers and his subsequent retrieval of a bag of white powder that sealed her fate. Her attorney made no attempt to refute the evidence and merely rolled his eyeballs skyward.

"What could he do?" he had said. "It was all there on tape in plain view," he had offered. "No one can question what you can see with your own eyes."

Karla tried to make the point that her bag was unlocked because of security checks. Anyone could have planted the drugs in her bag anytime the airlines had control of it. But such a simple explanation didn't seem to move anyone. It's as if I'm dealing with a group of stunned mullets, she had thought at the time.

Ten years in prison had been her sentence. Despair now consumed her these six weeks later as she sat on her bunk holding her head. *If my government doesn't help me out of this, I don't know what I'll do*, she thought.

There had been no word whether Germany even knew of her predicament. She wasn't even sure that anyone knew her situation. Her friends in New York City had known about her flight to St. Vincent. But her decision to fly to Vluchteling had been a spur of the moment choice.

A simple conversation on the flight from New York with her seatmate had led her to change her plans. Her friends expected her to be in Recife, Brazil after two weeks on St. Vincent. And no one in St. Vincent would miss the woman that never returned to the hotel after her quick three-day side trip.

No, no one is coming to get me released, she thought. Karla looked around her cell and contemplated a ten-year life here. A ten by ten-foot space of rock walls. A metal door with a small barred window was her only view of her fellow humanity. An open barred window to the outside world was seven feet up the far wall.

From her metal bunk, only blue sky was visible. She had lifted herself carefully on the small joints in the rock to look out. The sea lay right below her with about a one hundred foot drop down a rocky escarpment. To the left and to the right was only ocean.

At least the opening held only bars. The smell of the sea was her only pleasure in the bleak cell. Two foot prints on a metal fixture on the floor marked the squatter toilet she had to use. A small metal sink with only cold water was the final fixture to her world.

Karla flopped over onto her bunk and stared at the ceiling. She glanced over to the wall just above her head and looked again at the lines etched into the rock. Reminders of the other prisoners that had existed here and the rudimentary calendar they had kept.

And then the noise hit her again. The screaming from some far-off place in the prison. There was always screaming. Day and night, guards came and went with people. Some were unconscious and being dragged bodily. Some were mumbling incoherently as they passed.

Each time she heard steps, Karla would scramble to the small window. A blank wall on the opposite side formed the hallway through which the guards would bring their charges. Mostly other young women would pass by, but occasionally a man.

Many would have cuts and bruises from who knew what. This all was turning into a nightmare and Turkish prisons came to mind. In her world travels, the same tale of life in a Turkish prison would make its rounds. She remembered that she had been repulsed from something so awful. But now she was living through her own hell on earth.

A ten year sentence, she thought, staring at the ceiling. She placed her hands over her ears to block out new screams. *How could this be happening on such a beautiful island? Doesn't anyone know about this place?*

The tears flowed once again. They flowed each day since she had landed here. Karla knew she would go mad before her ten-year sentence was completed. A clank at the metal door broke her thoughts.

A small horizontal door was opened from outside and a plate of hot food shoved in. A short lip on the inside held the plate from crashing to the floor. Karla stood up and walked to the door and took the plate before it disappeared. She passed her empty lunch plate from yesterday out before the guard slammed the small door and latched it. In the moment, she saw her antagonist through the barred window.

It was the same one every evening. Unshaven in the same smelly t-shirt, her jailer came around each evening delivering food. And at least he was better than her breakfast and lunch jailer. He typically avoided any shirt at all and if he caught Karla looking at him, would make suggestive motions toward his crouch. The smile he offered made her want to vomit.

Once a week, after lunch, towels and soap were passed out. It would be time for her shower which consisted of wiping herself down with a hand towel. The cold water from the sink was her only shower. A towel for drying was provided but from the looks of it hadn't been washed since the last weekly shower.

And she had caught the guard looking in as she washed herself. They looked in even when she had to squat to use the toilet. Their leers were constant, and Karla wondered where they found such men.

Her only clothing consisted of a jump suit, with the arms cut off. Every other week she exchanged it for another one. They were supposedly cleaned in the interim. A small naked mattress and a wool blanket was the extent of her belongings.

Not that more things were unavailable. The guards routinely suggested that any number of items were available to make life more comfortable. The only requirement for such a luxurious life was some small favors she could extend the guard. Karla put her German mind to resisting anything so disgusting and stoically lived with what was provided.

She looked down at the food and her appetite disappeared. It was the same every meal. Oatmeal for breakfast. Some bread with maybe some fish for lunch. And thank God an orange, as it kept her fear of contracting scurvy away. Dinner was rice or potato soup with maybe a piece of chicken in it. If she was really lucky, maybe the soup held a piece of carrot or celery, but never both.

From the hip bones sticking out from her stylish jumpsuit, Karla knew she had passed too many times on the disgusting food. She had to eat to live so she sat with her wooden spoon and slurped down the lukewarm soup. No joy of eating existed as she dreamed of the times when life was full of tasteful wonders. Licking the plate clean, she absorbed as many calories as she was provided.

The plate was returned to the door to await breakfast. The light outside soon faded as another day in paradise came to an end. As soon as it was dark, she made her way to the toilet as it was the only private time she had. She grimaced as the rough paper she was provided rubbed her raw. *At least I have paper*, she thought as she finished. She crawled once more into her bunk, pulled the one blanket up over her head and cried herself to sleep.

Karla awoke in the middle of the night to someone wailing deep in the prison. The jail had its sounds each night and Karla had finally grown somewhat accustomed to them. They didn't soothe her torment, but she could sleep through most of them. But this screaming was more blood cuddling than the other times. She pulled the blanket tighter around her as she attempted to build a cocoon of safety.

Then she heard it. Faint and almost undetectable but definitely there, a scrapping noise. She tried to block out the screaming and concentrate on the tiny noise. *There it is again,* she thought. Karla pulled herself tighter into a smaller ball and listened.

The scraping sound was a little louder. It seemed to be coming from her metal door. She pulled the blanket back, revealing one eyeball. She scanned her door. Nothing.

But there was the sound again. Her one eye strained to see if anything was moving. The hairs on her neck stiffened in a primeval response to danger. If it was one of the guards at the door looking for favors, Karla knew her life would be over. She could never fight him off, she was so weak from lack of good food.

Then she thought she saw something. *Did the door just move?* she thought. Her ears strained for the metal on metal creak that the door emitted. It hadn't been opened often since she'd been thrown in here, but she remembered the last time it closed. There had been a noticeable screech.

With her ears straining and her one eye focused, she watched the door. There it was again. That sound and now light from the meager hallway bulb broke into her cell around the door frame. The door was opening, slowly. But it was opening. The faint creak of the door told her everything.

The blanket was pulled back so both eyes were now focused on her changing situation. Her arms were drawn tightly across her chest in defensive mode as she waited for the lecherous guard to emerge. There was nowhere to hide, no escape. He could take what he wanted, and she had no recourse. *Ten years of this, oh God, help me*, she thought.

Chapter 6

Stanley, Idaho

Kotone picked up a handful of snow and threw it at Jack. But instead of a tight snowball hitting him, the feather like flakes burst into a cloud and fell to earth harmlessly. Jack smiled at Kotone's attempt at picking a snowball fight.

"It's no good," Jack said. "Oregon snow will punish you badly. But Idaho snow is a pussy cat. Good for making snow angels." With that, Jack fell backwards like a kid into the snow and swept his arms and legs up and down. Once firmly compacted, he carefully sat up, planted his feet and gently stepped away from his creation.

He turned around to admire his handiwork, a perfect outline of an angel lay in the snow. Close by, Kotone picked her virgin snow and flopped backwards. She copied Jacks arm and leg motion, laughing the entire time.

Jack moved over to her spot, adjusted for landing, and fell beside her. His outstretched arms and legs swished back and forth. In his movement, he hit Kotone's hand. Their two hands stopped and gripped each other. Their mittens, for protection, dampened the feeling but not by much.

They both stopped laughing as their two hands explored each other in as intimate a movement as mittens would allow. The two of them lay quietly as if to project all their feelings through each mitten, into each hand and finally into each body. The hand dance continued as they stared into the blue sky above.

"Jack, this last week has been wonderful," Kotone said. "I wish it would never end."

"It doesn't have to, you know," Jack said.

Each hand moved up the opposite arm, pushing jacket material aside. The cold hit bare skin and the touch was enhanced.

After their one day ski trip to Lolo Pass, they had actually done some official dating. A movie was taken in, followed the next night with dinner. Since campus was closed for the winter holidays, each day they grabbed their cross-country skis and headed to one of Missoula's parks to ski.

The sunny weather added to the feeling of wonderment as the two grew closer each day. The trouble they had experienced was pushed deeper into their memories as new memories were created. Kotone headed home each night to her apartment near campus that she shared with her sister. Jack headed back to his motel.

But the waking hours of the week had been spent just being a couple. Things that they had never done before or hadn't done with each other in a long time.

It was Kotone who had suggested that they get away. With her sister at home and Jack not impressed with his affordable motel, a ski trip somewhere special was suggested. Time away to be alone to see where their new relationship was headed.

Jack knew the dangers of such an excursion. He had been down this path with Kotone twice before. And each time it had ended badly. *At least, not yelling I hate you, badly,* he thought. *No, it was always more subtle, as in, I need my space, badly.*

But he was willing to risk it once again. Kotone had held his attention since the first day he met her. Afraid and fearing for her life, she had been stuck on a highway in Wyoming. Jack, the retired police detective, had come to her aid. And not just because she was seventeen years younger and beautiful. Her beautiful Japanese-American heritage still captured his attention. And even though she was less toned physically then her bicycle days, there wasn't enough extra to worry about.

Their drive down from Missoula over Lost Trail Pass, past the town of Salmon into the Stanley Basin was noticeably quiet. Just holding hands, without mittens this time, Jack was clueless as to what was about to happen.

When Kotone had mentioned time away, his only thought was of a lodge in Stanley that he had seen the brochure for in the lobby of their hotel. She had volunteered to make the arrangements but had shared no details with Jack.

Their early arrival had forced them to take a break in the snow. The lodge had said that they would come and get them when the accommodations were ready. Jack's mittened hand play in the snow was interrupted by a lodge staff walking up to the two of them.

"Mr. Wesley, Ms. Butler, we are ready. You may check in now."

"Thank you for accommodating our early arrival," Jack-said as he carefully stood up. He turned around and offered to pull Kotone upright. Her snow angel was perfect when she turned around to check the two angels in the snow holding wings.

Brushing the snow off, they entered the lodge. Jack was anxious to hear what their sleeping accommodations were going to be. It would give him a clue at least to where Kotone was in their new relationship.

"Welcome Ms. Butler," the attendant said. "Your reservation specified the mountain view side of the lodge. Here are your two keys. The stairs right behind you will take you to the second floor. Have a nice stay."

Kotone took one key and left the other for Jack. *No answer yet,* he thought. Jack followed along behind Kotone as she climbed the stairs. He couldn't help himself as he scanned her legs and backside as she climbed. He had seen this view many times, but it was more typically when she was pedaling her bike. It still looked the same to him.

Jack glanced at his key and noticed a tab with the room number on it. He tried to look at Kotone's tab but it was hidden in her hand. Turning at the top of the stairs, they walked the short distance indicated by the sign marked with the room numbers. As Jack scanned the doors for numbers, he noticed Kotone doing the same.

He settled in to find out his answer. Were they moving on in their relationship, at least this time around, or was it friends having fun? Kotone stopped at a door and put her key in the lock. The door opened.

Looking quickly, Jack confirmed the number on the door was the same as on his key tab. *The first hurdle has been passed, we're in the same room,* he thought.

As Jack was considering the implications, Kotone turned around.

"What, you thought we had separate rooms?"

"Never assume. Its been my motto for a long time," Jack offered.

"Well, you're welcome. Come in and check out the view," Kotone said.

Jack walked in and noticed a king size bed. Good, another question answered. *In the same room in separate beds would have been worse than separate rooms*, he thought. *He would have to wait for his final answer.*

Kotone stood at the window looking out at the Sawtooth Range. Jack walked up behind her and wrapped his arms around her. She moved to snuggle close and rocked her head back. "It's beautiful, but not as . . ."

"As the Tetons," Jack interrupted. "And we know how special the Tetons are, don't we?"

"Very special," Kotone replied. "But we have time to make these mountains special. Get your gear on mister, we're not going to waste a beautiful day like this inside."

Jack ran to the truck to carry in their bags, thinking about plenty of things he could waste a day doing indoors. But he knew he had to be a good partner and let things come to him. There would be no rushing this trip.

They spent the rest of the day skiing the trails circling the lodge. Other guests experienced the same thrill as everyone stopped frequently to admire the view. The Sawtooths hovered over the resort, being only a short distance away. Wherever they skied, there were the mountains standing sentinel to the south. Jack and Kotone stopped frequently, always with Jack skiing up from behind, his skis outside Kotone's skis. They would stand and admire the view in each other arms. Then Kotone announced it was time to move.

By dinner time, their appetite was all consuming. They had missed lunch, only snacking on the drive. By the time they were showered and dressed, Jack's stomach announced its demands. A nice bottle of Idaho red wine was ordered, and the couple slowly moved through dinner. First a green salad followed by Kotone having trout, Jack going for the sirloin. When asked about dessert, Jack hesitated. At Kotone's offer to split one, soon a chocolate brownie with ice cream and fudge sauce appeared, two spoons on the plate.

Jack dove in first and worked the sticky fudge sauce off his spoon. On his second bite, he offered, "Hey, you said we were sharing. I'm not eating this all by myself."

Kotone smiled as her gaze shifted from Jack to the dessert. She also fought the fudge sauce battle as her tongue worked the spoon hard. Jack stared at her labor and was caught looking.

"No fair, this we do together," Kotone said.

They both took a spoonful and watched each other work the resisting fudge sauce off the spoon. Smiling, they both dove in for another round. By the time they were scrapping the edge of the bowl, both were equally aroused. Jack signed the bill, adding it to their room charges and took Kotone's hand.

Things were moving right along up to Jack's closing their room door. As he walked over and took Kotone's hands, he felt a certain resistance.

"Jack, please understand," she started. "Things have been wonderful, maybe too wonderful. My head is swimming from too much wine and too much fudge sauce."

"Kotone, stop right there," Jack interrupted. "We've been down this road before. You know me. If you aren't ready, I can wait. I want it to be right when it happens."

"You're so special," Kotone said. "Always the gallant one. Are you sure that spooning will be alright? I don't know if they have another room at this late hour."

"I'd be shocked if spooning wasn't part of our time together,' Jack said as he tried to inject a bit of humor. Kotone smiled weakly.

"I'll head into the bathroom first to get ready then."

Using the sink outside the bathroom, Jack was already in bed when Kotone stepped out of the bathroom. Pulling her t-shirt down over her panties, she climbed into bed next to Jack. The rustle of Jack's Big Dog shorts announced themselves as he leaned over and turned out the light.

In the dark, the moon lit Sawtooth Range loomed just outside their window. Jack stared at the mountains as he pushed his emotions aside. He had been through this before with Kotone, and he might be able to withstand it again.

His task grew harder as she snuggled in beside him, her breasts announcing themselves through the soft cotton shirt. When she swung her leg up onto his thigh, her pubic bone bumped into his hip bone. *Yes, it will take restraint tonight,* he thought.

Chapter 7

Stanley, Idaho

A beam of sunlight announced itself on the mountains as the first rays of the sun arrived. The growing light of the awakening day had stirred Jack from his slumber. With his eyes still shut, he moved his hand slightly. It was holding something, and it didn't belong to him.

He twitched his hand slightly and realized he held Kotone's breast. She had flipped to her other side and Jack had naturally followed her in the night. That his hand would move to embrace her was only natural. That his hand would find something soft and warm to hold was equally natural.

He let his hand linger as he slowly awoke. He had held Kotone's breast before, many times. They were still wonderful to touch. Large but not overflowing, above average breasts where Asians were concerned. And Kotone was taller than the typical Asian, the result of her Caucasian father, along with the soft features of her face. He couldn't see it now, but he remembered every detail. Softer than the sharp features of European women, but more distinct than the typical rounded Asian face. Altogether, he still consider ed her stunning.

As his hand moved, the nipple took on more substance. Soon it was poking into the palm of his hand. Jack debated whether he should back off, when he got his answer. Kotone reached up with one hand and offered Jack the other breast, its nipple pronounced.

The two lie in bed, Kotone's back tight against Jack's stomach. His hands holding her gently as both stared out the window. As the sun rose, the Sawtooths took on more majesty as the brilliant white reflection of billions of snow crystals all combined into one spectacular sunrise.

Kotone rolled over to face Jack, and offered, "It's going to be too beautiful a day out. We need to get outside and enjoy it."

Jack felt her hips pressing against his groin and moved to relieve any contact his growing interest would cause. He slid his left hand down her back to hold her ass as his right arm wrapped around her head to pull it close. He kissed her on the lips and noticed a warm return of his embrace. The he backed off.

"Yes, we need to be out in the snow. A good breakfast and then it's out on the skis," he announced.

Both of them climbed out of bed and while Kotone headed to the bathroom, Jack pulled off his

Big Dog shorts and pulled on his polypropylene underwear. Adding more layers of polypropylene, he left off his upper top layer. They would eat first and then hit the cold morning air.

A hearty mountain breakfast was quickly consumed as Jack realized that they were ahead of the other guests this morning. The front desk clerk had tipped him off about a special feature of the lodge. It required a longer ski than most of the guests were willing to do but the attendant assured him that the effort was worth it.

Finally suited up with their extra layers, Jack and Kotone each pulled on day packs holding emergency supplies as well as a lunch the lodge had made. They stepped into their mountain skis, slipped on their poles and adjusted their sunglasses. Having a rough map the front desk attendant had drawn memorized, Jack led out heading south.

The trail was easy going as the lodge ran snowmobiles early each morning to groom the cross-country routes that ran out from the lodge. Their trail would follow a tributary of the Salmon River for a couple of miles. Enough to get them away from all but the most heartiest skiers staying at the lodge.

Since the resort was a working ranch in the summer, all the land around the lodge was privately owned. With the main highway on the other side of Stanley Basin, Jack had been informed that they could be assured of solitude. That, and the attendant only offered his secret destination to a limited number of people.

Reaching a trail marker, one fork continued along the tributary that swung to the east. A second fork continued south as it wound its way around a large ridge. To their right, the valley spread out with the Sawtooths taking up the horizon. Kotone dropped her pack and stripped off her jacket, tying it on the outside of her pack. Jack had already dropped two layers from the exertion of the ski and now pushed off in just a polypropylene t-shirt. He led on as they left the stream and crossed a snow-covered bridge.

The snowmobile had left a solid smooth two-foot-wide track but Jack noticed no other ski marks anywhere. They would be the first to their destination as promised by the lodge staff. Others that knew about where they were going would respect the first arrivals and ski somewhere else.

Another mile or so of skiing brought them around a spur that dropped down off the growing ridge beside them. Nestled at the toe of the lope was an old fashioned windmill. It sat motionless in the still morning air. Steam rose from a large round galvanized tank that sat open on the ground.

The water tank had been installed for cattle that grazed here in the summer. About thirty feet in diameter and about forty inches deep, a pipe at the base of the windmill showed where the water was added whenever the wind blew. The bonus was that in this part of the world, hot water came up out of the ground to provide a large heated pool in the wilderness.

Idaho sits on numerous geographic faults that lend themselves to hot springs. The largest of these is Yellowstone National Park that takes up the eastern portion of the state. While mostly in Wyoming, Yellowstone itself was a super caldera, some thirty miles across. Described as a pile of high explosives thirty miles square by thirty miles deep, the potential existed for a catastrophic explosion during a volcanic eruption.

The closeness of the magma to the surface also meant that the surrounding area had numerous geothermal features. And Jack skied up to his personal hot tub with a million-dollar view. The Sawtooth Mountains loomed across Stanley Basin as Jack began to strip down. Kotone skied up to the tank and planted her poles.

"Jack are you planning what I'm think you?" she asked.

As he stepped out of his pin bindings, he leaned his skis and poles against the windmill tower. He hung the pack on the hooks that someone had provided and pulled off his remaining shirt. The cold dry air hit his chest as he stepped over to test the water.

"Feels wonderful," he announced.

Kotone continued her vigil standing on her skis as she watched Jack strip off his remaining clothes. With a white backside, he climbed the wooden steps that someone had added. A small bench on the top offered a ladder down into the tank. Jack slipped off the cold wood into the warm water. Kicking off the side, he glided on his back out into the middle of the pool.

"It's great,' he said. "Just needs a little mixing." Swimming and diving, he mixed the water so the cooler surface water blended with the warmer water at the bottom. He swam over to the edge. "I double dog dare you."

"Oh yeah, to do what?" Kotone asked. "Stick my tongue on the metal tower to see how cold it is? I've seen that movie and I'm no Flick."

"And I'm no Ralphie, so I still double dog dare you."

"Jack, it was twenty-five below zero this morning at the lodge," Kotone said. "It must still be close to zero. What happens when we get out?"

"We get dressed, unless you want the Finnish treatment and we roll in the snow for extra invigoration," Jack said.

"No, I'll pass on the extra fun."

"That's good. I was afraid you'd make me show you how it is done. This water is warm but not anywhere near as hot as a Finnish sauna. I think the extra heat load on your body makes the snow rolling more tolerable."

Kotone finally stepped out of her bindings and placed her skis next to Jack's gear. Hanging up her daypack, she began pulling off layers. She left her last top on as she stepped out of her long johns. Her panties were soon dropped onto the hook as she turned to face Jack.

He had been watching the slow strip tease as he rested his head on the wood platform, his naked body floating behind him. Kotone saw his gaze and stopped.

"Do you mind?" she asked.

"Oh, sorry," he answered. He rolled over on his back, his head still lounging on the wood.

He heard Kotone complain as she stripped off her last semblance of clothing. Then the crunch of boots as she stepped over to the base of the small wooden ladder. He heard each boot fall to the snow as she pulled them off and discarded her socks. Then he felt a whack on his head to get him to move as she climbed the ladder.

Jack swam away from the wooden platform and turned to see a naked Kotone crouched at the top of the platform. She stepped one foot on the ladder inside the tank and jumped into the water, swimming over to where Jack stood crouched so as to stay immersed.

The air was brisk if one rose out of the water, and frequently they had to go under totally to get their head warmed up. Jack swam under water and grabbed Kotone's legs, her knees bent to stay in the forty-inch-deep water. He slid his hands up her body, as his face rose up her front. Breaking the surface, he pulled her close and kissed her.

"Jack. You're just crazy. We're going to freeze to death when we step out of here."

"But what a thrill in between times," he offered. "Just look at the view. And it's all ours."

The two swam over to the edge that faced the Sawtooths. Jack placed Kotone between the tank edge and himself, holding her around the middle. His mouth kissed the back of her neck as his right hand slid up onto her breast.

"Jack, someone may ski up here," Kotone said.

"Not according to the lodge. Whoever gets here first has the place to themselves. Sort of the unwritten code of lustful mountain types."

"And you trust everyone's knowledge of this unwritten code?" Kotone asked.

"Sure, and if we get caught, who cares. From the sound of things, it happens frequently at this pool."

Jack slid his other hand lower and Kotone spread her legs. Taking that as an invitation, Jack began a lower massage as Kotone rocked her head back onto Jack's shoulder. Working her erogenous area over to get things stimulated, he slid both hands under her back side and lifted her up. As her body floated out into the middle of the tank, Jack slid up between her thighs, his mouth finding its target.

As he helped hold her afloat, the two slowly floated over to the wooden platform. Jack helped Kotone place the back of her head on the platform. Now with water spilling over the top of the tank walls, he held her hips with one hand so her sweet spot stayed near the surface. The other hand pushed warm water over her exposed head and chest. Her nipples grew tighter with each cold snap against them followed by a splash of warm water.

Kotone thrashed in the water as she felt Jack's attentions fulfill her. Sliding down off her perch, she took Jack in her arms and kissed him. They both dipped under the surface and lingered, the warm water bringing feeling back to their cold heads.

She reached down between Jack's legs with one hand and pulled his lower body to the surface with the other. She guided him to the same position she had enjoyed as her mouth found its mark. Jack felt the cold against his head and chest as both of Kotone's hands were needed to keep him floating. He splashed water on himself for relief from the cold.

Jack reached down and pulled Kotone toward him. Placing her on her stomach on the wooden platform, she bent forward, spreading her legs. Jack stepped forward and hit the spot offered as they joined together. More water thrashing and Jack fell off satiated. Kotone slipped off the wooden platform and swam to join him. They were content to squat in the water in each other's arms absobing the full effect of the natural setting.

Comparing wrinkled fingers from sitting in the warm water, they both looked at each other. The temperature might have gained another five degrees, but the noon time sun would never get the day hot enough for what they had to do.

"OK, mister double dog dare me," Kotone said. "I triple dog dare you to be first out of the water. I want to see how fast you can get dressed."

"I accept your challenge and I have a surprise for you."

"Good, you set up the heated tent while I just wait here," Kotone said.

"No such luck. But I have something that will make things better," Jack offered.

He hopped over to the wooden ladder leading out of the tank. He stopped and studied the logistics he had to perform to assure he was as efficient as possible before he turned back to a waiting Kotone.

"Ready?'

"As ever." she answered. She pushed off the bottom and floated over to the edge to watch. Her arms cradled her head on the top edge of the tank.

Jack pushed warm water onto the wood before climbing out. The ice that had formed on the outside steps crackled as it melted and dropped off. He stepped carefully onto the top and turned around, carefully lowering himself down the ladder. He purposely stepped with bare feet into his boots.

Protected from stepping in the snow barefoot, he lunged quickly toward his pack, dripping water as he moved. He yanked open the top and retrieved a lodge towel. Moving rapidly in one fluid motion, he wiped the majority of water off himself. He grabbed his first top layer and pulled it on. His hat was next as he felt his hair begin to freeze.

Shorts followed with his two bottom layers next. Using the towel, he dried his feet as best as he could and slipped on his socks. Jack picked up each boot and wiped out the extra moisture before slipping into them. He laced them up and finally pulled on his warm jacket. He looked up at Kotone's gaze of wonder.

"OK, your turn."

"You expect me to use that same towel after you've wiped out the inside of your boots with it?" Kotone asked.

"Am I that thoughtless?" Jack asked.

He turned and dipped into this pack again. This time he pulled out a larger towel from the lodge. He stepped over to the wooden steps and held it up between his two arms, inviting someone to wrap herself inside.

Kotone smiled at the gesture and said. "You always know how to treat me special."

Pushing water from the tank onto the wooden platform to warm it, she climbed out of the tank. The cold air hit her, and she moved faster to compensate. Jack admired the view once she was atop the platform and she turned to descend.

"Hey, no staring," Kotone said as she looked behind her and saw Jack's stare. The distraction caused her to miss one of her boots and one foot stepped into the snow. "Wow, it's freezing."

Retrieving her foot quickly, Kotone found her wayward boot. Jack smothered her in the towel as he wrapped his arms around her. Kotone scooted around to face him before pushing him away as she moved to get dressed.

"Just like all the others. Get what you want from them and then push them away," Jack teased.

Kotone said nothing but mumbled about the cold as she threw on her clothes. Jack watched the exercise as he stomped his feet to keep the circulation going. The dampness in his boots was reacting to the cold and he knew they needed to get moving.

Fully dressed, they packed up the damp towels in a plastic bag and pulled on their packs. Stepping into their ski bindings, Jack motioned to Kotone to lead the way back toward the lodge. The stint of brisk skiing brought their body temperatures back up and helped warm their boots.

Jack motioned that they should eat their lunch at the creek crossing. Knocking the snow off the low log that had been mounted as protection from falling off the small bridge, both backed their skis under the log. With their skis overhanging the stream flowing underneath, they sat down on the log. Kotone pulled out their lunch and passed a sandwich to Jack.

The Sawtooth Mountains continued to be their view south as they ate. Their warm hats worked on drying their hair as the wool wicked the moisture away. The sun baked them and they decided that they were quite comfortable as they sat enjoying life after a wonderful swim.

"Howdy," a voice said.

Jack and Kotone looked away from their mountain scene to see a young couple ski up from the lodge. The two sitting returned the greeting.

"Been to the water tank?" the man asked.

"We have," Jack answered. "Very refreshing, especially the get out and get dressed part."

Kotone elbowed him in the ribs to make sure he didn't offer anything more.

"Anyone else up there? We thought we'd take a dip if it's open," the man said. "We were here last winter and discovered the water tank."

Jack noticed the man get an elbow from the woman standing beside him, obvious a reminder to stop the story there.

"No, we just left, and it was wide open. We might have lowered the water level some though."

He received a sharper jab on his comment about splashing water and Jack took the subtle hint to watch his words.

"Not a problem," the man said. "We might be spilling some ourselves."

The man got an arm jab on his side for the comment from his partner.

"Well, have a nice day," Jack offered as the most neutral comment he could think of.

"We sure will," his male counterpart offered back. The man skied across the bridge and gave Jack a wink and a smile as he passed. The woman followed but offered no mutual adventure sign as she passed. Jack followed them as they skied toward the tank, the woman's Lycra ski outfit stretched tightly catching his attention. A sharp pain in his ribs brought him back to reality and he looked at Kotone.

"Hey, just looking," he offered.

"Well, concentrate on the mountain view, not hers," Kotone said.

They finished their lunch with gorp the lodge had provided. The nuts, chocolate and raisins a fitting dessert to their meal. Placing the food back in Kotone's pack, she closed the top and strapped the lid down.

"I just remembered, I think I left my gloves by the water tank," Jack said. "I'll just ski back and grab them."

"Like hell you will," Kotone said. "And check out how much water thrashing was going on, I suppose?"

"I promise, I won't look."

"You can buy some new gloves back in town."

Jack dug in his coat pocket and produced a pair of gloves. "Oh. look what I just found."

Kotone gave him a dirty look as she stood, pulled on her ski poles, and skied off in the direction of the lodge. Jack hustled to catch up.

Chapter 8

Vluchteling Island, the Caribbean

Karla Schmidt had endured the torment of being imprisoned for something she didn't do for two months now. As a German national, she thought that her embassy or consulate on near-by St. Vincent or Grenada would have offered help by now. This was a Dutch island she was locked up on and they had international rules. And between members of the European Community, surely something would-be worked out.

But her dismal life continued as before, locked in a stone cell in the old castle built to ward off pirates. She had caught a glimpse of her prison as she was transported from the municipal building on the waterfront to the castle. Her last view of the outside world had been from a car window had been of the stone fortress sitting on a rocky headland that jutted out into the harbor. At least her last view without bars. Her high open window offered a view of the blue Caribbean, but she had stopped looking. It only tormented her, the outside world that was now barred from her.

She had endured it all with her stoic German attitude until the screams in the night had hit her. Women's screams from other cells. Screams followed by crying through the night as the male guards roamed the corridors outside the cells. She had looked to see a guard emerging from the cell across from hers. Through the tiny window in the door, she saw him pulling up his pants, a sickening smile on his face, inside the cell, before the door was slammed shut, a ravaged woman lying on the cell floor.

The thought tormented her every night wondering what was keeping her safe from the lecherous guards. They had made their rude gestures toward her as they delivered food. Sometimes grabbing their crotch and other times running their tongue suggestively around their lips. Always the message was one of soon, soon they would have their way with her. She had even caught them spying through the small opening in her door as she used the squatter toilet. Karla had switched to using the toilet as little as possible during the day, saving the night for private activities.

And now, her privacy was about to be torn asunder. She shook in fear as she watched her cell door slowly creak open. The dimly lit hallway threw enough brightness into her cell that she could just make out a person. She wished for darkness, so she would have no visual memory of what was about to happen.

She tightened into as small a ball as her body could make. Clenching her arms around her lower legs in the only protective mode she could think of, she waited. Shadows played on the floor as someone moved into the cell. Karla closed her eyes to await her attack. As she strained her mind grasping for strength to endure the inevitable, a voice whispered in her ear.

"If you want to live, come with me."

The shock of what had been said stunned her. Before she could respond, the voice spoke again.

"If you want to live, we need to leave right now."

Karla threw the blanket back and stared into a partially obscured man's face. The man was standing right over her, bending down to whisper. Paralyzed, she still did not move.

The man reached and took her arm. Pulling slightly, he stepped toward the open cell door. His will finally got her moving as she stood up. The man led her out of the door and then stopped. He reached behind her and slowly pulled the door shut. Latching it with a key, he pushed her forward as he slipped the key into a pocket.

Karla reached a place where the corridor split and stopped. The man was right behind and moved to lead her to the right. Moving quickly past other cells, another intersection emerged in the dull light and the man took a left. The walls here were blank, offering no cell doors, the light bulbs rarer as they moved through the castle, deep in its innards.

Karla looked behind her to see if they were being followed and saw nothing moving. She turned forward to discover her rescuer had disappeared. She froze, standing alone against the rock wall. Panic welled up immediately at the thought of being alone. A hand grabbed her lower leg.

Looking down, she saw the man below her in a crawl space leading off the main corridor. She dropped onto her hands and knees. The man turned and led her forward before they emerged in a small room. With limited head room, he half stood, bent over. Karla, still on all fours, waited as she saw no other exit but from where they had come.

That was when the man lifted a metal floor plate and slid it aside. He stepped into the manhole and Karla heard water splash.

"Do you know how to swim?" the man asked.

"Ja," her voice finally responded.

The man motioned her to climb down into the manhole. Once inside, he reached up and pulled the metal plate back over the hole. Karla began to panic in the complete darkness until the man switched on a flashlight.

The space they were in was a confined area just big enough for the two of them. From a rocky shelf, the man grabbed a bag. He reached in and pulled something out.

"Put these on," he said and offered her a pair of swim goggles. She pulled them on her head. The straps were tight and dug into her skin, but she paid it no notice. The man pulled on his goggles.

Reaching back in the bag, he retrieved two strange devices. He handed one to her and placed the other on his face. Part of the device had nose plugs and part fit into the mouth like a snorkel. The man pulled the mouth part out and pointed to Karla. She placed the nose plugs on her nostrils and the mouth piece in her mouth.

"This is a breathing unit," the man said. "We need to swim a short distance under the castle walls to the open sea. Just breathe naturally like you would with a snorkel while diving. Have you ever snorkeled?"

Karla had snorkeled a lot on her travels. She loved swimming among the reef fish, as she preferred traveling to warm climates on her trips. She nodded to the man.

With one hand holding the flashlight, the man took Karla's other hand for support. The two dropped down into the water as the man made sure Karla was breathing normally before he gave her a thumbs up. She responded back with her own thumbs up that everything was good.

He turned and faced a long underwater tunnel that led off from the manhole. Using the flashlight, he began moving down the tunnel, more so walking against its sides than swimming. Karla worked her legs to stay up with the man.

The tunnel continued for some distance and Karla fought the panicky feelings she was experiencing being underwater with no surface to swim up to. Like cave diving, swimming in confined spaces was extremely dangerous. But she held on long enough to see the walls of the tunnel fall away.

The man flicked off the flashlight as he guided her up to the surface. An ocean swell met them as they broke into the night air, lifting them higher. Letting his breathing device drop to his waist, he removed Karla's device. It hung by its strap around her neck as they did a slow breast stroke toward a sandy beach, just visible in the star light.

Karla's cheap prison sneakers touched the sandy bottom and she caught herself with both feet. She took a couple of arm strokes and reached water where she could stand up. The man was already on the beach waiting as she crawled out of the sea.

Her eyes could make out shapes in the low light as the man led her off the beach after placing their swim gear in his carry bag. The warm night air cooled the wet prison jump suit as they scrambled up the rocks leading off the beach. She tripped on an unseen rock, coming down hard on her shin against something. A shot of pain racked her body, but the man was there, his hand yanking her back to her feet to keep moving.

The two soon reached a level stretch and the pace quickened. A stream came out of some trees and the man moved into the stream. The walking became more difficult as they made their way along the gravel and small rocks lining the stream bed. Again, Karla stumbled over a larger boulder, this time hitting her knee. And again, the man was there silently helping her to stand while taking her hand to guide her forward.

Exhausted by the effort, Karla finally succumbed to stress and fatigue. She slumped onto the stream bank. The man urged her on, but she resisted. Complaining she was tired with both legs throbbing, she refused to move.

That was when she heard it. Off in the distance, barking dogs. The prison had finally noticed that she was missing, and the guards had released dogs to track their escapee. Panic hit her, and she rose to continue. The man took her under one arm and half carried her forward.

As the stream continued through the forest, Karla could feel more than see the ground rising up on both sides. The right side was noticeably gaining height. Over the stream noise, the dogs continued their barking as they searched for the scent away from the castle. They had time still, but not much time. And with the ground rising, their progress would slow.

Moving around a bend in the stream, Karla heard the waterfall before she saw it. Growing closer, she perceived them being in a small glade, walls on both sides, a twenty-foot water fall in front of them. Panic returned as she thought they were trapped in a dead end as she tightened her hold on the man.

The man led them over to the right and higher ground. He began to climb the steep rocky bank as he scrambled up the nearly vertical rock for about fifteen feet. Backing down to Karla, he motioned for her to do the same. She grabbed a handhold and lifted her leg to a rock nub. Moving one extremity at a time, she mimicked the man's short climb. Backing down, she looked at the man in the faint light. The barking was now noticeable even with the waterfall thirty feet away.

The man took her hand as they walked toward thew waterfall. Just as the spray coming off the falling water hit them, the man just charged straight into the falls, Karla being pulled after him. The power of the falling water hit her in the head and shoulders and then stopped as they emerged behind the falls.

A dell about ten feet deep behind the falls hid them from their pursuers. Water falling from wall to wall kept any hint of the dell hidden from outside. Karla continued to hear dogs barking over the water noise.

The temperature was noticeably cooler in the naturally air-conditioned space. With her wet clothes, she began to shiver. The man walked to the rock face, turned and placed his finger over his mouth, the universal sign for quiet. Their pursuers were quite close and only a sound would give them away.

Karla turned to make sure the waterfall hid everything and as she turned, realized the man was gone. She looked left and right in the small space in panic. She knew she couldn't step back out of the waterfall to check, so she just stood, frozen.

A hand appeared out of the face of the rock wall and it waved her over. She stepped carefully across the rock as she followed the hand. A cleft in the rock opened up and she turned sideways to slip through. The man greeted her on the other side. He again held his finger to his mouth to emphasize the need for quiet. Karla nodded that she understood.

The cave they were in was even colder than behind the waterfall and Karla began to shake from the cold. The man took her in his arms to offer some warmth, but the shivering continued. Finally, the man motioned that they should sleep till the searchers had tired of looking for them.

Pulling off his wet shirt and hanging it on a rock outcropping, the man stepped out of his shorts and added them to dry. He reached up and pulled a wool blanket from its hiding place above the wet clothes. He motioned that they should wrap themselves up as he only had one blanket.

Karla moved to get close to the man, but he pointed at her wet prison jumpsuit. She knew the wet cloth would drain her body heat if she remained in it but was reluctant to strip down in front of the man.

He leaned in close and whispered in her ear, "You need to get your wet things off. Just leave your panties on like my underwear. You are safe with me."

Karla unzipped her coveralls, dropping them down. She stepped out of them and hung them next to the man's clothes. Prison had provided no bra, so she covered up her breasts with both arms. The man dropped down onto the rock floor and motioned her to slide in beside him.

She placed her back against his stomach as the two wrapped themselves in the one wool blanket. Their shoes were kicked off as they drew their legs up together to save body heat.

With the prison behind her and her head resting on the man's arm, she fell asleep. The quiet of the cave was a relief from the nighttime torments of the prison. The man's arm across her side kept its distance from anything intimate and she soon heard him sleeping soundly. His warmth relieved the cold as both of them shared body heat.

Awaking suddenly, Karla's quick movement awoke the man. He moved his arm off her side. She realized where she was and that a dull filtered light was coming in from the outside. Where they had moved through the cleft in the rock, a dull light shown into the cave. Karla stood, covering her breasts with her arms.

The man jumped up and turned around to give her some privacy. She pulled her damp jumpsuit back on and stepped into her Chinese made sneakers. The man wrapped the wool blanket around her as he grabbed his clothes. Once dressed, the two strangers faced each other.

"Thank you," Karla said. "But who are you?"

"My name is Alberto. I live here on the island even though I'm originally from Italy."

"But you risked your life to get me out of there. Why? You don't know me."

"I just see too many people that come to our island get imprisoned for crimes that in other countries are nothing. I just want to help," Alberto said.

"Well, I'm grateful you did," Karla said. "But what do we do now? They'll be looking for me."

"I have a place that is safe until we can figure out what to do with you."

Alberto took the blanket from around Karla and folded it. He placed it back in its hiding spot and took her hand. Expecting a return through the waterfall, she was surprised when Alberto led her in the opposite direction. With the flashlight leading the way, the cave extended back from the waterfall. Soon they were walking in a large tunnel as it snaked through the hill. At points, they had to drop to all fours as the cave narrowed.

Soon, Karla heard the sound of the ocean. A faint light lit the tunnel ahead as Alberto made a stopping motion. Karla waited and hugged the cave wall as Alberto dropped to all fours and disappeared. After a short period, his face reappeared as he motioned her to follow. Karla dropped and crawled out of the cave into the sunlight.

The cave opening was nestled in some rocks at the base of a cliff. They had to climb on the rock faces to extract themselves from their little hole and once on top, the sun beat down to warm them. Alberto motioned they needed to find some cover in case anyone was on the cliffs above looking for them.

A short walk along the base of the cliff gained some higher ground with trees. Once under the canopy, they moved through the tropical rainforest as they paralleled the coast. Following the coast, a headland reared out toward the ocean, its steep cliffs dropped straight into the sea. They would have to work thier way to the top and cross the headland from above. The hot climb in the tropical sun soon caught up with them and Karla dropped to her knees. She grimaced at the pain but said nothing.

Alberto motioned for her to stay out of sight as he disappeared into the forest. Karla sat tight against a tree but began to nod off from the warm sun hitting her. Combined with the exertion and her limited food intake, Karla drifted off to sleep.

She awoke with a start from a noise behind her. As she twisted to see what had caused the noise, Alberto stuck his head around the tree, holding a water bottle. She took it eagerly and drank the entire contents. Then realizing what she had done, turned to Alberto.

"I'm sorry. I didn't save you any."

"That's OK. I drank my fill at the stream when I got it. But we need to keep moving so we can reach our destination before dark."

The day was more hiking and scrambling over headlands as the two traversed their way around the edge of the small island. Karla had seen a map of Vluchteling before her arrival and had a rough idea of where they were. While the only small town lay on the north side along with the castle and airport, the south side was all-natural forest. It held the nature preserve for the black tufted marmoset and was the reason people typically came to the island; seeing the primates outside the Amazon jungle.

As the sun sank below the distant hill, Alberto announced they were almost there. He again had her wait while he moved cautiously ahead to check. Satisfied, he returned to lead her to his safe hideout. Crossing a long flat spot in the forest, the two came upon a break leading down to the sea. Standing at the top of a cliff, Karla could make out a beautiful sandy beach through the tree trunks. Waves broke onto the white sand as the blue Caribbean beckoned.

Alberto ignored the beach and led Karla off to the side as they traversed the cliff, heading into a small canyon. With the beach as its mouth, the steep sided ravine had trees growing along its flanks. Vertical rock outcroppings jutted out of the hillside in numerous places and it was one such outcropping they now swung under to avoid.

Nestled just below the cliff was a small cabin, its roof almost part of the cliff itself. A small level spot on one end of the cabin offered space under the trees. Water sprang from the cliff at the end of the patio-like space. Karla followed Alberto as he stepped onto the patio from around the cabin.

A feeling of close safety came over Karla. If one didn't know where this place was, one would have a hard time stumbling on it. Alberto opened the cabin door and stepped inside. An elongated room held everything necessary for comfort. Against the cliff face that made up one wall was the kitchen, a sink with cabinets arrayed on a counter. A small closet in the corner held a toilet with a door for privacy.

A wall of glass windows looked out over the valley toward the beach. A bed as well as a table and chairs sat along the wall. A book case sat beside a couch and filled the remaining wall space.

"What is this place?" Karla asked.

"It's my grandfather's old hunting cabin," Alberto said. "Before they turned this part of the island into a nature preserve for the monkeys, the locals used to hunt over here. My grandfather arrived from Italy many years ago and bought the rights to this little canyon we're in. But the government closed it all off to save the monkeys. Now only wildlife researchers are allowed on this side of the island. And they only come during mating season when the monkeys are at their most active."

"And I'm safe here?"

"Yes, very," Alberto said. "As you can see, there are plenty of books to read while we figure out what to do next."

The statement about Karla still being a wanted fugitive got her thinking about her predicament. She slumped onto one of the chairs and dropped her head. Alberto noticed the change in attitude and offered some relief.

"Hey, we can get you out of that jumpsuit. I should have some clothes here that might fit you."

Karla perked up slightly as Alberto rummaged in a box he pulled from the lone closet in the room. He grabbed out two things and threw them to her. He pointed at the bathroom where she could change. Emerging in a tank top and running shorts, Alberto looked down at her legs. She glanced down at them for the first time.

"I'm sorry. You must be in pain," Alberto said, the bruising on Karla's knee and shin noticeable in the gathering darkness. "I'm afraid I don't have any ice here for you. But I might have some pain pills. Let me look."

He opened a drawer as Karla sat down in the chair again. A sweatshirt was lying on the table and she slipped it on. Alberto hadn't provided a bra but she was grateful to be out of her prison garb. Some pain medicine was soon found and she washed them down with a cup of water. She sat back and tried to relax.

Much had happened in the last twenty-four hours. And as Alberto lowered the blinds and looked for something to cook for dinner, Karla had time to study her rescuer. A small kerosene lamp was lit that helped with her evaluation.

Alberto was mid-thirties and above average height. He had dark hair worn rather long but not long like Italian soccer players. An unshaven face added to his continental appearance. As he moved around heating some canned goods, the smell soon had her mouth watering. Real food, even from a can was heaven after two months of prison food.

As Alberto turned to dish up dinner, Karla stared into his face with a certain gratitude mixed with indebtedness. She owed her freedom to this man who risked his life to get her out of her cell. And who knew how long it would have been before she was violated by the guards. *Yes, I owe this man a lot,* she thought.

Placing food on the table, Karla held her poise till Alberto sat down. Once he grabbed his fork, she dove into the food. It was gone in mere seconds and as she looked up, she noticed Alberto staring at her. Embarrassed, she felt her face grow red at her behavior. He pushed his plate across to her and stood up to open another can. Slowing down on her second helping, she looked at the man who had just given up his food to feed her. She slowly chewed her second helping and was still eating when Alberto finally sat down with a full plate.

He looked at her and sort of offered his portion again to her. She smiled back at him and shook her head, the portion she had eaten would fill her nicely. They both broke into broad smiles as they ate.

Chapter 9

Missoula, Montana

Jack swung his Toyota Tundra pickup truck onto the side street off U. S. Highway 12. It would take them toward the University of Montana campus where Kotone and her sister rented half of a duplex. Taking a right onto South 6th St., he felt his studded tires bite into he snow-covered street. While the main roads were bare from sun and vehicle traffic, the side streets were packed snow.

The squeak the tires made on the cold surface as he slowed announced their arrival. Kotone's sister stood at the window awaiting their return. Jack pulled up to the curb and turned off the engine.

"Jack, let me tell her my way," Kotone said. "You know what she's been through. She's very fragile."

Jack knew the fragile nature of Kotone's sister. She had been abducted onto a sailboat on the pretext of a modeling job. Driven to be a model, she had accepted the risk involved. At the time, she was reaching the age were models were either accepted in the business or not, and she had gone out on a limb to get accepted.

The client had been a pervert that proceeded to kidnap her and head across the Pacific Ocean with her as his toy for the voyage. Kotone had called Jack for help and only with luck had, he tracked the sailboat down and rescued the sister. Kotone had taken her to Montana to find a new life away from modeling.

An accomplished computer programmer with an advanced degree from Berkley, the sister had landed a job at the university. And now the sister's life was about to undergo another convulsion. Jack followed Kotone to the door as he followed her into the house.

"How was Stanley?" Komatsu asked.

"It was fun Sis," Kotone said as she pulled off her coat and hung it by the front door, Jack followed suit and removed two layers. They stepped into the small living room and sat down where Kotone continued, "We have something to tell you."

"You guys are getting married," the sister answered.

"How did you know? We just decided on the drive back from Stanley. We haven't told a soul."

"You two have been dancing around the whole issue for how many years now?" Komatsu asked. "On again, off again, then back to being on again. Get on with it finally. Get married, live happily ever after."

"But that's where you come in," Kotone said. "I don't want to leave you."

"Look, big sis. You've been trying to take care of me since Hawaii. I'm fine now. I like my job and the people I work with. I like my neighbors and the friends I've made here in Missoula. Things are good."

"But I'm still worried," Kotone said.

"Well, where are you planning to live after you get married, Jackson?" Komatsu asked.

Jack finally spoke up. "No, we thought Missoula would be a good compromise. Jackson was a little too small when Kotone lived there before. And Carl and Stacey are here."

"Well, that settles it then." Komatsu said. "You won't be leaving me at all. Just giving me a little space. And besides, I'm gaining a brother-in-law."

"Then you don't mind?" Kotone asked.

"Go forth with my blessing. But when's the big date?"

Kotone sat silent for a long time at the question. Neither she nor Jack were ready to spring the other news.

"What is it?" Komatsu finally asked.

"We decided not to have a big day. You know my two failures at the marriage thing and

Jack has one. We decided to do it quietly. No big event."

"But can we have a party afterward?" Komatsu asked.

"Sure, a party would be nice. But first a quick drive to Jackpot, Nevada and then we want someplace warm for a honeymoon," Kotone said.

Komatsu jumped up, startling the betrothed. She ran to her room and returned with a magazine. She quickly flipped through looking for an article.

"Here it is," Komatsu offered. "Sounds very romantic and with wild animals too. Warm water and sandy beaches are thrown in extra. It's a little island in the Caribbean that just opened for tourists last year. Up until then it was sort of a private island owned by some Dutch guy. Says they just built a new airport and set aside half the island as a nature preserve."

"And what wild animals do we get to deal with?" Jack asked.

"Monkeys," Komatsu replied. "Black Tufted Marmosets actually. It's the only place outside the Amazon jungle that you can see them."

"And where is this place," Kotone asked.

"It's part of the Dutch Antilles, but not really. Something about the grand Duchy of Luxembourg getting the island by marrying some

Dutch guy back in the 18th Century. But it's part of the Grenadines. You know, Dutch, French, and British islands all mixed up. The place is called Vluchteling.

A trip to Jackpot, Nevada provided the marriage ceremony while a return to Boise gave them the plane they needed to catch to get to Miami. A day shopping for tropical island wear left them at the airport catching a flight to St. Vincent the next day. An overnight stay and finally a short plane flight got them finally to Vluchteling.

Jack sat with a local having a quick chat about his home. Kotone sat two rows back in the small twin engine prop plane. With only fourteen seats on the Twin Otter passenger plane, they knew they were lucky to get two seats on short notice.

"Yes, our island didn't have air service until last year. A ferry used to run twice a week between St. Vincent and Vluchteling."

"And what's your history? Something about Luxembourg with a Dutch guy?" Jack asked.

"Actually, the entire island is owned by the Dupong family. Emile Dupong is our Governor, as the English would call him. In Dutch, the word implies a more possessive state."

"And he owns the whole enchilada?"

The man gave him a quizzical look until Jack offered a translation. He smiled at Jack's translation.

"Yes, as you say it, the whole enchilada," the man said. "The houses you will see have a ninety-nine-year lease, which was signed many years ago. Some have run the ninety-nine years and have been renewed. Our Governor hasn't thrown any residents off the island yet."

"But still, he is like a dictator, isn't he? His word is final."

"Oh, you Americans, you place much too much emphasis on what you call personal freedom," the local man answered. "We are Europeans, we consider ourselves more in Europe than North America, and we have a different view of life. Our lives are shaped by this man. He built the airport with family money and opened up the tourism business for the benefit of the residents. But the visas to visit are limited as we have limited hotel space for visitors. As you will see, we have no mega-resorts or high-rise hotels. Our island will remain simple like it has been since our founding in 1722."

"That's a long time. I'm surprised the locals have never risen up and asked for their independence," Jack said.

"But why?" he asked. "We have all we need. You Americans value stuff too much. We value the good life. I guess our dictator, as you call him, is a benevolent dictator. I've often heard that a benevolent dictator is the optimum style of government. So maybe we have something the rest of the world needs?"

"Well, I just want to relax on the beach, see your monkeys and soak up the sun," Jack offered.

"And we offer all of that like no one else," the man said.

"By the way, I'm Jack."

"Roland's the name. When you get settled, come and see me. I live over the Belgian Waffle shop on the Promenade. Everyone knows me."

"Glad to meet you Roland. And I'll stop by and say hi first thing," Jack offered.

The small plane settled suddenly, and Jack's stomach reacted to the drop. He looked out the window and saw a few specks of land in a broad ocean. He felt another dip as the flaps were adjusted for landing. He swiveled around and caught Kotone talking with her seatmate. Jack faced forward as the plane went into a slight dive.

Jack stared out the window at nothing but ocean, the only indication of their height was when they passed over a small skiff on the water. Jack realized the plane was very low by the two fishermen waving up at the plane. Still, nothing but ocean was visible out the window. Concerned that the plane was landing in the water, Jack tensed up and craned his neck to look as far forward as he could see.

Off the starboard wing a small bit of land was visible. He looked out the lee side of the plane and saw the harbor with a castle-like fortress sitting on the other side. Just as he looked out his side, the ground came up and the wheels hit. The two engines raced as the plane slowed and the seatbelt pulled tight across his waist. Turning to Roland, his new friend smiled.

"It might be a new runway, but it's short. They didn't have much room to squeeze it on this side of the harbor."

"I see the waterfront," Jack offered.

"That's about the extent of the houses. Two streets are it," Roland said. "Most of the island belongs to the monkeys."

"Nice looking fortress over there though. Looks like it stopped a pirate attack or two."

"Actually, that's where the island gets its name. Vluchteling, in Dutch, means refugee. We have always been a safe port from pirates and hurricanes."

The plane stopped by the terminal and the engines shut down. The passengers filed off the plane into the warm tropical breeze. On the hillside above the airport, palms swayed in the trade winds famous in this part of the Caribbean Sea.

Kotone joined Jack as they followed behind the others into the small terminal building. As the passengers gathered at the closed sliding door marked for baggage claim, Jack put his arm around his wife. *Feels special somehow,* Jack thought. It was the same Kotone that he had held in his arms many times, but with the ceremony behind them and the official paper from the State of Nevada, things felt different. A nice different.

The crew slid the garage like door up and began tossing bags from their cart onto the metal fixture sitting low off the floor. Passengers grabbed their bags and headed toward the two desks marked Customs.

Jack waited as Kotone retrieved her bag. Following the crowd, they each took their place in opposite lines. The line moved slowly ahead as the Custom officials did a cursory job inspecting each piece of luggage and stamping passports.

Reaching his official first, Jack threw his bag and carryon onto the inspection station. Confirming that they were his bags, the official rummaged briefly through each one. Examining Jack's passport, the official stamped the page and waved Jack toward the exit.

The exit door stood a short twenty feet away and Jack noticed two armed police standing to one side. He took up a spot on the opposite side of the exit and leaned against the wall. Kotone stepped up to her inspector and hefted her bags up for examination.

"Are these your bags?" the Customs official asked.

"Yes, sir," Kotone shot back.

"Please open them for inspection then."

Jack looked around as Kotone complied with the request, his police instincts were always processing any scene. He noticed multiple video cameras aimed at the inspection tables. *Strange*, he thought. *Seems a little overkill for a back-water place like this.*

From the corner of his eye he saw the police take up a more focused stance. Gone was the chit chat that they had been carrying on when Jack first took up his position against the wall. *They are standing ready and focused on where*? Jack thought. He studied the angle of their attention and saw it was on Kotone. The hairs on the back of his neck stood up as he pulled himself off the wall.

The official's arm and hand were deep inside Kotone's checked bag searching. His demeanor changed suddenly, and he withdrew his hand. In its grip was a plastic baggy with a white substance inside. Jack saw Kotone's face turn to shock as she stared at the bag now held high.

"What is this?" he asked.

Kotone was speechless at the question and continued her stare. The official opened the top of the baggy and stuck his pinky finger into the powder. With a small sample stuck to his finger, he rubbed it on his lower gum.

"Bringing illegal drugs into Vluchteling is a very serious offense," he said. "We take these matters very seriously here. This isn't Amsterdam where such things are tolerated."

"But that isn't mine," Kotone finally said. "I've never seen that before."

"You admitted this was your bag." The official waved the police over. Jack moved with the two officers toward Kotone. Kotone looked up at Jack's approach.

"Jack, what's going on?" Kotone asked.

"Sir do not interfere," one of the policemen said. He grabbed Jack's arm and stopped him from approaching the Customs area. The second officer stepped over to Kotone and took both her arms and pulled them behind her. Placing handcuffs on her wrists, he led her toward a door marked 'Official Only'.

"Jack, do something," Kotone yelled.

Starting to move toward her, the policeman redoubled his grip on Jack's arm to hold him. Jack turned to the officer, rage building quickly.

"Unless you want to join her in custody, I'd suggest you leave the area now," the Vluchteling cop said. He emphasized the word now for Jack's benefit.

Roland stepped over and grabbed Jack's free arm. He pulled his fellow passenger toward the exit and Jack moved with him, the police officer letting his grip go.

Once outside, Roland pulled Jack toward a spot on the seawall overlooking the harbor. Roland took up a spot between the terminal and Jack in an attempt confine the situation.

"You don't want to get arrested yourself," Roland said. "They are very serious about illegal drugs on this island. They won't hesitate throwing you in jail if you show any sign of inferring."

"They just took my wife away," Jack stammered. "You expect me to do nothing?"

"Come, my friend. We can contact a lawyer and see if we can help your wife," Roland said.

The two picked up their bags and started walking toward town. The distance was short, and it gave Jack time to process what had just happened.

"Where are you staying tonight?" Roland asked.

"We hadn't made a reservation yet," Jack said.

"Then you'll stay at my house. And tomorrow we'll be on your wife's case, first thing."

* * *

"Your Excellency," the Customs man said. "I don't know how that happened. Our man in St. Vincent is supposed to screen for only women traveling alone."

"Well, he was bound to make this mistake sometime," Emile Dupong said. "We don't give him much time to fully screen the passengers."

"But look here, her passport says Kotone Butler and no others with that last name were on the plane," the official said. "And her passport has her listed as single. And we know she sat with a man from Vluchteling on the plane. And she has no reservations on the island so that wouldn't show if she was traveling with someone."

"We've been lucky up till now," Emile said.

"Should we drop the charges with an excuse then, your Excellency? There will be others."

Emile Dupong, heir to the throne of the Duchy of Luxembourg stood and contemplated that idea. *Yes, there will be other good-looking single females flying to his little island soon enough,* he thought.

He considered that course of action and then changed his mind. The Asian woman intrigued him. The European women that floated through his net were fun, but he was looking for something different. He had been with Asian women before in his travels and he had always been satisfied by their seductive ways. Maybe this woman would stir those memories for him.

"No, we shall proceed," Emile ordered. "This old man she seems to be attached to will not interfere. He will run home to get his government involved. By the time all the bureaucrats get involved, I will be done with her. She'll have escaped off the island and who knows what her fate would be when they finally come calling."

"Very well, your Excellency," the Customs official said. "The usual preparations then."

The official bowed and exited the small room that overlooked the interior of the terminal. As the door shut, Emile stood and stared at the now empty terminal. *Yes, Asian women have always been like tigers in bed,* he thought. An excitement coursed through his body at the thought of a new conquest.

Chapter 10

Vluchteling Island, the Caribbean

Karla Schmidt was relaxing in the stone hot tub that sat a short way from her cabin. Finally alone, she felt safe enough to take a relaxing soak and attempt to wash the memories of the past two months out of her soul.

She stared up at the rock cliff that sheltered her hiding spot. Besides the cabin that almost grew naturally out of the rock face, a small flat patio led to this bathing area. Two pipes led to a clawed-out depression in the natural rock where a large tub had been chiseled into the rock outcropping. Two plastic pipes funneled water from somewhere off in the forest.

Looking back toward the water source, she saw the pipe that emptied hot water into the tub ran several hundred feet along the steep hillside and up the hill slightly. Somewhere over there was a natural hot spring that someone had tapped. The cold-water pipe came from a spring just twenty feet away. A small cascade of water tumbled down the cliff and was gathered in a spring box and fed into the pipe.

Mixing the two water sources provided a pleasant temperature for soaking. Karla moved the hot water pipe and directed more into her bath. The splash mixed in as she felt the hot water swirl around her body. Thoughts of prison and all that went on there melted away.

Her thoughts moved to the man that had rescued her from her private hell. Alberto was gone this morning when she awoke. He had played the perfect gentleman last night and had taken the couch in the small cabin while she had spread out on the queen size bed quite alone. A note form Alberto told her he would be gone for the day checking on how to get her off the island. It also instructed her to stay near the cabin to avoid any patrols that might be out looking for her.

Alberto had said that it might be necessary to hide out in the cabin for a while as the authorities would be watching closely for any boats leaving. Things needed to settle for a bit, he had written.

Karla was fine with enjoying her current spot on earth. She had food, books to read, warm sunny weather and what appeared to be a well concealed hideout. Her mind eased with each tick of the clock as the hot water did its job.

Then she heard it. Or, at least, thought she heard something. With the nearby pipes splashing onto the patio, it was hard to tell. She sat up, grabbed the pipes and pulled them under water.

Their noise disappeared. In the stillness, just the overflowing rivulets of water made a small sound. Karla strained to hear as she cocked her head from side to side for direction.

She heard it again, a small crunch of boot on twigs. She swiveled her head and detected the direction. It appeared to be coming from the other side of the cabin. Another louder snap of a dead branch being stepped on brought her fully upright. She looked around for escape but it was too late.

A man came around the edge of the cabin and walked straight toward her. Alberto smiled as he caught sight of her sitting in the rock tub. He waved slightly, and his smile grew bigger. Realizing she was naked and her top half was out of the water, Karla covered her breasts quickly with one arm and slid down, the water covering her slightly. Alberto stopped a respectful distance away.

"I see you found our tub," he said. "And you figured out the pipes for mixing?"

Karla nodded that she had, all the while trying to maintain her modesty. She had been naked with men before, so it wasn't that holding her back. And Alberto certainly had saved her life, literally. She studied the man as he talked.

Very good looking, tanned, fit and certainly young enough. But not too young. She had enough of those men her own age. They were interested in only one thing and when that was satisfied, all they wanted to do was get back to whatever stupid stuff young men did.

Alberto however, had something else, just standing there and smiling. Her body went funny in that way she remembered when the juices started flowing. And she knew where that typically led to. *I'm OK with that,* she thought. *If not for him, some prison guard might be* . . . she shuddered at the thought of what had almost happened to her.

"Have you had dinner yet?" Alberto asked. "I brought some fresh food from town. How about I throw something together?"

"Sounds wonderful," Karla said. She glanced at her towel laying on a chair a short distance away. She noticed Alberto catch her glance. He stepped toward the chair and grabbed the towel.

Holding it up, he held it between his two hands as he held his arms out. He stared at her in anticipation of watching her climb out of the tub before she wrapped the towel around her. She hesitated.

Alberto recognized the hesitation and like a gentleman, flipped the towel over his head as he twisted around to face the cabin. With both arms pressed behind and over his head, the towel was still offered, but giving her privacy now.

Karla smiled at his gesture and stepped carefully out of the tub. She took the towel being offered and wrapped it around her, tucking one end just over her breasts. Alberto turned around and smiled at her, then walked off toward the kitchen area. She felt her knees shake slightly from the look he had given her.

Dinner was fresh chicken with a salad. After the previous day's heavenly meal of canned goods, this meal was off the scale. Alberto pulled out a bottle of French white wine for the occasion. They both offered repeated toasts to Karla's release from prison. With the bottle drained, Alberto pulled a second bottle out of his backpack.

"No, too much," Karla protested.

"But this wine goes with the dessert I selected," Alberto explained. "We don't have to finish it tonight."

"Just one glass then," Karla relented. Her head was already spinning after her long soak, the dehydration combining with alcohol. The first bottle had seemed to disappear as she sucked in liquid.

Alberto pulled a cardboard box that held a large piece of chocolate cake from his pack. He placed it on a plate and gathered two forks.

"Now, chocolate cake and red wine, the perfect nighttime treat," Alberto said. He took a fork full of cake and slid it into his mouth. Karla took her own bite. Holding his wine glass high, Karla clinked her glass against his in another toast to freedom.

Yes, I do owe this man a lot, Karla thought. She took more cake as Alberto seductively ate his bite. She stared at the man's mouth as he slowly chewed. His gaze was riveted on her as she felt the moisture between her legs increase. As he sipped his wine, his gaze never wavered. The moisture grew.

When they were down to the last bite of cake, he scooped it up and offered it to her. Karla opened her mouth slightly as Alberto slid the fork in. Closing, her mouth pulled the last bit of chocolate from the fork. He carefully pulled his fork out, continuing his stare.

Reaching over, he took her head in his hand. Leaning forward, he tipped his head to one side and kissed her on the lips. Returning to his spot, his tongue wiped the chocolate residue from his lips into his mouth. Karla felt the spot between her legs go from moist to wet. She shifted in her chair to try and ignore the distraction.

When Alberto leaned in for another kiss, Karla put her hand behind his head and pulled him tighter. The kiss lingered as the two moved slightly to increase their closeness. When Alberto slipped his hand onto her breast, her legs moved instinctively further apart.

Continuing their kiss, Alberto's hand found its way lower. Karla's legs spread to welcome the attention as Alberto pushed her shorts aside. His fingers found the wetness and slid around in the lubrication. Karla leaned back into her chair as Alberto slid down to kneel on the floor. As his head moved lower, her legs moved higher. The two met halfway.

After some careful attention, Alberto scooped her into his arms and carried her to the bed. As she was placed onto the covers, Alberto slid her shorts and wet panties down her legs. With full access, Alberto pulled her legs sky ward and bent over.

* * *

"I'm sorry to be the one to tell you Mr. Wesley, but this case is very difficult," the lawyer said. Jack and Roland had headed first thing in the morning to one of the four attorneys on the island. Roland had explained that the one they were seeing was the only one that took criminal cases. The other two typically handled estates and business dealings.

"What are you saying. There's no chance?" Jack asked.

"The prosecution usually has a very convincing case," the attorney said. "They have the video feeds. They show the jury footage of your wife admitting that it's her bag just before the official pulls out illegal drugs. Very simple and the jury usually finds the defendant guilty. We are a very conservative people here on this island. We see the outside world and all its problems. They naturally resist any such thing getting a foothold here."

"Yes, Roland has said the same thing," Jack said. "But her bag is unlocked the whole time the airline has it. Anyone could place the drugs in her bag."

"But for what purpose?" the attorney asked. "There is nothing to gain for anyone to see your wife imprisoned here. No one knows your wife here. So, what would be the purpose of entrapping her?"

"I don't know that. But I know she didn't have any drugs. Someone somewhere planted them on her,' Jack said.

"But how do we prove that? Justice happens quickly here I'm afraid," the attorney said. "We have a court date tomorrow. Can you provide some information to me by then?"

Jack sat back. There was no way he could accomplish anything that fast. He didn't know the language and he was in foreign lands. His police detective skills would be next to useless here.

The attorney added. "Mr. Wesley, I'm afraid you need to prepare yourself for the fact that your wife will be sentenced tomorrow. And from past cases, you can assume it will be a ten-year sentence."

Hearing the probable fate of Kotone, Jack slumped in his chair. A wave of despair washed over him while he contemplated her fate.

"Where will the sentence be carried out, if she's convicted?" Jack asked.

"The fortress on the point that you saw. There is a prison on the lower levels I'm afraid."

Jack's despair turned to rage at the thought of Kotone being held in a cell in an 19th century rock fortress. As his temper grew, Roland placed his arm on Jack's back.

"Be careful my friend. The authorities here are very careful where security is concerned. They will not tolerate any dissension. Remember, this island is owned by one man. And he is very connected to the powers in Europe. He and his family have been doing what they choose with this island for over two hundred years."

"And you people put up with that?" Jack asked "Doesn't the injustice bother you?"

"But Mr. Wesley, we have our justice," the attorney said. "Your wife will have a trial in front of the good citizens of this island. Evidence will be presented. If you have any contradictory evidence, we can offer that in her defense."

"And with less than a day to find any, what are my chances?" Jack said.

"Just because we are not like your American justice system, doesn't mean ours is wrong. From what I read, your trials can take years. Where is the justice in that?"

The man is right, but I'm in no mood to discuss our two different legal systems, Jack thought. Jack stood and shook the attorney's hand. Opening the door, he left without saying any more. Roland scrambled to catch up. Once outside, the two sat on the seawall by the harbor.

"I know it's not what you wanted to hear, Jack. If there is anything I can do, please let me know."

"No, thanks Roland. I just need to get my head around the fact that Kotone will be locked up after tomorrow. Maybe I can find some information on what happens between here and whereever the drugs are planted. We can get a new trial on appeal."

"Appeal where?" Roland asked. "As I said, this is a one man owned island and quite independent. There are no higher courts to take your case to."

Jack tried to maintain a stoic front the next day at the trial. When Kotone was led into court, he attempted to go to her but was stopped by two policemen. Her look of fear that she passed to him said all he needed to know. *Whatever the outcome, their little island justice would not stand*, Jack thought

The proceedings moved along quickly, the case built entirely on the video tape of the search and the subsequent discovery of drugs. The Customs official swore he had found the drugs in Kotone's bag after she admitted that the bag was hers.

A lab tech was sworn in and added testimony that he had conducted the tests and determined that indeed, the evidence the Customs official had recovered was methamphetamine. The jury all looked at Kotone at that announcement. Jack knew from thirty years of attending trials that this one was moving quickly to the wrong conclusion.

When the defense was allowed to present a case, Kotone's attorney called Jack as a witness. Jack held his emotions in check as he faced Kotone at the defendant's table.

"Mr. Wesley, could you describe the circumstances that brought you to our island?" the attorney asked.

Jack proceeded to describe how he and Kotone had been married the previous week and traveled to Vluchteling for their honeymoon. Then the attorney asked the pertinent questions.

"And was your luggage in your possession the entire time?

"No sir. We checked our bags with the airlines," Jack answered.

"And the bags were locked and secured when you turned them over to the airline?"

"No, no bag can be locked. The security officers require unlocked bags for their inspection."

"So, you contend that anyone could have planted these illegal drugs in Ms. Butler's bag at any time?"

"Yes, of course. There are reported thefts from people's bags all the time. By the same measure, someone could place an item in someone's bags."

Satisfied at the argument he had presented to the jury, the attorney turned Jack over for cross examination. The prosecutor stood up and adjusted his suit.

"Mr. Wesley, do you or your wife have family here on Vluchteling?"

"No sir."

"Friends perhaps?"

"No, we know no one on Vluchteling," Jack answered.

"But it is your contention that someone planted drugs in your wife's bag. For what purpose would anyone do that? You admit you know no one here. So, there would be no one that harbored ill toward you."

"I don't know why someone would do such a thing."

"But you expect us to believe this tale of a mystery person planting drugs so we can lock your wife up on our island, wasting our poor citizen's money."

Jack held his temper at the prosecutor's comments. *How the hell do I know who or why someone's doing it?* Jack thought. He fought for self-control and tried not to look at Kotone. Her sitting in the dock at risk only made him madder.

"Is there a question in there?" Jack threw back at the prosecutor. "I just know that my wife does not do drugs and would never knowingly have such things on her person."

"You say you have been married to the defendant for a little over a week now," the prosecutor continued. "How long did you know her before you married?"

"We've known each other for over four years."

"So I guess you overlooked the two homicides she committed in the United States?"

"Those were judged self-defense and . . ." Jack started to say.

"Thank you. That will be all. The witness is excused," the prosecutor said.

"But there were . . ." Again, Jack was cut off by the presiding judge.

"Mr. Wesley. You are done. Please return to your seat," the judge ordered.

Jack stood and walked slowly back and took a seat, careful not to look at Kotone. He knew if he did, he would fly at the policeman, take his gun and shoot it out to free her. He sat down, his head hanging. He awaited the final outcome.

The jury was released to determine Kotone's guilt or innocence while Jack and the attorney waited just outside the courtroom. They were soon called back. As Kotone stood next to the attorney the jury pronounced Kotone guilty. Jack slumped in the chair as Kotone was sentenced to ten years in prison.

When Kotone was led out of the courtroom after the jury had been dismissed Jack's heart was ripped apart.

"Jack, please, do something!" Kotone yelled before she was pulled through the side door. He sat motionless. Finally finding the will to just stand and leave the building, he walked along the seawall by the harbor, deep in thought.

Other tourists walked by, gaily recounting their excursion to see the island monkeys that morning. With ice cream in one hand and a drink in the other, they ignored Jack as he walked along by himself.

The bastards will die for this, Jack swore to himself. *I will come back and burn their little island playground down.*

Jack's mind raced as to what needed to be done and who he needed to ask for help. One name popped up. This would be a job for his Marine Corps partner that had always been there for each other. *Lamarcus won't fail me now,* Jack thought.

Reaching the end of the seawall, the beach along the harbor gave way to the rocky promontory jutting out, Jack sat down. He looked up at the looming fortress above him. Its thick rock walls shouting impregnable to him. Soon Kotone would be encased in rock deep inside. *But not for anything close to ten years,* he thought. He didn't know how long it would take, but he wouldn't rest until she was free.

As Jack continued sitting on the seawall the sun slowly set into the Caribbean. The night time scene took on a romantic flair as the lights lining the promenade came on. Tourists strolled down to where Jack sat but turned around before reaching him, his sullenness evident to the strollers. They all realized walking back toward town was a more appropriate direction.

As he sat, staring at the fortress, a voice found him. Jack ignored it. But it was insistent. Looking down to the end of the beach, Jack saw someone he knew, one of only two on the island.

In the low light, Jack made out Roland more by his body than his face. A little gesture to join him got Jack off his rock ledge. Dropping down onto the beach, Jack walked over to where Roland had motioned them. The two men stood next to a rock outcropping away from the seawall.

"Jack, I had to meet you. No one must see us together."

"Why?' Jack asked.

"I wasn't at the trial today because they got to me. I've heard others on the island talk of such things, but I'd never experienced it."

"Who's they? And what did they get to you about?" Jack asked.

"For helping you," Roland said. "I got a carefully worded suggestion to stop associating with you."

"By who? What is going on?"

"Let's just say that a certain important person on the island suggested that my business would suffer if I offered any more help to you."

"Jesus, what kind of hellhole have I been transported to?" Jack asked.

"Worse than I ever knew," Roland answered. "Now I'm beginning to believe what people have been whispering."

"For God's sake, Roland, tell me."

"Well, ever since our new governor took over, things have been different here. He's the son of the family that has owned the island for centuries. He considers himself one of the most eligible bachelors of Europe. Has quite the reputation back on the Continent."

"And you think he's setting up tourists?" Jack asked.

"When the airport was finished a couple of years ago, all of a sudden, young women were being arrested for drug smuggling. Never men, always women. And always young."

"What are you telling me?"

"And Jack, the women are always alone," Roland admitted "The trials are handled quickly, and the women never have someone here to speak for them. Just lost souls thrown to whatever fate. Your wife was a first. The first time someone stood up for any of the women. You two having different last names and not being seated together probably threw them off. The attorney told me that this afternoon."

"What happens to them after the trial?"

"No one knows. I suppose they are jailed. But the jailers are mute on what goes on inside. And the jailers are all hired in Europe, ex-military. There are no islanders working inside the fortress. As for the prisoners, we all assume they are serving their ten-year sentence. Since its been going on for just two years, no one has been released."

Jack looked up at the fortress as he processed everything Roland was saying. If true, Kotone was in more danger than he originally thought. If someone was trapping all these women, they were doing it for a heinous reason. Jack now would have to work fast to keep her from falling into whatever abyss someone had created.

"Jack, you need to leave the island right away. It's too dangerous for you here. You know too much about what they're doing," Roland said. "I have a friend with a boat that can take you to St. Vincent tonight. And one other thing."

Roland passed a slip of paper to Jack. It would mean everything. But first, Jack had to retreat. The fight would resume another day.

Chapter 11

Cambridge, Massachusetts

"Cap'n, there's a phone call for you. Sounds long distance," the clerk yelled across the police station. The Cambridge Police Department was located off Massachusetts Avenue as it run from MIT to Harvard. Having two of the premier universities situated within its jurisdiction contrasted with the lower socio-economic sections of Cambridge near the Somerville Town Line.

It was this local police station that Captain Lamarcus Lewis commanded. His job was to keep the Somerville and Everett undesirables from infiltrating into Cambridge and upsetting the college professors. Rich residential neighborhoods around Harvard University had to be protected at all cost. And now he had a phone call interrupting his weekly morning inspirational talk to his troops. He walked in his office and picked up the phone.

"Captain Lewis here."

"Lamarcus, Jack. I need your help."

"Jack Wesley. What a thrill it is to hear from you, not. And what's with the shitty phone you're using?"

"Shut up and listen," Jack said. "I'm in St. Vincent. That's in the Caribbean."

"Good place for you. The further the hell you are away from me the better. You know the last time you got me involved, you almost . . ."

"Lamarcus, they have Kotone," Jack stopped him from finishing.

"Who the hell is Kotone?" Lamarcus asked. "Oh, she that women you talked about. The one that whacked the sheriff."

"Shut up Marine and listen. I married that woman a week ago and now she's been sucked into some bad shit. She's in an island prison down here that makes Papillion look like Rebecca of Sunny Brook Farm."

"Christ, Jack. What do you want from me?"

"I'm going to war. I'm looking for someone to watch my backside."

"You know I've always been there for you. But Jesus Jack, I'm a Captain. I've got responsibilities. I can't just drop things and run off to the Caribbean."

"Fair enough," Jack said. "I was just asking."

A long pause followed as the line crackled with static. Lamarcus knew his friend was desperate and desperate people got killed. He needed to be with his friend to settle him down and get his mind right. Going to war meant serious things had to happen. And key among them was clear thinking. That's what got the jarheads to live another day.

"Jack, this is a department phone line. Call me tonight at home. I'll see what I can do," Lamarcus said. He knew he couldn't let a fellow Marine go to war by himself. Lamarcus started putting things together in his mind as to what Jack would ask for when they talked later. Logistics to the Caribbean would be the first hurdle. *I hope Jack has the Navy ready as I can't swim to wherever the hell he is,* Lamarcus thought.

* * *

Jack's second call was to another old friend. After a quick greeting, Jack jumped into the business at hand. A third call was necessary to finish his preliminary work.

Satisfied that the wheels were in motion, Jack caught a flight out of St. Vincent bound for San Juan, Puerto Rico. A brief stopover in the airport and a second flight took him to Tortola in the British Virgin Islands. A taxi delivered him to a gated compound that sat high on a hill overlooking Tortola Harbor

Jack scanned the gate area for an intercom among the ivy. Locating the button, he buzzed.

"Yes, who is it?" a female voice squawked out of the speaker.

"Jack Wesley to see Donald French."

The hiss of the cheap speaker mounted in the rock wall surrounding the compound continued. Jack waited for a reply. He looked behind him at the view over the houses across the street. The Caribbean Sea lay below in blue splendor. Tall palm trees swayed in the gentle trade winds. The smell of lush vegetation flowed to his nose. The speaker came back to life.

"He doesn't know any Jack Wesley, mate," a male voice announced through the speaker.

"Bridget on Vluchteling sent me" Jack said.

Another long spell passed with nothing but a light hiss from the wall speaker. As Jack waited by the gate, he watched three sailboats that appeared to be locked in a race below him. The spinnakers announced the wind direction at the sea's surface as all three big colorful sails pulled their boats down wind. Jack jumped slightly in response to a voice behind him. He turned around to face a man stepping around the rock wall on the other side of the wrought iron gate.

"Bridget sent you now. Why ever would she have done that?"

"Mr. French. Bridget thought you might help me. I have a problem on Vluchteling and she seemed to think you were the one to supply some answers."

Jack noticed the man's reaction at the mention of Vluchteling island. In his fifties he appeared a cautious man. Wearing shorts and a sleeveless shirt hanging loose, the man looked as if he worked out regularly. And from the bulge Jack noticed in the small of his back, he was armed. *Yes, a very careful man,* Jack thought.

"That bloody place. I'm sorry mate. I've spent the last year making sure those types were out of my life. And that you found me here doesn't make me happy. Bridget needs to keep her yap a little tighter."

"I think I understand your reluctance to help," Jack said. "But just some information, please. Ten minutes of your time is all I ask."

"And the bloody ten minutes of my life could get me killed. No sorry mate, I can't help you. So just bugger off to where you came from." Donald turned to leave but stopped short.

"They have my wife," Jack offered. "If what Bridget said is true, you're SAS, Britain's finest. No wonder you left them.

Donald turned back and stared at Jack. His hesitation spoke volumes.

"I spent four years in the United States Marine Corps. Duty, honor, country. You left

Vluchteling because you could not abide what they were doing."

"But I'm retired now. Just trying to stay alive in my little corner of heaven. I don't need those silly bastards raining on my parade here. No, I'm still sorry. I can't help you."

Donald again attempted to leave but Jack offered one last comment. Jack knew it was a long shot, but he had tried every other enticement for the man.

"Last year, the Albert Hall in London," Jack said. "Cypriot terrorists attempted to kill the Queen and the British Prime Minister."

The statement caught his attention and Donald turned back around. He grew closer to Jack.

"Other people died. So, what?" Donald asked

"All masterminded by the Russian mob," Jack finished.

"Who are you?" Donald asked.

Jack knew the Cypriot connection to the assassination attempt was public knowledge, but the Russian organized crime connection was very hush hush. The four governments that had been the subject of the attack wanted the Russian connection kept under wraps. Affairs would be evened in the quiet of clandestine operations. Jack assumed that an officer in the British Special Forces would be privy to the information.

Donald asked again. "How do you know about the Russian connection. Only . . ." He stopped and stared at Jack. "You're him, aren't you?"

Jack let the question linger and stared back. Donald reached behind the wall to punch in the code that controlled the gate. The iron gate began to swing open and Jack walked in. Donald hit the control again and the gate closed.

Once inside the house, Donald offered Jack a drink. Over water with ice and lemon, the two resumed their conversation.

"They spoke of a man and a woman that stopped the whole thing. Both disappeared to Germany soon after. But they never mentioned who it had been," Donald said. "Just that Australian cop ran up for the credit. What was his name now?"

"Graham" Jack offered.

"Yes, Graham, hero of the day," Donald said. "Knighted by the Queen six months ago. Amazing what he did all by himself."

"Yes, good man Graham. Deserves all that he has received for his service to Queen and country."

"But the mystery man and woman. Whispered about but never mentioned. A bloke I know in Scotland Yard mentioned to me a man was picked up that night with a gun.. Had the bloke dead to right. One phone call and it all disappeared."

"And I'll guess that gun had a silencer on it, sort of like the CIA might use."

"Now that you mention it, my friend might have mentioned such an accessory." Donald increased the intensity of his stare as he realized who was sitting across from him. "Now, what kind of call could make such a thing just disappear."

"Shit flows downhill is a favorite excuse in my country," Jack said. "I guess it flowed the right way that day."

"Yes, I guess it did," Donald said. "So, you were there?"

"Not saying, one way or another. But I am here now, and I'd like your help."

"I'm listening. But mind you, if you're CIA, you don't need my help."

"I'm hardly CIA," Jack laughed. "Just retired police after a stint in the Marines. But as I said, they have my wife. I'm thinking you can help with recon."

"For Queen and country, you have my undivided attention. I guess I kind of owe you one," Donald said. His smile helped Jack realize that things might work out after all.

Chapter 12

Vluchteling Island, Caribbean

Karla Schmidt awoke with a headache from too much wine the night before. Her head swirled from what had happened afterward. Now, lying beside Alberto, she regretted what had happened. Still captive on the island, she realized this man held her life in his hands.

Getting naked with him had just changed the dynamics of the whole situation. Where before, she was a damsel in distress, now she was a naked intimate damsel in distress. She wasn't sure but the difference was important. How important soon became evident.

Alberto awoke at his partner stirring next to him. He reached over and took her in his arms and kissed her softly on the neck. Her reaction didn't set well. There was a certain revulsion at the touch he offered and that was dangerous for her. She pushed the feelings aside as her life depended on it.

"What's for breakfast?" She asked, trying to change the subject.

"Let me see," Alberto said as he moved in with his mouth on one of her breasts. She cringed slightly as his lips took her nipple in and his tongue gently massaged it to erection. His hand drifted lower.

But where it was met be a welcoming moist spot the night before, this morning she kept her legs together, her body not releasing the lubricant to love making. His fingers worked, attempting to stimulate the area to excitement but Karla resisted.

An annoyed Alberto came up for air to look into Karla's face. His expression was of mild frustration mixed with strong desire. Karla began to panic from his stare.

"I'm sorry," Karla said. "Last night must have worn me out."

"Yes, it was quite invigorating," Alberto offered. "We shall just lie here and enjoy this beautiful morning then."

He rolled over onto his back and slid his arm under her neck. Karla moved to cuddle close to the man that held more than her body. She was suddenly aware that her safety and future freedom hung with this one man. Taking his hand in hers, Karla slowly caressed it. That was when she first noticed it. She was holding the hand not of a fisherman, but of someone that had never seen hard work. She moved her fingers around Alberto's hand feeling for calluses or cuts that surely a fisherman would have.

Karla felt nothing but the soft manicured hand of a gentleman. Palms soft to the touch and fingernails neat and trimmed, she saw no cuts or scars from hooks or fishing lines. No marks from a life of hard work.

She moved her head so she could see Alberto's. With her face close, she now noticed that his hair was styled, not as a barber would cut it, but the work of a stylist, his hair in perfect layers on his head. His face she now realized was not sun streaked as a fisherman's would be. A careful tan had been cultivated with the nose the same tone as the rest. And no raccoon eyes showed from sunglasses.

A fisherman would wear sunglasses for the glare off the water as he pulled in his catch. The ocean sun would bake him unless he covered himself, but he would not have a nice even tan over his entire body as if from a lounge by the pool. The fisherman and workers Karla knew had tan arms but white bodies from wearing shirts while working. Not like this golden boy next to her. As she realized that Alberto was not who he said he was, her tension projected through to her bed partner.

"What? What is it?"

"Nothing. I think hunger pains just hit me,: Karla said. "Too much fun last night, I guess."

"Yes, time for breakfast. Then a relaxing soak in the tub," Alberto offered. "You noticed last night it's is big enough for two."

Karla shuddered at the thought. Naked and afraid in the tub? Who was she cavorting with? That question hung in the air as the two climbed out of bed.

* * *

On the other side of the island, someone's personal trip through hell was just starting. Kotone had been dragged out of court crying for Jack to help her. But no one had come to her aid. As that terrible day progressed, she was transferred to the fortress prison. There she was handed her prison jumpsuit and told to change on the spot.

With guards looking on, she slipped out of her shorts and pulled on her prison garb. The guard barked at her that her top and bra had to be removed which she did quickly with her back to the guards. Now, just in panties and a short-sleeved jump suit, she was led down into the cell blocks. Screaming could be heard as she passed down three levels, each one darker than the one before.

An iron gated cell creaked open and she was unceremoniously shoved into her hold. A coarse blanket was thrown in after her and it landed on the only accessory in the cell, a metal bed with a stained mattress on it. In the corner was a squatter toilet for relieving herself. The guard placed a bucket of water in her cell and closed the door. A key grinded as the lock was thrown, ending her freedom.

Kotone collapsed on the floor. The tears flowed as she sobbed. She sat sprawled against the wall, her eyes closed as the tears ran down her cheeks until she had no more tears. That was when the smell hit her. A musty smell mixed with human body odor. She pinched her nose as she lifted her head to see her enclosure.

The rock of the fortress was everywhere. The walls and floor and ceiling were all made of stone. The ceiling had a barrel vault to hold the weight of the floors above. High off the floor was an opening to the outside world. Kotone needed to look and she stood up and walked to the outside wall. The opening was at about seven feet off the floor near the ceiling. Iron bars were set in the opening to rule out any escape.

Kotone felt along the wall above her head and grabbed the small ledge that separated the large stones in the wall. She brought one foot up and the sneakers she had been given with her prison garb searched for purchase. Again, a small joint offered support for the rubber edged sneakers. She pulled herself up and located a second place for her other foot.

She felt the ocean breeze before she lifted her head even with the opening. Her gaze took in the expansive view out over the Caribbean Sea. Looking left and right no other object came into view. Remembering that the fortress sat on a promontory at the end of Vluchteling harbor, she moved to the right carefully, one hold at a time. Now she could just see the end of the airport runway where it jutted out into the sea.

She slipped and fell the short distance to the floor. Again, she just collapsed all the way down into a heap. Seeing the airport brought the horror all back, the excitement of being with Jack flying to an exotic island on their honeymoon. The anticipation of fun as they landed. And then the nightmare. *How could this all be happening?* she thought. *Jack has to save me. Please Jack.*

Kotone drifted off more in futility than being tired. She wasn't going anywhere and she knew it. She just sat on the floor in a numbed state as the day moved on. A scraping sound caught her attention and forced her to look up. In the dim light, she saw a small metal door just big enough for a bowl, open and something was shoved in. A metal ledge held the bowl as the small door was shut.

Finally moving to investigate, Kotone walked across the cell and picked up the bowl. The metal bowl was warm but not hot and the food inside the bowl announced dinner. Outside the sun was sinking although she could not see it. But the small patch of sky in the opening grew darker and changed hues from bright yellow to a subdued purple.

She picked up the wooden spoon stuck in the food and first smelled it. It seemed to be a stew of some sort. She pushed the food around and noticed a fish head loom up out of the broth. She gagged slightly at the eye staring back at her. She placed the bowl back on the ledge.

With the setting sun a coolness began to infiltrate into her cell. The stones continued to hold the warmth from the day's sun but the air was cooling. Soon the cell was dark with only a stray beam of light from the light bulb in the corridor seeping in through the small window in the door. She picked up the blanket for warmth but threw it back down when it got near her nose.

She surmised that the blanket hadn't been cleaned since the last prisoner and it held residue from unimaginable numbers of bodies before her. But as the coolness continued she knew it was her only warmth. As she wrapped it around her body she wretched slightly. Sitting down on the metal bed, the smell of the mattress hit her. It was worse than the blanket.

Her situation finally overwhelmed her to the point she just lied down wrapped in the blanket and tried to cry again. But her eyes refused to comply, and she just lay there whimpering. And thats when her consciousness recorded the sounds around her. Muffled crying and the occasional low screams followed by cries for help. Exhaustion took over finally as she fell asleep.

Chapter 13

Miami, Florida

Jack waited at the marina on the south side of Miami. Sitting beside him was his Marine Corps friend, Lamarcus Lewis. While Jack had done his information gathering in the British Virgin Islands, Lamarcus had loaded up his Cadillac and driven from his home outside Boston to Florida. The two-day drive gave Jack time to catch a flight back to the United States and meet his friend upon arrival.

"Where are we going again?" Lamarcus asked.

"It's a small island near St. Vincent in the Caribbean," Jack said.

"And this place doesn't belong to anyone, like you can't call the authorities?"

"I told you," Jack said. "It's one of those weird island possessions from the 18th Century. It's the playground of a Dutch aristocratic family; their ancestors won the island by supporting the Dutch King in some war."

"Those white people were always doing shit like that, weren't they? Grab a place and give it away to some prince dude or something. And to hell with the locals."

"Generally the locals died off from disease."

"I'm glad I don't have that guilt clogging up my life like you do. us Africans dodged all that shit," Lamarcus said. Jack knew his friend was pulling his chain. It had been the same when they were a sniper team in the Marines. Generally, Lamarcus spotted and Jack shot. But it was always the debate who was a better shot that kept them at each other constantly. And it hadn't ended with them both moving into law enforcement. It was just that they worked on opposite ends of the country, so they didn't have many opportunities to flick shit at each other.

"Oh sure. Africans never had slaves or anything like that." Jack said.

"Hey, we didn't give the poor bastards small pox."

"And remember that the Native Americans gave us Europeans syphilis in return. It was just that our disease killed you faster." Jack said.

"Ones a lot more fun to catch though."

"At least until you go blind and crazy before you die."

"So, when is your friend due?" Lamarcus asked.

"I got an email off to her from St. Vincent and she was in the Bahamas. Said she had to settle a couple things but she'd be here today. She said she'd call when she hit the three-mile marker."

Just then Jack's cell phone began to play music signaling a call. He pulled it off his belt and answered. After the normal greeting he was quiet. A couple of ah huhs and he clicked off.

"Everything good?"

"We're good."

They had stashed Lamarcus' car in the long-term lot of the marina where other sailors left their rigs during trips into the islands. Their gear was in bags at their feet as they looked out over the entrance to the marina watching for their ride. Soon a twin-masted catamaran swung into view as one sail was lowered for docking. Soon the second sail on the mizzenmast went down leaving just the head sail aloft.

The roller reefing mechanism on the front shroud soon took in the sail as it retracted into its housing. Now under outboard motor, the catamaran moved up to the main dock where the two men stood. The woman on board kicked her rubber fenders over the port side of the boat and eased back on the throttle. The 38' sailboat eased into a spot on the dock as she threw the outboard into neutral. Jack and Lamarcus grabbed lines and tied off the boat.

"Hi Jack. And Lamarcus too. Must really be trouble somewhere for the two of you to be at it again," the woman said.

"Misty, thanks for coming on short notice," Jack said.

"I'd say it's been too long, but it hasn't," Lamarcus said.

Misty Duran walked over and stepped off onto the dock. She gave both men a hug. "How long has it been? Three years?" she asked.

"Has it been that long?" Jack asked.

"Yeah, although our friend here hasn't kept out of trouble. I'm just glad he did it on the other end of the country," Lamarcus said.

"Yeah, and what were those rumors of you in Europe?" Misty asked.

"Can we load up and be gone? Time is moving and so should we." Jack said.

"Hold on," Misty stopped Jack. "Do I get an explanation before we do this?"

"On board. I'll explain everything once we are moving."

Misty looked at Lamarcus and shrugged her shoulders. She had been around Jack before and knew what he was capable of. But not to offer an explanation to either one of them stretched their friendship.

Seeing the hesitation of the two others, Jack offered a quick answer. "They arrested my wife on a trumped-up charge. I'm going to get her released."

Misty and Lamarcus both stared back at Jack. Their expressions they exhibited spoke volumes. Jack didn't wait for any more questions and began lifting the gear bags aboard the sailboat. The two others, jolted into action, grabbed a load and carried it below.

Fifteen minutes later they were untying the sailboat as Misty eased the throttle forward making way. The catamaran soon left the confines of the marina and Jack helped Misty raise all sails. The outboard was turned off and the mechanical lift pulled the heavy motor out of the water. It was lashed down for the trip.

"Misty, have you been down to the Grenadines?" Jack asked.

"Last year, after hurricane season, why?"

"Set a course to get us there as quickly as possible."

Misty descended down the hatch to the chart table. She searched for her large chart and her book on passages. The book offered the best route after considering the prevailing winds and currents. It was critical to serious sailors.

Thirty minutes later Misty returned with her notes. Jack sat holding the tiller that ran to both rudders. The Wharram Tiki catamaran had been built in England of fiberglass. He had been with Misty when she received it from a company crew that sailed it across the North Atlantic. The boat was a replacement for Misty's boat that had sunk in a storm on Lake Huron in the Great Lakes.

Jack and Misty had sailed the Tiki down the East Coast before Jack had left to return to Wyoming. They had stayed in touch as Misty continued sailing solo down into the Caribbean. And when Jack needed transport back to Vluchteling, Misty was the first person he thought of. And luckily she had been close by in the Bahamas. Misty took over the helm and Jack moved to the cushioned seat nearby.

"Still sails like a dream," Jack said.

"Yes, and now can you tell me where our dream is taking us?" Misty asked.

Lamarcus arrived from the starboard hull where he had grabbed a berth.

"Yes, I want to hear this too," Lamarcus said. "Start at the beginning, when you got married. I thought you'd have been done with that shit."

Jack began his story of running into Kotone at his son's wedding and how things just went from there. He added the tale of landing on the island looking forward to his honeymoon and how the nightmare dropped on them. His two friends sat and listened as they learned what their mission was going to be. Little did they know just what was about to happen. Things that Jack didn't even know.

* * *

Alberto eased naked into the hot tub that sat against the cliff. The water splashed over the rim as his body displaced the heated water. More water poured into the hand chiseled tub from the pipe running along the cliff from its source. A cool water pipe that protruded from the nearby cliff could be mixed with the hot water.

Alberto pushed the cool water pipe so it ran onto the terrace and flowed over to the edge. There it joined the other water flow, as it headed down the hill toward the small valley and the creek along its bottom. The sea was off to the left with an inviting white sand beach where the creek met the sea. Alberto had been having his way with the German woman now for three days. They had frolicked in the ocean and snorkeled off the headland nearby. Each evening they had finished off with a long soak in the hot tub.

With the cool water source removed, the pipe bringing the hot water began to heat the tub water. Sweat beads emerged on his forehead as the water temperature rose. He looked as the tall German walked out of the small cliff dwelling that had been their love making cabin. She was wrapped in a towel and her bare feet slapped the tile terrace. As she reached the hot tub, Alberto sat waiting for the prize.

Karla dropped her towel onto the settee nearby and stepped on the small ledge to climb into the tub. Alberto's gaze never wavered from her exposed sensuous areas. Karla tried to cover things as best as she could and bent her leg to give her some privacy, at least down there. Her breasts swayed as she bent down as her one foot found the tub bottom. Swinging her other leg over the lip, Alberto was given a full view of her womanhood.

Not that he hadn't been even closer than this over the last few days. She sat down on the rock seat opposite Alberto and looked out over the valley toward the sea. No words were spoken. There hadn't been many words spoken after their first love making. Alberto had experienced this before.

After he helped the distressed damsels escape the awful prison, they all showed gratitude in the right way. But then the situation changed. Once the women realized they were no longer being tormented by their cell and all that happened around them, they would become more aloof. Some worse than others. But through it all Alberto got what he craved. He didn't really care if the women grew regretful as the sex happened.

He could live with that. So far almost all had willingly opened their legs for him, some just took longer than others.

And the fun part was, when he was satisfied that he'd played with them long enough, he got them loaded onto a sailboat and deposited on any of the nearby islands. And all got the same warning on leaving. He reminded each woman that he was risking a lot helping them escape the island and if they said anything to the outside world not only he would be in trouble. He always reminded the women that there was an outstanding drug conviction hanging over their heads, and they could be extradited back to Vluchteling to complete their sentence.

And so far, all the women had been happy to get away. No blow back had come to any of the island officials. And Alberto knew that the German was ready to be sent on her way.

"Karla, I've finally arranged a fishing boat for you to leave on. It is an old friend of mine and he will make sure you get safely to a nearby island from where you can get home."

"Thank you, Alberto. I don't know what I would have done without you." Karla said.

Alberto leaned back and closed his eyes. He knew she didn't really mean it, but she was playing the part. That's what he loved the most about his little spider web of sex. The prison traumatized them so badly that they were willing to do anything not to go back. And he offered the only way off the island for them. And the only price he asked was a little slutty fun in return. *Actually, a lot of slutty fun* he thought. He chuckled inside at his little joke.

As he relaxed, he slid his body forward toward Karla. With his eyes still closed, his legs found her across from him. He let his legs move up the tub wall until his male appendage broke the surface just in front of Karla's face. He slid his feet, so they forced her body forward while he used his free hand to encourage her. She had done this before and soon her mouth found the willing target. *Yes, life is good* he thought, his eyes still closed. *I'll send her away tomorrow after a fulfilling night then go see who's next back at the prison.*

* * *

Kotone snapped up in bed at a blood curdling scream. She had no idea what time it was or how long she had been sleeping. The smells hit her and she stepped off the metal bed. She walked over to the cell door and looked out the window into the hallway. The bowl of food sat cold and alone still on the shelf.

Another scream made her crane her neck side to side to try and see something. A similar

177

iron door lay across the corridor. Off to both her left and right sat two more doors. And that was the extent of her view. Three single light bulbs illuminated the space as the corridor led away from her view.

She heard footsteps and turned towards the sound. Soon a jailer walked into view. He was more rotund than tall and had a filthy shirt over torn shorts. The stubble on his face only accented the stringy dirty hair hanging down to his shoulders. He caught her looking out the door and stopped. Turning to confront her, he smiled. A smile of yellow teeth with gaps where teeth were missing..

Kotone drew back into the dark and away from view of such a creature. She heard footsteps as he continued his march and the light beam returned from where he had blocked it. Shaking in fear more than cold, she grabbed the blanket and wrapped it around her. She laid back onto the mattress but could not sleep. Every little sound was carried through the rock cavern walls to her ears.

Crying, whimpering, yells for help. All the sounds of women in trouble and trapped in the stone hell. As she stared at the small lighted area cast from the hall light, it seemed to waver. The only visible spot of stone floor held her attention as the remainder of the cell sat in dark. Suddenly the light disappeared, and she heard heavy breathing through her cell door window.

Now terrified in the total blackness, Kotone reached deep into her soul for strength. Strength to endure. She drew on the training she received while obtaining a black belt in Taekwondo to light a fire inside her. *I will survive this* she thought. *I will survive, at least as long as it takes Jack to come for me.*

A grunt, and suddenly the light returned to the spot on the floor as the guard left. Kotone rolled onto her back and pulled her legs up. She organized her thoughts into survival mode. It would take all her strength to endure her existence. At least until, until when? She thought, *How long before Jack returns an rains hell onto this island?*

Chapter 14

Vluchteling Island, the Caribbean

"But your excellency, it is too soon," the guard said.

Alberto had seen the German woman off after an all-night sex romp. He knew she had changed her mind about being intimate with him but she had wisely chosen to fake it. And Alberto congratulated her on her faking. She was very good at it, and he assumed she had experience having sex with someone she didn't really want to be with. *Such as an old boyfriend she had grown tired of* he thought. *Woman and sex were much different then men and sex.*

Alberto smiled remembering the joke he had heard about men screwing mud if that was all that was available. Men didn't care as long as they got satisfied. But he knew women were different. He had seen all types in his little island playground. And enjoyed them all, at least as long as they serviced him. Some were good for a couple of days and some for a week or two. But none lasted more than two weeks as Alberto soon grew bored. A new conquest was needed and he would move on, leaving the women glad to be away from their horrors.

"The Asian. She intrigues me."

"But she has only been here a week. You know it takes at least three weeks to mentally prepare them."

"You've done the regular things I take it?"

"Standard stuff. It works, but three weeks is the minimum. Longer is even better."

"So, how is she reacting?"

"Like the others. We play the noise tapes with the screams and yelling. We lurk in her window. It took her two days to realize she needed to use the squatter at night since we always caught her in the daytime using it."

Alberto didn't really want to hear the sordid details of what his guards did to traumatize each woman. It was all designed to scare her so badly that Alberto would be seen as a knight of shining armor as he rescued the woman. The empty cells held speakers to imitate tortured women. The guards entering her cell at night to lurk, but never to touch. That was all Alberto's territory.

"Do we have another plaything then that I can use in the mean time?" Alberto asked.

"No your excellency. That German was the last one until we got the American."

"Then she'll have to do. I'm due to head back to the Netherlands soon and I don't want this one lingering in her cell too long."

Alberto knew that beautiful women did not take to being locked in a stone cell for too long. The damp stones and cool nights meant unhealthy conditions. Added to that was the bad food and the bloom would leave quickly. And Alberto was totally taken by the bloom the Asian woman had given off. For him to risk doing his little intrigue while her husband knew of her whereabouts spoke to his desire for her.

While there was little the husband could do since Alberto's family owned the island, there could be trouble. He had never taken a married woman before, at least not ones traveling solo. He relied on single travelers showing up that could expect no outside help. By the time anyone might figure out the traveler was in trouble, a month would have passed and he would be finished. Their loved one would have show up by then and be busy adjusting to the experience.

"As you wish, excellency." the guard said.

"We will make our escape tonight. Pass the word to the guards to stay clear."

The head guard nodded he understood and left to inform his crew. Alberto walked back to his living quarters located high on the fortress. The trade wind blew in off the ocean and he pulled on a warm coat. He took a short nap to prepare himself for the fun.

* * *

Kotone slept fitfully on the disgusting mattress. She had taken on the habit of scratching a mark on the stone wall as she went to bed. It denoted the days she had endured in this place. From the assorted other scratches, she surmised other women had done the same. What intrigued her was that none of the marks represented long stays.

While there were some obviously very old scratches that matched the vintage of the fortress, the newer marks all seemed to stop with about 22 marks. Three weeks seemed to be the norm. She wondered what happened after three weeks that whoever had been confined here no longer made any marks.

She shuddered as she contemplated the unknown. *Did the people escape? Did they all die?* she thought. She let go of things she had no control over. The week of her incarceration had left her compartmentalizing such ideas. Some thoughts were too horrible to think about, so they were put in a box in her mind and locked tight. Other thoughts were free to linger.

And thoughts of Jack sailing to her rescue rose above any others. Her days of confinement were spent in a fantasy world of boats racing across the sea straight at her. Then her new husband, her protector, descending to her cell and freeing her. It kept her sane while everything around her tore at her sanity. The noises every night would drive any one to madness. And not seeing what was being done to those other poor women had to be locked away constantly. Whenever an especially blood curdling scream rang out, Kotone pulled the blanket tighter around her as she took a fetal position.

With the blanket covering her face, Kotone heard a noise. A metal scraping sound. The sound she had heard before when one of the guards let himself into her cell. They would linger in the full light of the open door. No one had touched her yet, but they would get close enough, so she could hear their breathing and smell their bodies. Kotone would keep her head and body wrapped tightly in the blanket and they would always leave.

Tonight, the same noise startled her. The key turning to release the lock followed by the rusty groan of the door moving open. Through a small slit in the blanket one eye caught the guard moving into her cell. But this guard was taller and leaner than the others had been. He crept forward without a word. Suddenly a hand touched her shoulder.

"Oh God, please, no." she screamed.

The hand flew across her mouth to stifle her screams.

"Quiet, you fool. Don't let the guards know."

Kotone opened her eyes fully and saw someone totally unlike the guards. Clean shaven and thin, this man had clean hair hanging down and smelled wonderful. After nothing but filth smells, his hand let off an aroma that was heaven.

"I've come to help you escape. Come quickly."

Kotone felt the man grab her left hand and pull her out of bed. The blanket fell to the floor as she was led to the open door. Her heart raced as she stepped into the corridor. The man stopped and Kotone took her place right behind him. They were both bent over, and she breathed his scent. He turned to the left and pulled her with him.

In the corridor with the full light she saw that the man was about Jack's height but thinner. Dressed in simple clothes, she did notice his tan. But she didn't care. She would follow any one to escape this place. The two made their way to a side corridor and the man lingered listening. Without a word, he turned right and after a short distance dropped down onto his knees. Kotone was forced down with him as his grip on her hand made no other option possible.

Needing his hand to crawl on all fours, he led her down the narrow passage until they entered a tight space where the two of them could sit side by side. A hole in the stone floor revealed water and the man lowered himself into the space. Looking up at Kotone, he handed her a pair of swim goggles and then put a pair on himself.

Kotone quickly slipped the goggles over her head and pulled them over her eyes. They were loose, so she took them off and quickly adjusted the straps. Now fitted properly, he handed her the breathing device with a quick instruction on its use.

Kotone slipped into the water next to the man. The tight space forced their bodies together and she felt something at his touch.

"We need to swim about fifty feet under the water. I have a small light to help you see. But we will be outside the walls when we surface. So be very quiet."

The man dropped down under the water while Kotone followed. A flashlight lit the pipe they were in, and she pulled along the walls to move toward freedom. The man kicked just ahead of her as the pipe continued. Just as she was about to panic from the confined space, the man disappeared upward. She felt the pipe stop and followed the man to the surface.

The man had turned off the flashlight and began swimming toward shore. In the starlight, a sandy beach lay off in the distance, the white sand standing out from the surrounding dark. Looming over her right side were the walls of the fortress. Kotone swam the breast stoke as it was quieter then the crawl. She matched her strokes with the man as they both moved closer to shore.

The fortress fell away revealing a moat between the shore and the fortress. While the fortress had been built on a promontory, a moat of water had been dug for added protection. The two swimmers swam by the moat to the beach on the far side. A small wave carried Kotone up onto the sand with the man right beside her.

He grabbed her hand again and without a sound led her up off the beach. The rocks soon gave way to ground and they picked up their pace. Her wet clothes and shoes caused her to shiver slightly as they climbed away from the fortress. Soon they were in the trees and moving fast. Kotone began to sweat at the exertion and stumbled over a tree root. She fell, the man's hand slipping out of hers. Her knee caught something as she hit the ground and pain hit her.

The man grabbed her hand again and pulled her up. With her left knee screaming in pain, she tried to keep up with the taller man. She collapsed again. Her confinement had weakened her muscles. Normally this type of workout would be nothing. A former triathlete, she was realizing how little she had worked out recently. But her guide would let nothing stop their escape. He pulled her along as they moved further into the depths of the island. He finally switched the flashlight on again, feeling they were away from any humans.

That was when they heard it. Dogs. Dogs on their trail. The man pulled harder as they practically ran through the forest. The ground was uneven and hilly. They climbed up one hill and descended the opposite side. A stream. ran along the bottom of the hill and the man led her up the stream Her sneakers once again were soaking wet as they kept to the water. Kotone knew dogs could not follow any scent in water and put her knee pain aside. *Anything not to go back to prison* she thought.

The valley they were in began to close in on them. Soon it turned into a gorge of shear walls on both sides. Impossible to climb out, Kotone worried that they might become trapped in such a narrow place. As they continued up the stream, a loud noise began to echo down the canyon. As they moved around one rock out cropping a water fall came into view. It appeared to be at least fifty feet high as it tumbled over the cliffs ringing a small glade. They were trapped.

The man stopped and motioned Kotone to wait. He then walked over to the rock wall and began climbing it. There were enough outcroppings for hand holds to gain a certain height. Kotone had rock climbed before and saw that this wall had enough fissure sand cracks to lead a route to the top. Her confidence rose that they would escape the trap and the dogs would be unable to follow.

Just as she was getting ready to start climbing the man climbed back down to her. Without a word, he took her hand and led her toward the waterfall. She looked up at the volume of water coming down as the spray at the bottom wafted out to soak them. The man kept walking and disappeared into the water, Kotone followed as the water pounded her head and shoulders. Once behind the falls, the man took her hand again as he slipped through a cleft in the rock. One minute he was there and then not. He led her through the same tight fissure into a chamber. She noticed the cave inside the cliff was large enough for many people as the flashlight flickered around the chamber. The man reached up on a shelf and pulled out a large wool blanket. He held it up.

"We need to rest now. The search party will run the dogs all around while we hide in here. Take off your wet things so you don't freeze."

The man started disrobing, hanging his pants on a rock nub with his jacket and shirt next to it. He pulled off his wet shoes and socks and lay down on the rock with the blanket under him. It was large enough to cover both of them. He held it open.

Kotone hesitated disrobing with only the jumpsuit on. The man had left his underwear on and she had on her panties. But her breasts would be exposed without the jumpsuit. She began to shiver in the cool cave and she knew she had to stay healthy to survive. Turning her back to the man she stepped out of jumpsuit, hung it up and removed her prison sneakers. Kneeing down with her arms across her chest to cover herself, the man moved slightly to allow her to lay down.

She slid in next to him as he wrapped the blanket over both of them. Now spooning, she moved as close as she dared to this stranger with her back. He placed his arm over her but did not pull her closer.

"I don't even know your name," she said.

"Alberto. Now go to sleep."

Chapter 15

Off St. Vincent

Jack Wesley was in a hurry. He had pressed Misty to run as much sail as possible to make the big cat move. They had made a fast passage according to Misty's book. But it wasn't fast enough for Jack. His wife was now in her second week of imprisonment and he needed to reach her. He and Lamarcus had laid out their plans for interdicting the island from Jack's rough map of Vluchteling. Some was from his own memory, but a lot had been information gleaned from David French.

As the former security chief of the island, he had lasted a little less than a year. When he found out what really happened on on the island, he begged off on being part of it. But the Dupong family threw a lot of weight around in European circles and David French knew he had to be careful. Having Jack show up in Tortola was not in his game plan. But Jack's past had come back to help him with the former SAS officer. Now it was just a matter of pushing the Wharram catamaran as fast it would go.

"Jack, we need to reduce sail," Misty yelled over the noise of the wind. The water rushing through between the two hulls was the other indicator that they were going too fast. The danger with any catamaran is carrying too much sail when a gust hits. Lifting one hull out of the water looked exciting on the racing cats, but on a cruiser, it screamed danger.

Once a cat was on one hull, it didn't take much more to push it over all the way. And unlike a conventional single hull boat with its heavy keel, a cat didn't right itself. A conventional sailboat would lay over onto its side releasing the pressure on the sails. A well-designed boat would then right itself as the counter weight of the keel worked under gravity and sought to head to the bottom. Once a boat righted itself, the sails once again took over and the boat regained its speed.

But a knock down in a cat was much different. Once one hull left the water it was in a very unstable state. A little more force on the sails and the cat would go over. Depending on its design, it might stop at the point where the sails hit the water. The hull would be perpendicular to the sea. But nothing really prevented the boat from continuing all the way over. Once the mast and sails entered the water, the stable state of the catamaran was totally upside down.

And once a cat was turtled, it took another motor boat and a lot of effort to right it again. For a cruising cat to flip meant the crew was now floating on a large inverted raft. Without the heavy keel to pull it down, a light weight catamaran could float indefinitely upside down. Meanwhile the crew would be sitting on the hulls out of the water and they would have someplace to await rescue.

And now the freshening breeze was building, and Misty was worried. Jack had noticed the wind increasing but his desire to get to Vluchteling outweighed his judgement.

Finally Misty had had enough, "Lamarcus, get up here and help me shorten sail, now."

Jack seemed to come back to reality as he looked at the woman holding the tiller and the facial expression she carried. He knew that the look was somewhere between frustration and fear.

"I'll get it," Jack said as Lamarcus climbed the ladder from the port hull. "Lamarcus, get the line here."

Jack pointed to the shroud that would lower the main sail as he scrambled out of the cockpit onto the deck between the hulls. While the starboard hull was wanting to lift out of the water the cat held steady. The large flat deck between the hulls left room for Jack to walk quickly to the forward mast. He signaled to Lamarcus to uncleat the main line and lower the sail. Jack stood by the boom and gathered in the sail.

"That's good," Jack yelled. He grabbed the reefing ties and began to tie them off around the boom. With about half the forward main sail now tied off, Jack moved to the rear main sail. He directed Lamarcus to the line controlling the second main sail and again as the sail was partially lowered, Jack gathered in the material. He quickly tied off his reef points.

The catamaran was much happier now with the shortened sail. Both hulls were firmly settled in the water and their speed was only reduced slightly. Catamarans were famous as fast sailors and this one continued to make a quick voyage. Jack stepped down off the small doghouse that sat just in front of the cockpit. The doghouse was the only obstruction on the deck and held a small berth to shelter the crew while sailing but still on watch. Unlike most catamarans, the Wharram design did not have a large salon between the hulls.

Wharram Cats were designed to mimic the original Polynesian catamaran that sailed the Pacific Ocean prior to Westerns showing up. The design consisted of two hulls with a open deck in between. The deck consisted of a net in front of the front mast and a slatted deck aft. Any water washing over the cat would flow right through and the cat would float. Two shorter masts of equal height meant there was less pressure to overturn the boat but significant sail area to move the big boat. And the real magic was in the flexible connection on the cross beams which let the entire boat flex with the waves and not fight them. The Wharram was world famous for its safety record on long ocean crossings.

"Should I take in the head sail?" Jack asked.

"No, it's feeling good now," Misty answered. "I know you want to get there but Kotone won't be helped if we flip trying to get there too fast."

Lamarcus' eyes grew wide at the mention of flipping. Being a city boy all his life and African-American besides, he wasn't totally happy to be out on the ocean. Ever since he stepped on board he had been happy to remain in his small cabin and avoid time on deck. And the forward cabin he had chosen had room for a single berth in between the narrow hull.

Even further aft where the galley sat the hull narrowed. There was room for a small counter holding a sink and a stove where one person could stand and cook or clean dishes. Forward was the table where they could eat which because of the narrow hull meant two narrow bench seats with a narrow table in between. At thirty-six inches at its widest spot, neither hull offered luxurious conditions.

But the boat offered a quick passage with enough comforts to make it pleasant. And with the warm weather of the Caribbean, life mainly revolved around sitting on deck. While each had their three hours at the helm, the next six hours was for sleeping or relaxing. Cooking was shared although Jack took Lamarcus' turn as he knew cooking was not his favorite. And cooking in a tight space for the big man was even less fun.

"Sorry, Misty. I don't want to risk you or your boat. I'm grateful for the help," Jack said.

"What about me? You're not worrying about your old war buddy?" Lamarcus asked.

"No, Lamarcus, I need you too."

"Damn straight."

"Jack, I checked the weather on my satellite phone. Downloaded the weather map and put it in my computer I use for navigation. This breeze is the leading edge of a tropical storm headed our way."

"What's that mean?" Lamarcus asked. "We're not talking a hurricane, are we?"

"Slow down big guy," Jack said. He knew he didn't need his partner going into a panic attack. But if a tropical storm was on the way. that could build into a hurricane. "Hurricane season ends in November so we're fine."

"Just a spring storm," Misty said. "But it might complicate getting onto the island if the surf is up."

"So it will hit about the time we get to Vluchteling then?" Jack asked.

"Two more days and we should be there at just the same time as the main storm."

"Ah, how big a storm are we talking about?" Lamarcus asked.

"Don't worry, we've got a life jacket for you when we head to shore." Jack said.

"Oh, thanks."

* * *

Kotone woke with a start. She had been awake most of the night laying on the rough wool blanket. It must have been just before first light when sleep finally overtook her. As her eyes scanned the dark cave they slept in, her mind raced as to who was sleeping right behind her.

The man had laid down with her and had kept a respectable distance, at least as much as sharing one blanket would allow. His arm had rested on her side and no attempt had been made to move a hand where it didn't belong. Even now as she lay quiet,ly the man's hands were not touching anything they shouldn't. One hand was in front of her where his arm was under her head. She had accepted that arm as a pillow last night.

The other arm and hand ran across her side and hung down over her stomach. Just the part of the arm touching her side where nothing personal was involved. He had even kept his distance where her back was against his stomach. While she welcomed the warmth through the night, he had kept his groin area away from her rear end so that nothing would be stimulated. *Yes, he hadn't taken advantage of me last night,* she thought.

"Good morning," the voice behind her said quietly.

"Good morning," Kotone offered back.

The man moved his arms as one would to get blood flow circulating again. Kotone rolled out of his grip and placed both arms over her exposed breasts as she stood up. She took her orange prison jumpsuit and turned to dress. She shivered as the cold damp orange suit hit her body. She turned around to face the man quickly dressing. Once his pants and shirt were on, they stepped into their shoes and laced them up.

"Can we get out in the sun? I'm freezing." Kotone asked.

"Yes, but we must be careful. They will still be looking for us."

Kotone turned and started towards the cleave in the cliff that led out to the waterfall and warmth. The man grabbed her arm to stop her. She turned to question why he had grabbed her.

"No, this way."

The man folded the blanket and placed it back on the rock shelf. He turned on his flashlight and headed deeper into the cave. Kotone walked closely behind as she tried to look around the man to see where they were going. The cave narrowed to where just one person could move and forced them to continue single file further inside the mountain. The cave twisted as the roof came down and Kotone felt a wave of claustrophobia come over her. At two spots they had to drop to their hands and knees and crawl forward. But always the cave offered spaces where larger rooms let them walk side by side.

As they walked along, Kotone said, "Thank you again Alberto for rescuing me from prison."

"That is quite alright. The man who owns this island is a very bad man. He should never lock up tourists that come to visit us."

"So you live here on the island?"

"Yes, I am a fisherman. My father and his father have all been fishermen here. And it was always a pleasant place to live until he arrived. Now, it's very bad."

Kotone moved behind Alberto where the cave narrowed again. Soon they were on their bellies crawling as the cave roof closed down. With little light Kotone's fear rose up. The rock walls were close, and she tried to keep up with Alberto. Just when she thought she would panic, she emerged into a cave much the same size as the one they had slept in. A small glow of daylight near the floor announced that they might be at the end. She looked at the small spot and dreamed of the warmth on the other side.

"Wait here, I'll check first."

Kotone watched as Alberto dropped to his hands and knees and crawled out of the cave. The cavern she was in grew dark as he blocked the light. As he disappeared, the small light returned. She waited impatiently to see what was on the outside and for a chance to feel the sun. Kotone grew anxious as Alberto failed to return and she was just getting ready to drop down and crawl out when the light disappeared and a body emerged from outside.

"It is clear, but we can only move out a short distance. Please follow me."

Alberto disappeared again with Kotone right behind him. She stood up once outside and found herself in a tight space surrounded by rocks. Her body was forced against Alberto's side before he climbed the short distance out of the pit they were in to the top of one of the rocks. Kotone climbed up beside him and that's when she heard the ocean.

She looked but the sea was out of sight, hidden by a jumble of rocks. One large one sat over their heads forming a roof. The two sides sat on other rocks but the opposite sides were open. They stepped carefully down onto some beach sand laying between the rocks. Alberto took her hand and led her to where the sun hit them, but they were still under the rock.

"This is a safe spot. You can sit in the sun and get warmed up without anyone seeing you. Unless they walk by right in front of us. You stay here while I go scout to see if anyone is about."

Before she could agree, Alberto walked down the sand and climbed one of the rock walls. He disappeared over the lip of the small ravine they were in. Kotone sat down against the smooth rock and felt the warmth of the sun hit her. The rock added its warmth as well and soon her orange jumpsuit was dry. As she became hot, she moved into the shade and relaxed. As she waited for Alberto's return, she dozed.

Soon she was fast asleep. Relieved from her cell and her tormentors, sleep consumed her. The ocean smell combined with the noise of the nearby sea hitting the shore kept her mind in a pleasant place. Her dream carried her back three years to when she and Jack had first met. While there had been wonderful times back then, their time together had been troubled. Kotone felt she was the cause of the trouble and had always held back where Jack was concerned.

Jack had been accepting of her and had been the perfect gentleman. Kotone had struggled with why she had left Jack and fought her guilt when she had called him two years later to help her find her sister. Luckily they had rescued her sister but their relationship during the rescue had not led them back together. It was only a chance meeting in Montana that had sparked the fire inside both of them for each other.

And once again she needed her man to rescue her. It seemed to be the story of her life. Just when things were wonderful between them, something stepped in to take it all away. As she dreamed of Jack swimming ashore on this island and sweeping her into his arms a noise startled her awake. Alberto dropped down the cliff onto the sand. He turned and walked to where she was seated.

"Here, I found these. They won't stand out as much as that orange jumpsuit."

He handed her some clothes and she held them up to inspect them. They were a pair of khaki men's shorts and a denim man's button shirt. Both looked as though they had been last worn in the the 19th Century. *But he is right, they blend in better than orange does* she thought.

She turned to undress and put on the new clothes. As she did her mind raced. *Where did he find these clothes* she thought. Something clicked in her mind that didn't feel right. But she pushed it aside as all she cared about was being free. Free from the rock cell that awaited her if she got caught. *And what about Alberto, what would happen if he got caught with me?* she thought.

"We need to wait here until night fall. It's too dangerous to move during the day time."

Kotone took that as reasonable. But hunger began to hit her and sitting all day with nothing to eat would take will power. But the alternative was worse. She sat back down and leaned against the rock.

Chapter 16

Vluchteling Island, the Caribbean

The weather off Vluchteling was building as the Wharram cat swung around the lee side of the island. Away from the populated north side of the island, Misty took the sailboat closer to shore. Now on a broad reach as they sailed along the west coast of the small island, the sun was setting into the Caribbean Sea. There were only about two hours of daylight left and they had to make a decision.

"Do we go in tonight Jack?" Lamarcus asked.

"If you don't, tomorrow may be too rough to get near the island," Misty said.

"Yes, we go as soon as we reach the southwest promontory," Jack said. He stood and scanned the coast looking ahead to where the west coast turned the corner. The longer south coast lay just around the corner.

"So we will check the cabin first?" Lamarcus asked.

They had discussed where to land and what to check first. Jack had learned about the love cabin where all the women were taken after their rescue. They were closer to that than to the fortress on the northeast corner of the island. And the fortress was near human habitation so they would have to land on the unpopulated south side and walk to the fortress to avoid detection.

Donald French, former island security officer, had given Jack all the information they needed to find Kotone. And when Jack learned of the real purpose of Kotone's arrest, his desire for quickness was doubled.

The two men headed below and changed into their tactical clothes. Jack pulled on his black pants and black top. He laced up his black boots and then snapped on his web gear. Both he and Lamarcus had experience with what they were about to do. Having been on a Marine Recon team, they had frequently practiced island invasions and missions of a similar nature.

A grease pen blackened Jack's face and they slipped knives into their leg sheaths. A waterproof bag that had been set up long ago was opened and the contents double checked. Satisfied that they were ready, they grabbed their two packs and swung them over their shoulders. Lamarcus grabbed the waterproof bag and stepped up onto deck where Jack was moving the inflatable dinghy over to the side.

The dinghy normally rode upside down and partially inflated on the deck. Stuffed with emergency water and food, it acted as one of the life rafts in case of trouble. The real life raft was held in a fiberglass container strapped to the deck in front of the small doghouse. It held a real life raft and supplies in case they had to abandon ship. The dingy acted as a backup. But tonight, fully inflated with its small outboard attached, it would be their way onto the island.

As dusk moved over the island, Misty changed course and brought the cat around the rock promontory. A small beach came into view with a valley leading away from the beach.

"According to my sources, the cabin is on the right side of the valley," Jack said. He scanned the area with his binoculars. "I don't see anyone out and about. Lets do it."

Lamarcus pulled on his life jacket and attempted to snap it on over his webbing. Jack turned and loosened the life jacket straps, so he could fit. He double checked his friend before turning and pushing the dinghy over the side. As Misty luffed the sails to slow the cat down, Jack slipped a painter through the toe rail and held the other end in his hand. That would hold the dinghy against the hull of the cat as they climbed in. Jack went first and once balanced in the bouncy rubber boat, Lamarcus handed him the gear bag. Jack placed the waterproof bag in the bottom of the boat and turned to grab the first backpack. The second backpack was snatched and placed alongside the gear bag.

Lamarcus sat down on the cat's gunwale and slid his legs over the side. As the dinghy bounced, he found the bottom and stepped into the small boat. He immediately sat down in the front while Jack handed him the painter. Jack turned and pulled the start cord on the outboard and the engine caught. Motioning to Lamarcus, Jack sat down on the rear tube and gripped the throttle as Lamarcus let the painter slide off the catamaran's cleat.

The dinghy lurched free of the big boat and Jack gunned the outboard and turned the motor, so they were now headed toward the beach. Jack looked back and saw Misty pull the sails in as she tacked onto a southerly heading. She would ride out any storm in open water to the south and await the rescue.

Keeping his view of the beach, Jack kept their speed at a safe rate. They rode over the swells and spray hit Lamarcus at the bottom. Their next challenge would be if the surf on the beach had built to a dangerous level. From the sailboat it looked to be reasonable, but Jack knew from experience that looking from the sea did not give one a good view of any waves. Too much wave height and the dinghy would capsize, losing all their gear.

Jack crept closer to the sea side of the waves as he motored along just outside the break. He was looking at the froth that was visible just over the tops of the waves where they had crashed. Too much foam and white meant big crashes. He was looking for darker water indicating smaller crashes. Half way along the beach he noticed where a creek entered the ocean. While a sandbar partially blocked the creek's entrance to the sea, enough sand had been deposited under the water to break up the waves here. Gunning the motor, he shoved the outboard to one side, turning inland.

"Hang on." He yelled at Lamarcus who was already white from his death grip on the dinghy.

Jack spotted the next swell building and lowered his speed to stay just in front of it. Now riding between rollers, he slid down towards the beach and hit the white froth. He gunned the motor to stay in front of the wave crashing to his right. But he had hit the sweet spot on the beach where the swells simply rolled over the sand bar, while to either side the wave broke in a booming roar.

The dinghy hit the beach and stopped suddenly. Jack killed the engine and lifted the motor up. Lamarcus was already out of the boat and pulling it ashore when Jack stepped into the water and grabbed the hand rail. The two of them lifted the dinghy and slid it up onto dry sand.

"Take these," Jack said. He pulled his pack on and handed the other to Lamarcus. Lamarcus unsnapped his life jacket and pulled on the pack. He heaved the gear bag onto his shoulder as he grabbed the dinghy with his free hand. The two dragged the dinghy across the beach to the brush growing near the creek. They pushed their boat into the brush and Jack went to cut some branches to conceal their craft.

Soon, with the dinghy camouflaged and their weapons out, Jack took a compass reading on the spot where the cabin should be. In the low light, they slipped on their communication gear and then they put their monocular night vision gear on their head strap. Jack lead off heading along the creek bank. He would head inland before moving up slope so as to attain some elevation and hopefully come into the cabin from above. But first they had to find it.

"Jack, hold up," Lamarcus whispered into his microphone a short distance later.

Jack turned to see his partner move off the bank as he unzipped his pants. Soon a tinkling noise gave him away. Returning to his place behind Jack, Lamarcus whispered, "I've been holding that for too long."

"Are you ready now?" Jack asked over the comm link.

A shove in his back was his answer. The shove was the barrel of a Lupua Magnum .338 Cal rifle. It held a Leupold scope with a Barrett Optical Ranging System for precision shooting. Jack carried a Smith and Wesson M&P AR-15 semi-automatic rifle in .223 caliber. Both had handguns strapped to their vests. Lamarcus had a 9mm Glock while Jack had a Ruger .22 with a suppressor on the front. They carried two days of supplies as well as a guillie suit for concealment for Lamarcus. Jack carried a rope and grappling hook in his pack.

At what Jack figured to be a reasonable distance he headed up hill away from the creek. Donald French's description of the location of the cabin they sought was below the cliff at the top of the valley. They needed to locate the base of the cliff and then work their way along it to the spot where the cabin lay nestled into the rock. Jack had been told it would be hard to spot from any distance and they might actually walk right up to it before they spotted it.

About an hour later, they ran into the cliff. Jack looked with his night vision monocular and saw no sign of human life. He turned and with his normal eye, judged the distance back to where he could just make out the white foam of the beach.

While everything else lay in darkness, the night time reflection off the surf let him know where they were.

"The cabin should be back toward the beach." Jack said.

Lamarcus again nudged Jack forward. The two walked carefully through the tropical forest keeping the cliff base on their left. At a couple of spots they would have to drop down the hill to maneuver around an obstruction of boulders that had fallen off the cliff. As they reached the cliff base again something caught Jack's eye. A white pipe protruded from the cliff and water was running down the rock. There was a slight sulphur smell to the water and Jack felt the rivulet. He pulled away quickly from the hot water.

He knew the cabin lay at the end of the pipe. He followed the white pipe slowly as he scanned for any sign of human life. The forest sat quiet as they stepped forward. Off in the distance the crash of waves announced the building storm. Jack noticed another obstruction to their forward motion, but this mass had a manmade shape.

He reached for Lamarcus and with his touch, Lamarcus knew to take up a shooting position while Jack moved forward to investigate. Lamarcus tapped Jack's back and Jack moved forward. The sound of splashing water was heard over the ocean in the distance. Jack walked up to the back of the hot tub and looked over the rock it was carved into at the small cabin across a tile terrace. He swept the area and saw no one.

Walking around the hot tub he kept below the terrace wall, stepping across the small stream of water flowing off the tile. He moved silently up to the lower side of the cabin before he raised himself up to look into the side windows. No sign of life. His heart sank that Kotone was not here. If she wasn't at the cabin, then he would have to go into the fortress to find her. That risked much more than if they could have snatched her from the cabin. Jack stepped up onto the terrace and walked to the front door. He opened the glass paneled door and walked in.

"There is no one here. Move up and take a position below the cabin while I search the place."

Jack got two clicks on the radio in acknowledgment. He took out his flashlight and began to search the cabin. More like a large room, except for the door for the toilet, everything was in one space. Pulling out drawers, he found no evidence that Kotone had been there. Just routine kitchen ware and some canned food you might find in a hunter's cabin. Some clothes in a dresser gave an indication that more than hunters used the place.

Negligees and camisoles in various sizes announced that seduction was the main use of the place. A few other sex toys in drawers made Jack more determined to find his wife. Whatever happened here between the prisoners and the hero, he knew he didn't want his wife to be any part of it.

Jack closed up things as he had found them and stepped to the door. Looking one last time, he prayed that Kotone had not been brought here. The place had a sinister feel to it and Jack shuddered at the thought of what took place here.

He stepped onto the terrace and closed the door. Stepping downhill, he saw Lamarcus' shape in the night vision and moved to his position.

"No sign of anyone." Jack said.

"What do you want to do then?"

"According to French, the fortress is a five-hour hike from here. We could be in position before dawn if we hump it."

"You don't want to take the dinghy to the other end of the island?"

"Surf is getting too rough. And we don't know what the beaches are like down there. Better to walk."

"No argument from me. I prefer land myself," Lamarcus said.

"How did they ever let a landlubber like you in the Marines anyway?"

"Affirmative action, I guess."

Chapter 17

Vluchteling Island, the Caribbean

Kotone was shaken awake. She fought the intrusion as sleep continued to hold her as Alberto stood over her.

"Time to move. We have a couple of hours before its pitch black to make some distance."

"How far are we going?" Kotone asked. She had no idea where they were headed. She was putting her trust in her rescuer. But she hoped that there was food at their destination.

"Its about a five-hour hike. You'll be totally safe there until I can arrange to get you off the island."

The news that he intended to get her off the island boosted her spirits. *Maybe Jack won't have to rescue me after all,* she thought. For once I can take care of myself. I'll find Jack and just walk in and surprise him.

Alberto moved out and Kotone fell in right behind. The first part of their hike was along the rocky coast, the waves crashing into the shore and blowing spray into the air. They walked close enough to the ocean that they were slowly getting wet again. But the energy from moving increased her body temperature to offset the cold.

After about an hour Alberto headed inland and started climbing a large promontory that stuck out into the horizon. As the night settled over them, Alberto retrieved his flashlight to help with their route finding. Kotone worried that the small light would be spotted.

"We should be OK. This side of the island is uninhabited. Only the monkeys are over here. And we would hear the dogs if they were on our trail. They always use dogs."

"Alberto, you sound like you've done this before. Helped people escape I mean," Kotone said.

"Yes, a few times. Its the right thing to do."

Kotone relaxed a bit more. The man she was with was saving her life, literally. *I would probably have died in that prison if someone hadn't rescued me* she thought. *And he knew about that underwater tunnel to escape through. Jack wouldn't know about that. How could he ever get into the fortress to rescue me?*

They gained the top of the ridge that led out to the promontory and moved inland along the ridge. The forest here was open enough that they made good time. And as the moon had come out, Alberto put his flashlight away.

Suddenly Alberto stopped and Kotone ran into his back. She stepped back and listened.

Alberto stood frozen, and she could make out his head turning side to side as to listen carefully.

He grabbed her hand and they dropped down off the ridge into the tropical forest. He switched on the flashlight, as the forest canopy kept any moonlight from reaching them. Moving quickly downhill they reached the bottom where the land leveled out. They made good time. But hunger was consuming her as the hours ticked by.

Alberto stopped and produced a water bottle from his pack. It was the first water she had and she gulped it down. She handed the bottle back to Alberto and he took a long swig. Almost empty now, he shoved the bottle back into his pack. He pulled out two oranges and handed one to her. Kotone dove into peeling the tart skin off and wolfed the orange down in three quick bites.

"I'm sorry I have no more food. I picked those oranges when I left you by the rocks." He started to offer her his orange, but she refused his generosity.

"No you need your energy too. You eat."

Kotone stood while Alberto more slowly peeled the orange and then separated the sections piecemeal. He ate two before he lifted one section to Kotone's lips. She initially resisted but he pushed, parting her lips. She pulled the fruit into her mouth, juice running down her chin.

"Thank you," she said.

Alberto ate two more sections and again pressed a section against her lips. With a protest before she accepted, she chewed vigorously. The sugar in the orange gave her the energy to carry on. The last section was politely refused as Alberto shrugged and ate it.

The two hikers moved out as the ground slowly rose. The climb added to their work as the hill gradually continued to rise. Soon it leveled out and they walked easily along a flat plateau. The moonlight filtered continuously through the trees before disappearing as clouds moved in. The sudden darkness was enhanced by an increase in the wind.

While the wind blew fairly steadily in this part of the Caribbean, the new wind was more malevolent. It was obvious that a storm was moving through the islands as the cloud cover kept the moon hidden.

Alberto stopped and Kotone stepped up beside him. Ahead lay a large valley with a surf line off in the distance through the trees. Motioning her to be careful, Alberto led them down off the plateau on a trail that wormed its way down a cliff. With open steep spots they lowered themselves down holding onto root balls for support. Once they were about one hundred feet lower, the cliff gave way to a slopping hill that led down to the surf.

The trail turned right and followed the base of the cliff away from the surf and ocean beyond. The trees grew thicker as Alberto led them down slightly to maneuver around an obstruction. On the other side he led them up onto a tile terrace. The flashlight shone on the water flowing across the tile, as Kotone noticed a small cabin built into the base of the cliff. Opening the door, Alberto found a kerosene lantern and lit the wick. Lowering the glass down, the bright light illuminated the room.

"Oh my, is this safe, having the light and all?" Kotone asked.

"Perfectly safe here. No one comes to this side of the island. Since the monkey preserve was established, no humans are allowed here."

"But this cabin, wherever did it come from?"

"My grandfather built it," Alberto lied. "He would come over here hunting. Before the monkey preserve such things were permitted. Then my father joined him, and I was brought here as a child. Then it was all locked away for those monkeys."

"Well, I'm glad it's here." Kotone said. She looked around and noticed the toilet room. "May I?"

"Be my guest. I'll see about some food."

Kotone closed the door to the little toilet space and sat down. relieving herself she lingered, contemplating her escape soon from the island. She finished and stepped back out into the room. Alberto had candles lit on the two-person table near the windows. Off in the distance you could just make out the surf hitting the beach. He was standing at the one burner stove stirring a pot.

"I found some canned soup. Nothing exciting I'm afraid. See if there are crackers in one of those tins."

Kotone moved to the small pantry set against the rock that made up one wall of the cabin. Part of the cliff, the rock overhang sheltered part of the room before a roof took over to shelter the rest of the cabin. It was truly almost a cave with windows. She found a large tin can and popped the lid off. A package of crackers was inside and she pulled them out and placed them on the table. Pulling at the wrapper and tearing it,. she took one cracker and placed it in her mouth.

The cracker tasted wonderful. After all her prison food, she was happy to be eating a fresh cracker. *But how could it be fresh out here where no one came anymore?* she thought. The soup was soon ladled into bowls and placed on the table.

"I think I can find a bottle of wine," Alberto said. He started to open the few cabinets until a bottle of red wine appeared. "I hope red is OK?"

"Sounds great. Thank you again for all you have done," Kotone said. She pulled the chair out and sat down. She looked out the windows and saw the white surf hitting on the beach.

Alberto used a cork puller and poured a glass of wine. He handed it to Kotone and poured himself one. "To freedom." He held his glass out and Kotone clinked gently against Alberto's glass in a toast.

"Yes, to freedom." She took a spoonful of soup and tasted it. After prison fare it tasted wonderful. And there were no eyes staring back at her. "Tastes great Alberto. Thank you so much."

"No need to thank me. Just getting you away from that evil place is gratifying enough for me."

The two ate and drank in silence. Alberto refilled Kotone's glass and she sipped the wine as she ate. The crackers completed the simple meal. She suddenly felt the wine going to her head and taking over. Before she knew it a second bottle of wine appeared, and her glass was refilled.

Kotone suddenly drew back at what was happening. The man that said he was a fisherman was getting her drunk and she was accommodating him. And the man who claimed to be a fisherman sure didn't have the hands of a fisherman. As they ate and drank she began to focus on who her rescuer really was.

She had noticed his hands before and knew they didn't belong to a fisherman. And his styled hair was not the hair of a working person. The bright white teeth that were perfectly aligned would never appear in a fisherman's mouth. Whoever Alberto claimed to be, there was something more that made Kotone stop to take a breath.

When her third glass of wine didn't disappear, Alberto noticed the change. He lifted the bottle and held it out towards her.

"Come on. You need to help me finish this one."

Kotone's head was swirling from the two glasses she had already drunk. And now he was wanting her to plow through two more glasses. She sat and looked out the window as if contemplating her freedom. Anything to gain time to think. And her head was too compromised by the alcohol to do that properly.

"I think I've had enough Alberto."

She noticed the look she received on response to her statement. A mix of disappointment and anger. Kotone's mood swung to one of caution. *This man is not as he appears. And I'm at his mercy* she thought. She wanted desperately to get off the island and she knew Alberto was the only option. *At least that is what he had said* she thought. *But at what cost do I get my ride to freedom.*

A year ago Kotone had encountered such a man when her sister believed a modeling career was hers. But the man turned out to be interested in other things. It had been necessary for Kotone and Jack to track them down and rescue her sister. Alberto showed more and more that he was the same kind of man. But Jack was not here to rescue her, so she had to be very careful. She decided to change the subject. Looking around the small one room cabin she saw the queen bed nearby, the only one visible.

"I'm tired from our hike Alberto. I'm just not good company tonight I guess. Maybe I should turn in."

"Yes, of course. It was a workout getting here. I'll just clean up dinner."

"No, let me do that," Kotone said. As she grabbed the dishes and headed to the sink she said, "I only see one bed."

Alberto was quick with an answer. "Yes, I'm sorry it is not a big cabin. But I don't mind sharing. We did it last night with just a blanket."

Kotone didn't respond as she washed the dishes. She kept her back to Alberto as she thought of what she was going to do. Sleeping a second night with this man would not be good. Finishing, she wiped her hands on a towel and turned around. In one corner of the cabin sat an old couch.

"Alberto, I'm a married woman and I don't think it would be appropriate for me to sleep in the same bed as you. I'll just grab a blanket and sleep on the couch."

As she moved to take a blanket off the bed, she glanced at Alberto and saw the look she received at her pronouncement. Again, anger mixed with rage shown on the man's face. It was a look that many women experience in their lifetime at the rejection of unwanted advances. But he didn't say anything. Alberto stood and went to the toilet room. He soon returned and without another word took off his shirt and climbed into the bed.

Kotone was already wrapped snuggly in the blanket and feigned sleep, her eyes shut tightly against her companion. With the candles extinguished and the kerosene lamp turned to low, a dull light held the cabin. Kotone peered out carefully and saw the man on his side in bed. She hoped he stayed there.

Chapter 18

The Grenadines

Situated between St. Vincent and Grenada sat a string of small islands called the Grenadines. Vluchteling was one of the Grenadines and lay at the north end of the island chain. It was the next island to the south that Misty headed to as soon as she dropped off Jack and Lamarcus.

Sailing solo required sustaining a grueling schedule. While autopilots could be set to sail the boat while one slept, no one was watching for trouble. And in a storm, the autopilot did less than perfect work. It took a human to adjust to the swells and wind conditions to safely make a passage. Misty had done many solo passages out of necessity and didn't relish another one.

Especially since she wasn't really going anywhere but was just waiting to extract Jack, Lamarcus, and hopefully Kotone. All she needed to be was within range of the CB radio Jack carried to call her. And from her chart, a small island south of Vluchteling met her needs.

Jack had purchased detailed nautical charts of the area around Vluchteling and on one Misty had spotted an island with a bay. It was located on the leeward side of the island so it would provide shelter from the storm. A easy two-hour sail gained the island, and in fifteen minutes more she was off the mouth of the bay. Sailing around the headland the anchorage came into view. Two other sailboats were taking refuge there and she pushed the tiller over to enter the calm waters.

Dropping the motor into the water, it fired up to give her headway. She ran the roller furling and the motor took in the head sail. She climbed onto the doghouse with one line in her hand. She lowered the sail and wrapped bungee cords around it to hold it in place. The forward sail soon joined the other as Misty took in all her sails.

The chart showed a sandy bottom, so she slowed the outboard as she went forward to the small locker on the forward portion of the deck. Opening the locker, she retrieved her Danforth anchor along with the length of metal chain attached. She walked forward on the port hull, and as the big cat came up to the other two sailboats, she let the sailboat move past the others. When she was about one hundred feet in front of them, she dropped the anchor overboard and threw the chain with it.

As the anchor line played out she rushed back to the outboard and threw it into neutral. She was now moving over her anchor as the anchor line continued to run out. She hit reverse and carefully backed straight back, making sure she kept in line with where her anchor would be. Soon the line ran out in front of the boat as she returned to where the other sailboats swung at anchor.

She felt the anchor grab bottom and plow into the sand. The boat stopped as the outboard tried to pull the anchor. She switched off the outboard and walked forward to make sure the line was clear. With two hulls, the anchor line ran off both bows until it met the single anchor line. Noticing everything was set properly, Misty walked back and dropped down the ladder into the galley. She was hungry.

* * *

"Jack, I'm hungry." Lamarcus said.

"You're always hungry," Jack flipped back. But his friend was right. They had been walking all night and had finally gained the east coast of the island. Looking carefully out through the dense forest, they saw the fortress lying just to their north in the early morning light. Sunrise would happen in about an hour which gave them just enough time to get into position overlooking the fortress.

"Grab something quick. We have just enough time to get to high ground and get set up before the first rays hit us."

Lamarcus reached into his pack and pulled out some crackers. He swung the pack onto his back as he pulled the wrapper loose. He threw a cracker in his mouth and grabbed his rifle. Jack followed suit, and they were off, crackers disappearing as they walked.

The night walk across the island had only one eventful moment. They were up on a ridge when Jack picked up movement out in front of them. They went to the ground as the movement turned into two humans moving fast down the ridge. Suddenly, they switched and dropped off the ridge. While the two had been just visible in the night scope, they had been too far away for any detail. Jack was just glad they hadn't been spotted.

With the threat gone, they resumed their hike. The whole time they would walked under trees with monkeys above them. Sometime the monkeys would raise a ruckus over their presence and other times they would just chatter loudly. Jack knew all about the Black Tufted Marmoset from Kotone's talk about them. She had been the one excited about a honeymoon with the monkeys. Now, they just tormented him as they hiked east. Their noise would attract attention if any humans were nearby.

As they approached the fortress, the hill climbed. There was a ravine with a stream, and as soon as they crossed it, the ground rose significantly. The two former Marines humped up the hill, grabbing roots and small trees for leverage. By the time they reached the top, sweat poured down their faces, their clothes wet from exertion. The wind from the approaching storm cooled them quickly as Jack wondered when the full storm would hit. If it arrived at night, it would help him in his attack on the fortress.

"Jack, there's a good spot over here."

"Ok."

The hill they were on overlooked the fortress by about two hundred feet in elevation. Jack pulled out his range finder and shot a distance to the fortress.

"Five hundred yards," He said. "You ever hit anything at that distance?"

"Shit, Marine," Lamarcus chuckled. "You always thinking you were the better shot. Why don't you sit up here and I'll go inside that fort?"

"And miss all the fun, no way Marine."

The two stood under the trees and glanced out through the foliage at the fortress that was just visible. The sun was struggling to break the sea surface and the cloud cover glowed bright pink.

"Red sky in morning, sailor take warning," Lamarcus said.

"Yeah, but we aren't sailing. We be on solid ground, so red sky in morning may be our best friend."

They both moved into position before the daylight hit them totally. It was a good spot that gave them full view of the fortress while still being within rifle range. It would be a long shot, but not too long. The Lupua Magnum round would make quick work if it hit anyone at this distance as it was lethal at much longer distances.

They spread out a ground cloth and laid out their rifles. Pulling on their guilly suits for concealment, they lay down for the day. They would observe the fortress and wait for nightfall. Then Jack would enter the jail and retrieve Kotone. If anyone interfered in Jack's mission, Lamarcus would be Jack's back-up. At least until he went into the castle. Then Jack would be on his own.

Jack took first watch with his binoculars. He watched as the lone guard patrolled the top of the fortress. The two of them had eaten a MRE and Lamarcus was fast asleep. Jack wrote in a small notebook about the activities he observed. And there wasn't much. Two vehicles crossed the wooden bridge that spanned the moat. Like castles in Europe, the chains on the bridge indicted that it could be drawn up in times of trouble.

The fortress itself was fairly typical from what Jack knew about 18th Century stone fortresses. The walls had a slight slope to them and appeared to be about thirty feet tall. The top deck was open with the normal cannon slots along the parapet. No cannon were visible which would be antiques if they had been there. Jack knew more modern guns protected the fortress.

And from his talk with the former head of security, if things hadn't changed since he had left, Jack only had to worry about two guards. The one that patrolled the top and one that kept the jail down two flights. *Easy enough* he thought. He knew there were more guards available inside their living quarters, but they would be off duty when he went into the fortress. So unless there was an alarm, they would not be involved.

Four hours later Jack nudged a snoring body next to him. Lamarcus awoke with a snort. He looked at Jack as he wiped the saliva off his check.

"Four hours already? Seems as though I just fell asleep."

"Rise and shine sleeping beauty. Or at least shine since you can't rise," Jack said.

"Well, excuse me a minute."

Jack knew what was coming. They had been in this position many times before. A sniper team never moves from their position, even for vital body functions. Lamarcus pulled out an empty water bottle and rolled slowly to one side.

Jack heard the sound of a zipper followed by water running. The smell soon hit him as he waited for his partner to finish. Lamarcus rustled slightly as he screwed the cap back on the water bottle. He twisted slightly and placed the full bottle at his feet.

"Don't go mixing up that bottle with a water bottle now." Lamarcus snorted as he said it. He loved giving Jack a hard time.

"No, I think I can tell the difference."

"Maybe now, but tonight when its dark I don't want you cussing me out."

"Look big fella. I've got my own bottle at my feet. I was considerate and did my thing while you slept."

"Yeah sure. Always the cultured one. Me, I was brought up with no Daddy to teach me right." Lamarcus said.

"So, how'd you get time off from Cambridge anyway?" Jack asked.

"What, I'm a hero if you remember. And my captain position comes with four extra weeks of vacation."

Jack knew Lamarcus had been promoted from lieutenant to captain of the Cambridge, Massachusetts Police Department. Lamarcus had stopped a school shooting and was a national hero for his efforts. Jack was glad to shine the spotlight on others and gladly remained anonymous.

"Well, I'm thankful you could join me. Good to have someone I can trust looking out for me."

Lamarcus laughed. "You, shit, I came for the Caribbean vacation. Laying on the beach, catching rays, and sipping adult beverages."

"Like you need a tan." Jack threw back.

As they both watched the fortress and whispered insults at each other, the day moved toward noon. Soon Jack took his four-hour sleep break and Lamarcus was on duty. Just as the shadows grew from the hill onto the fortress, a car came into view and swerved onto the wooden bridge. Lamarcus nudged Jack awake.

"Car." It had been the only vehicle all day. The road from the main village ended at the fortress and only people having business there would use the road. Since the local population avoided the fortress, no one had driven close earlier.

Jack grabbed the binoculars and focused at the courtyard inside the walls. The black sedan swung around and stopped on the far side of the courtyard. A man stepped out of the sedan and quickly made his way into the redoubt. The redoubt on a castle consists of the central tower where the important people all sat during a battle. It was a fort within a fort and if the walls were breached, the redoubt was capable of carrying on the fight.

This redoubt was only two floors higher than the regular walls and measured maybe twenty by twenty. Not a very large redoubt, but considering the small island it protected, reasonable size. As Jack continued to watch, a small group of men gathered in the courtyard. They held rifles and Jack counted six of them.

"I don't like the looks of this," Lamarcus said. "If they don't leave, they'll be hard to get by."

Jack stayed silent as they both watched the courtyard. Soon the man returned from the redoubt and stood in front of the men. He was issuing orders, but they were too distant to hear what he was saying. When he finished, the man climbed into the car and drove quickly out the gate and across the bridge. Soon, a pickup truck appeared and entered the courtyard. The six men climbed on board the truck and left the fortress.

"That's good. Less bodies to worry about." Lamarcus said.

"But where are they going? And that guy driving the sedan matched the description of the island's owner. This Dupong character."

Just then the wind increased, and the first drops of rain announced the arrival of the main front. Within minutes a steady rain fell as the wind lashed at their position. High on the hill, they were catching the full force of the storm. Jack and Lamarcus fought to keep their concealment from blowing away. Finally, Jack moved carefully and pounded metal stakes into a tarp he pulled out from his pack.

The rain pelted the camouflaged tarp as the two men huddled under it for safety. Darkness washed over them as the cloud cover drew the day to an end. Soon total blackness gripped them as the storm continued. They both ate and drank.

At midnight, Jack announced it was time. He borrowed Lamarcus' 9 mm and along with his Ruger placed both in a water proof bag. He stuffed that into his pack, leaving everything he didn't need. Jack pulled a balaclava on his head as he strapped on the night vision monocular.

Over their comm gear he said, "Stay sharp."

Jack crawled out from under the tarp and made his way back toward the ravine they had crossed. He made good time although the rain made the hill they had climbed earlier slippery. But he found his handholds and made it to the creek. He checked and then moved downstream to where the creek entered the ocean. Low walking across the beach, he watched the fortress off to his left at all times.

"Clear?" He asked.

"Guard is hunkered down on the northeast corner out of the weather."

"Roger, tell me if he moves."

Jack took off his night vision and placed it in his waterproof bag. At this spot the ocean was blocked by the fortress from the full fury of the storm. Small waves rocked him as he swam across the moat. Reaching the other side, he climbed onto the rock promontory that the fortress was built on. Twenty feet away the rock walls loomed above him. He reached in his waterproof bag and pulled out his silenced handgun and shoved it into his vest. Next, he retrieved Lamarcus' 9 mm and shoved in into the holster on his chest harness.

Placing his night vision over his head he scanned the wall above him. Hearing nothing from his top cover, Jack retrieved his climbing rope and grabbed the grappling hook. He gripped the hook in his right hand as his left held the coiled rope. The grappling hook swung back and forth until Jack had good momentum and he flung it skyward. It clanked against the rock wall and fell down beside him.

Quickly recoiling the rope, he again gripped the metal hook and swung back and forth. Another toss and the hook went over the walls. Jack looked up at the line and saw it was on the tall portion on the wall. He wanted it running out one of the gun slots. He flipped the line as it crept toward the slot, finally falling into place. Pulling slightly on the line, he felt the grappling hook catch on the rock wall.

"Climbing," Jack spoke to Lamarcus.

"Climb, you are clear."

Jack placed two Jumar ascenders on his rope. Ascenders were metal devices that gripped the rope but would slide up the rope freely. With nylon stirrups for his feet, it was a matter using one ascender after another to move up the rope. As long as the grappling hook held. If it slipped, Jack would find gravity working fast with him smashing into the rocks.

He reached the parapet and lifted slowly so he could see the deck. Grabbing the inside ledge he muscled his way over the top and onto the deck. He put his ascenders in his pack and then untied the grappling hook. After placing it back in the pack, he coiled the rope and stuffed it in his pack.

Scanning the upper deck, no human activity was visible. From his sources, Jack knew there was a set of stairs to the right that led down to the jail. He kept low and close to the parapet as he crossed the short distance. The rain drove into his face as it continued its deluge. He reached the top of the stairs as water was running down into the fortress. Jack checked once more that the lone top guard was still hiding out from the weather across on the other side.

Looking down the stairs, he moved cautiously toward the courtyard level. A set of arched pillars held up the upper deck and separated him from the courtyard. The rain was leaving a large puddle at the bottom of the stairs, but Jack moved quickly around to the next set of stairs down. Now protected from the rain, the dry stone squeaked slightly from his wet boots.

Jack stopped and pulled his balaclava down over his face. With just his eyes showing, He took off his night vision as he saw the interior lights below. He stepped carefully on the top step and took in the lower level. *Somewhere down here is the second guard* he thought. *And he won't be hiding from the storm.*

He knew that the prison lay on the other side of the fortress so as soon as he reached the bottom of the stairs he located the passage way under the courtyard. He stayed close to the walls and now had his silenced Ruger in his right hand. As he approached the end of the passage way, he could tell it intersected with a corridor. The cells for the prisoners lay to the left and right. He crept up to the intersection and looked down one way. No guard was visible. He stepped quietly to the other wall and leaned slightly out to look down the other direction. Nothing that way either.

He had a fifty-fifty decision to make. He went left. Cell doors came up at regular intervals and they were all open. He passed a low door like entrance, but it was too short for regular walking. He passed it by. He smelled the guard before he spotted him. Moving to the opposite wall, Jack saw an antechamber ahead on the corridor. It sat opposite the cells with a brighter lighting.

Sitting at a makeshift wooden desk was a guard. And the guard was asleep, his head resting on the desk. Jack stepped carefully up behind the guard and moved his Ruger up to the base of the man's skull. His left hand grabbed the guard's neck firmly. The guard immediately sat up.

"If you want to live, just stop." Jack demanded as he pushed the suppressor into the man's neck.

He froze. Jack grabbed a bunch of the man's shirt so he had a good handhold.

"I don't want to shoot you, but I will if I have to."

The man sat perfectly still. Then in broken English he asked, "What you want?"

"I've come for the Asian woman. Where is she?"

The man made no sound. Jack knew that Dutch was the native language of the island and that any locals would not know English. Since Jack's Dutch was nonexistent, he decided he needed to search the cells himself. He shoved the pistol again to announce to the man not to move and swung his pack off onto the floor. With his left hand he searched in his pack and came out with a roll of duct tape.

Once the man was duct taped to his chair and his mouth was taped shut, Jack took the keys off the desktop and searched each cell. A flashlight showed that each cell was empty. Some had speakers in them which made sense from what Donald French had said.

The women were subjected to sounds of torture and other women suffering. While each victim was never touched, the emotional stress of other women being abused forced the victims into a fragile state. Then Mr. Wonderful would swoop in and save them Jack thought.

He stepped back to the guard and pulled the tape off his mouth. He had to find out about Kotone. He placed his index fingers on the outside of his eyes and pushed them back. His eyes narrowed representing Kotone's more oriental eyes. The man looked at him dumbly.

Jack placed both hands over his chest and made the universal sign of women's breasts. Then he immediately moved to his eyes and repeated the motion. A light bulb went off in the man's face. He nodded vigorously and spoke in Dutch.

Jack pointed at the first cell nearby and the man shook his head no. He pointed to the next cell and got a similar response. He pointed down the corridor at the third cell and the man nodded. Jack raced to the cell and pushed the metal door all the way open. He stepped inside and scanned the cell with his flashlight. Besides a metal bed with a disgusting mattress on it, a blanket was all the cell contained.

As he stood there he eyes caught the wall markings. Scratches of prisoners marking their time in confinement. He searched carefully ignoring the obviously old scratches. As he methodically went about the cell he spotted one fresh one. There were twelve marks and above that was a faint KW. *Kotone Wesley* Jack thought.

He went back to the guard and pulled his knife from the sheath. The guard's eyes grew big at the commando knife in his face. But Jack used the knife to cut the duct tape and free the man. He grabbed the guard by his shirt and yanked him to his feet. With the knife point poking his back, he shoved him into the cell. He pointed at the scratches with the knife.

"Woman. My woman." Jack said.

"Volwassen?" the guard said.

Jack didn't know what that was so he tried another word. "Girl"

"Jongedame?"

"Yes, dame."

"Ja, ja, dame." the guard lit up on recognizing something.

He needed to know how long she had been gone. Jack knew that each woman rescued would be taken to the cabin where the man would take his reward. He sat the guard down on the bed, so he could communicate better. The corridor light shown through the doorway making things visible.

Jack mentioned dame again and then made a pantomime of a bird flying away. After a minute the guard got the message. Jack knew a little German and added, "Tag." Then held up one finger for one day.

The guard shook his head no and held up two fingers. Then he said "Morgen" and he made a flying motion.

Jack surmised she had left in the morning two days ago. But he wasn't sure. And he had no way of getting any better information from this guy. He motioned the guard to stand up and took him by the neck back to his chair. Duct tape again strapped him to the chair and a piece over his mouth kept him silent.

Retracing his steps back to the courtyard, Jack was thinking the entire time as to how he could find out more information. Kotone had left two days ago, which should have put her in the cabin yesterday. Unless she had been moved somewhere else which didn't fit the guy's normal routine. He climbed the steps to the courtyard and noticed that the rain was slackening.

"Where's our guard?" Jack spoke to Lamarcus.

"Jack, he's roaming now. He's fifty feet west of your stairway heading east."

"Roger." Jack moved to the bottom of the stairs and looked up into the night sky above. He debated what he should do. *Take down the other guard and maybe he would know English. Then what to do with him?* he thought. *They'll know shortly that someone is on the island anyway when they find the other guard.*

"Tell me when he passes the top of the stairs."

Two clicks told him Lamarcus understood the message. Jack waited tight against the wall, constantly looking up for the guard. But if the guard kept to the courtyard side of the deck, Jack would not see him. Lamarcus would warn him then. He gripped his knife in his right hand and placed one foot on the first stone step.

"Now."

Jack moved quickly up the stone steps until he saw the back of the guard. He held his rifle across his chest and Jack knew that a harness held it there. Easy for patrolling but not fast for response. Jack stepped out onto the deck and rushed to the guard. In one motion he grabbed him around the harness while his other hand moved the knife up onto his throat.

"Don't move." Jack said.

"You have my attention, mate." the guard said.

"Lets get those hands behind your head and fingers interlocked.

The man complied as Jack quickly realized he had an English mercenary, unlike the local down below. Jack moved him backwards toward the steps and the man complied. Shoving the man down the stairs, Jack moved out of sight of Lamarcus. At the bottom of the stairs he forced the man down onto his knees, keeping the knife tight on his throat.

Jack added "Stay very still while I unsnap your weapon."

He took the man's rifle and threw it up the stairs. Then he took the man's handgun and added it to the rifle. Lastly the man's knife was removed from the sheath on his leg. It rattled on the stone steps. Next, Jack took his left hand and took out his duct tape. Then forcing the man to lay down on the stone floor, Jack placed his knee on the man's back and moved his knife to just below his rib cage, the point aimed at his kidneys.

Jack had the guard move his hands behind his back and they were duct taped. Next the man's ankles were taped and attached to his wrists. Once trussed, Jack rolled him onto his side.

"The Asian woman, where is she?"

"Oh, bloody hell, that's what this is about."

"I won't ask again." Jack applied pressure on his knife and the man squirmed to move away from the pain.

"She escaped two days ago mate."

"And she's not at the secret cabin, so where did she go?"

The guard's eyes showed the surprise that Jack knew about the cabin. The knife drew more pain.

"Stop, stop. She's at the cabin now."

"You lie. I was just there and it was empty." Jack said. His anger was building as he was not getting the answers he wanted. Blood trickled down the man's back from the knife point digging into him. He attempted to move away to relieve the pressure but Jack pulled him back tight. "Where were those six guards headed?"

The guard swiveled to see Jack's face. "You saw them?"

"Yes, so where were they going?"

"To arrest the woman you're looking for. Who is she anyway? You know the boss always returns his captives when he's through with them," the guard said.

Chapter 19

Vluchteling Island, the Caribbean

As Jack and Lamarcus had moved across the island to arrive at the fortress at daybreak, Alberto had slept alone on the bed. The woman was nearby sleeping on the couch. He had caught glimpses of her in the moonlight as she was wrapped tightly in her wool blanket, now more of a cocoon. Alberto debated about pressing the issue during the night but decided he would try the soft approach in the morning.

As the light grew in the cabin as the new day began, he rolled over to see her still wrapped tightly in the chair. Her face as well as the rest of her was firmly hidden.

"Good morning," he called softly to see if she was awake.

A soft good morning came back in reply.

"Oh good, you are awake. I hope you got some sleep. That was totally unnecessary you know. The bed was very comfortable, and you were perfectly safe, I assure you," Alberto lied. But he would try to be the accommodating male and see where it got him.

A face appeared out of the cocoon. Alberto marveled at the beauty still in her face. Her Asian features were softened by what must have been European blood. The results were the best of both races. Soft eyes with a rounded nose. No narrow slits of Asian eyes and no sharp beaks of European noses. A warm mouth filled out her face which was surrounded by long black hair.

Alberto had never had such a mixed woman and his desire grew. He threw the sheet aside and climbed off the bed. Standing in a pair of nylon shorts with no shirt on, he knew his beautiful tanned body showed his attributes that had melted many a woman's resistance.

"So, what shall we have for breakfast? I'm famished."

Kotone crawled off the couch and threw the blanket onto the bed. Standing in her outfit from the day before, she was disheveled. She swept her hair back and tied it in a loose knot behind her head. Alberto stared at the motion.

"What do we have?" Kotone asked.

"Good question. Let me look. No eggs, I'm afraid." Alberto looked in the cabinets and came out with a metal tin of oatmeal. A second tin was examined and pronounced to hold raisins. A container of honey was found.

"Looks like oatmeal is as good as it gets."

Kotone agreed that oatmeal was fine and Alberto grabbed a pan to cook with. A spigot of cold water had been plumbed in from the spring in the cliff and Alberto filled the pan. He lit the propane burner and placed the water on to boil. He turned to see Kotone looking out over the beach and the ocean beyond.

He walked over and stood beside her, their arms touching slightly. He noticed her move away slightly to keep them apart and he knew she would be difficult to win over. His resolve grew that no matter what, he would get his reward from this woman. No woman had ever denied him his reward for being rescued from the dreaded prison. He was not about to let this one ruin his record.

"It's a beautiful view isn't it? My grandfather loved coming to this place."

Kotone offered, "Yes, its wonderful being able to see. Thank you again for getting me out of my cell."

That's more like it he thought. *A little gratitude and maybe we can get down to business soon.*

Kotone continued. "So, there's no chance that the authorities will find me here?"

"You are perfectly safe," Alberto lied. *You are safe as long as I say so and you better figure that out soon* he thought.

Alberto returned to the stove and dumped the oatmeal and raisins in the water. He stirred the mixture and turned the heat down. The woman showed up beside him and grabbed bowls and spoons to set the small table. Soon oatmeal was ladled into their bowls and honey squirted on the top.

"Tastes wonderful. The oatmeal we got each morning didn't have raisins and honey."

Yes, I know he thought. *I know everything about your incarceration.* He was beginning to agree with his headguard that he had rushed this one. She needed more pain in the prison before her will would be agreeable to his loving advances. But it was too late now. And he was scheduled for his annual return to the old country so there was no time to return her for more manipulation. He would just have to press the issue which he had done before. Alberto as Emile Dupong, playboy of the Netherlands, had a reputation for forcibly persuading European woman to accept his advances.

That is what has been so much fun about my little island arrangement all these years he thought. *Scare a woman with jail time under horrendous conditions and then be the white knight rescuing them. Works great, every time.*

"So, how about a bath this morning? You must feel like crap after your cell and that swim in the ocean while escaping."

"I don't see a tub in here," Kotone said, looking around the cabin.

"Right over there is the best thing about life here. A natural hot spring feeding a stone tub just over there." Alberto leaned slightly and pointed to the hot tub.

Kotone turned around and spotted the water running over the lip onto the terrace. "Oh, that's what that is. A bath sounds great."

Eating quickly, Alberto grabbed the dishes and offered Kotone first dip. He stood and washed the dishes as Kotone walked out onto the terrace. She tested the water temperature and then just climbed in, clothes and all. She sat down and leaned back, a look of relaxation on her face.

Alberto stared at the stupid woman that had just climbed in with her clothes on. *What an idiot* he thought. Determined to move things along no matter what, he finished his dishes and stepped to a chest of drawers nearby. He retrieved a large bath towel, and dropping his shorts, wrapped the bath towel around his waist.

As he walked out of the cabin, he noticed the woman was paying no attention to him. She was leaning back, her eyes closed, relaxing. As he drew closer to the tub she sat up. She smiled slightly until he realised his towel and placed it in a nearby chair. Now naked in front of her, her eyes grew big.

That's more like it he thought. *She's seeing me in all my glory and we can get better acquainted.*

As he stepped toward the tub, the woman drew back into the farthest corner of the stone tub.

He ignored her as he stepped over the lip, his male parts swinging in plain sight. Putting his other leg into the water, he sat down opposite her.

"Wonderful, isn't it? Not too hot for you? I can add some cooler water." Alberto said as he stood up and moved across the tub in Kotone's direction. His private parts were out of the water and plain to see. As he neared the cliff side to change the position of the cold-water pipe, Kotone stood up suddenly.

"Excuse me." she said and stepped around Alberto's back and climbed out of the tub. The water splashed over the tile as she sloshed into the cabin.

"What are you doing?" Alberto called after her.

"I'm clean and want to change now."

Alberto sat down in the spot Kotone had vacated and stared as Kotone found a towel in one of the drawers. She then pulled out each drawer and saw various women's frilly things that a woman seducing a man would wear. Alberto watched as the woman searched each drawer and finally found a pair of shorts and a t-shirt that fit her. She stepped into the toilet room and soon emerged in her new clothes. Walking onto the terrace, she hung her wet clothes on the stone bench. She disappeared back into the cabin and sat down on her couch.

Alberto fumed slowly at the total disregard the woman had shown him. Not interested in sitting in the tub alone, he stepped out of the tub and wrapped the towel back around him. He was ready to confront this woman and take what was rightfully his. Stepping into the cabin, he walked over to where the woman was ignoring him, staring out the window.

Alberto moved to where his male member was just to the side of the woman's head. He released his towel and grabbed Kotone's head with both hands. Pulling her head toward his manhood he tried to guide her mouth.

The woman was ready. Unknown to Alberto, Kotone had earned a black belt in Taekwondo years ago. Jack had found this out one day and learned that her brothers had taken up the martial arts. In defense against her brothers, Kotone had joined them. Now her training took over.

As Alberto struggled to get his desire into Kotone's mouth, she twisted to her left and jumped to her feet. Alberto immediately lunged at her, pulling her T-shirt neck down, and ripping the fabric. Her left breast was exposed, and he latched onto it with one hand. The other hand went behind her neck as he attempted to shove his tongue into her mouth.

Suddenly he screamed in pain as Kotone stomped down hard on the top of his left foot. As he staggered back, she swung in a twisting motion and slammed her elbow into his solar plexus, knocking the air from his lungs.

"You bitch," he gasped.

"Back off asshole. Whatever you have in mind is not happening," Kotone yelled.

"You slutty bitch. After all that I've done for you. This is my thanks."

"Just stay back. I've thanked you over and over for getting me out of prison. But that's where it ends."

The two slowly maneuvered into the center of the cabin. Alberto recovering as he pulled in oxygen from his blow to the chest. His foot ached but his lust drove him forward.

"Without me it is futile for you to think you'll ever get off this island," Alberto said. His voice snarled out each word.

"Maybe so. The more I think about it, I think you are the one who set me up with that phony drug bust so then you could be my big hero. Well, screw you."

Alberto moved slowly as he decided how he would take her. He had taken what he wanted many times and had enjoyed that also. He didn't really care if it went hard or easy. But he would get what he wanted.

He lunged at the woman just as she spread her stance to put power into her right arm. Her right hand flew at his face, her flat palm aimed at his nose. Alberto dodged the blow but caught it in his right eye instead. His head twisted but he succeeded in wrapping his arms around her. Now her arms were immobile and with his weight he could overpower her onto the bed.

He lifted her off her feet and carried her toward the bed. He was going to throw her onto the bed and then tackle her as she landed. But Kotone was ready for the release and twisted her body to hit the bed and roll before he could get on top of her. She quickly rose to her feet, standing on the bed, as Alberto landed on the bed face first. She jumped off the bed as Alberto rolled off the bed and stood up.

As he turned to take another lunge at her, his balls were lifted up into his waist by a massive knee striking him. Alberto screamed, grabbed his private parts, and fell to the floor. The agony was excruciating as he screamed and writhed on the floor. His world went dark as the oatmeal pan was slammed into the side of his head.

Chapter 20

Vluchteling Island, the Caribbean

While Jack could not guess about Kotone's plight the morning before, he did know that the Emile character had shown up yesterday afternoon and rallied the troops. That could only mean bad things for Kotone. Donald French had given him the routine of how each woman was seduced. And the normal seduction did not include rounding up extra bodies. Whatever had happened, Jack needed to find his wife.

But before he could begin that search, he had unfinished business in the fortress. Standing over the British security guard, Jack had to make a quick decision. While he still had maybe three hours of darkness, eventually he and Lamarcus would be dealing with the entire security detail. While he had counted six people leaving yesterday afternoon, that left at least three in the fortress.

He knew there was a top guard, a gate guard, and a radio operator. Jack discounted the sloven specimen down in the cells. He was an untrained, out of shape local who would vanish in any fight. Jack was concerned about the professionals. With French leaving, Jack surmised that Dupong had hired men with less scruples who chose money over morals. Those were the ones that were a threat.

And the fewer he had to deal with the better. He pulled out his silenced Ruger, pointed the barrel at the man's knee, and pulled the trigger. The duct tape on the guard's mouth keep the screams muffled and the low pop of the round barely echoed in the arcade. He moved the gun to the man's other knee and as the man's eyes grew white in fear, Jack again pulled the trigger.

"You won't be tracking me down any time soon."

He left the man writhing in pain and climbed the stairs headed toward the radio room. He had its placement memorized from French's hand drawn map but called to Lamarcus before stepping on the top deck. Receiving an all clear, Jack scooted along the walls as he made his way toward the redoubt. He located the door into the redoubt and climbed the stone steps to the upper level. A lighted room announced his goal and he peered around the corner to see a man sitting at a shortwave radio. He was reading a magazine.

Jack moved quickly into the room. Shoving his handgun behind the man's ear, he grabbed his shirt collar.

"Don't move and you'll live."

"What, who are you?"

"On the floor, hands behind your back."

Jack shoved the man out of his chair onto his stomach. Again, with a knee in his back he pulled out his duct tape and soon had him trussed up. A strip over his mouth kept the screams down as Jack shot him on the left knee. Jack then smashed the radio set so that there would be no communication between the guards except for hand held units and their limited range.

A quick trip down into the courtyard and Jack was ready to take out the gate guard. He caught the man reading and forced him to the floor inside the gate house. Taped up, the man received a bullet in the knee to keep him from joining the fight.

With no one to watch, Jack ran across the bridge and climbed the hill towards Lamarcus. He reached his friend out of breath.

"Pack up. We need to get back to the cabin."

"What's going on, Jack? You just came out over the bridge. What'd you do?" Lamarcus asked.

"No time. That creep Dupong has sent those six goons after Kotone. We need to find her first."

"Jack, they have at least an eight-hour head start on us."

Jack quickly packed up all their gear and then pulled out the night vision monocular. He pulled off his balaclava and placed the head strap on his head. Picking up his rifle as Lamarcus finished stuffing his gear in his pack, they headed out with Jack taking a compass reading as they walked.

"Jack, it's going to be light soon. We'll never get back to the cabin in time."

"We'll have to chance it in the daylight.

The two men moved quickly through the jungle forest, disturbing clutches of monkeys as they went. The noise the monkeys made as they entered their territory would give them away to any reasonable tracker, but Jack knew time was critical. He also knew that he might have to go assault the fortress a second d time.

If Kotone was captured and retuned to her cell, he was ready to take on anyone to get her out. He was at war with the island's owner and only one thing would satisfy him now. They stopped for a water break and a check of the compass. Jack had kept track when they traversed the island the first time and was now keeping a reverse direction so they would hit the top of the cliff just above the cabin. Then he would know if they were too late or not.

A second stop allowed them to put their night vision gear away. The daylight was breaking and soon the sun would appear. The storm that had aided them during the night had blown off to the west. Clouds lingered but it appeared that it would be a hot sunny day.

Two hours later and Jack noticed the tree canopy disappearing a short distance ahead. That would indicate the cliff and the valley beyond. He dropped down onto one knee as Lamarcus squatted beside him.

"What's the plan?" Lamarcus asked.

"Stay concealed up to the cliff and see what's happening at the cabin."

The two moved out in a low stance keeping as much concealment around them as possible. Thirty feet from the cliff edge, Jack lowered himself down and began to crawl the remaining distance. Lamarcus was right behind him and moved up beside Jack to peer over the edge.

They had missed the cabin by one hundred yards but could still see the hot tub through the forest below. The cabin was obscured from view, but Jack pulled his binoculars out and trained them on the terrace. Lamarcus scanned the area around them from their position under some brush. They were well hidden unless someone walked close by.

After a few minutes, Jack said, "There's a guard with a gun. He just walked out of the cabin onto the terrace."

"That's bad."

"No, that's good. If they had Kotone they wouldn't be here." Jack said.

"Maybe they got her and took her back to the fortress when they discovered that we are on the island. This guy is probably stationed here in case we show up."

Lamarcus is right Jack thought. *I have no real idea where Kotone is.* Jack began to panic that Kotone was back in her cell and that she was being punished for the damage he had caused at the fortress.

"I'll go ask him," Jack said.

"Are you crazy? There's at least six guys with guns somewhere out here. And you're just going to ask this one guy you happen to see."

"You got any better ideas? I'm all ears."

Silence from Lamarcus let Jack know that his friend didn't have any other ideas. Jack didn't find the prospects of going in alone to his liking either. But the only way to see if Kotone had been taken was to ask one of the guards. Then Jack remembered the handheld radio he had taken off the second guard. He reached into his pocket and pulled it out. He turned it on with low volume as he and Lamarcus listened.

"Gee Jack, you're getting old. You forgot you had this thing?"

"Be quiet."

Soon, one of the guards announced that they had finished searching the upper valley and were returning to the cabin. Jack's resolve grew at the news that Kotone was still being searched for. He motioned to Lamarcus to move closer to the cabin, so they might hear more of the conversation when the men were together.

They moved one at a time, keeping one person watching while one moved. They got to a spot directly above the cabin and slid out to the edge of the cliff. The terrace lay one hundred feet below them. They could see the lone guard sitting on a rock bench. Next to him were clothes laid flat.

Soon two guards showed up as they pulled out cigarettes and lit up. Jack listened to the normal griping of men about being hot and tired. They had obviously been searching all night and wanted to take a break. Two more guards showed up and the five all began griping about the long stint of searching.

As the sixth guard showed up, they all stopped complaining. Jack figured he was the head guard. A quick decision was made, and three guards disappeared into the cabin. *They must be grabbing a sleep break* Jack thought. The men had been removing gear as they entered the cabin as if to lay down. The three on the terrace talked a bit and then one more guard headed in to take a rest.

That left one guard and the boss. But the boss soon left, heading down hill. Jack hadn't quite caught onto what the boss was up to, but figured he was continuing the search while the rest of his men took a break. One guard remained outside and would provide security for the others.

Feeling tired himself now that he knew Kotone was uncaptured, he suggested to Lamarcus that they take turns sleeping. Lamarcus offered first watch and promised to wake Jack if anything changed. Jack was soon asleep.

Chapter 21

Vluchteling Island, the Caribbean

Kotone had realized that she would not be leaving the island when she cold cocked Alberto with a cooking pot. With her tormentor unconscious on the floor, she debated what to do. Her only chance was to wait for Jack to come to her rescue. But she had no idea how or when that would take place. It was her job to remain hidden on the island till he showed up.

She ransacked the cabin looking for supplies she would need to go into hiding. She grabbed all the food she found and threw it in a pillow case. She folded one of the wool blankets and stuffed it in the second pillow case. She found a six-liter plastic bottle of water and added that to the blanket.

The kitchen had a long knife and she shoved that into one pillow case, being careful to wrap some cardboard from a box around the sharp blade. A flashlight and some rope were discovered in one cabinet. She made a sling to go over one shoulder and tied each pillowcase to her sling, leaving her hands free if she needed them. The rope cut into her shoulder and would need to be changed to the opposite shoulder frequently, but it helped to carry her gear.

Checking that Alberto was still out, she left the cabin heading down hill. She knew from her initial escape that they had dogs to track her. She made her way to the valley floor where a creek flowed, stepping into the creek and heading up the valley away from the ocean. When she had gone a moderate distance, she stepped onto shore to leave her scent and then returned to the creek. Now she retraced her route, being careful not to touch any dry object.

She hoped the dogs would spot her scent upstream and figure she was in the upper valley while she intended to await Jack near the ocean. As she neared the beach, the stream grew deeper and lost its current. A sandbar held the water back and the sluggish water held plant growth. Just before she reached the beach a shiny object caught her attention. She moved to the left bank to investigate what was hidden in the brush.

Carefully moving a branch, she saw the inflatable dinghy. Her heart soared as her mind raced to the conclusion that Jack was already on the island. *But where on the island?* she thought. *And how do I tell him I'm here?* As she debated what to do, she knew the weather was changing and that a storm was moving in. She quickly dropped her shorts and stepped out of them. Then she pulled off her panties and placed them in the bottom of the dinghy. She pulled her shorts back on and moved out.

She crossed the beach, keeping in the small rivulet of water and which joined the beach below the surf mark. Keeping her feet wet the entire way along the beach, she reached the far side where a short cliff denoted the end of the sand. While not difficult to climb, the vertical rock led up and away from the beach. She had stayed in the water the whole time and should have avoided leaving any scent a dog could follow.

Leaving her panties was the quickest way to warn Jack that she was around. She had replaced the brush so that anyone following her would not have seen the same shiny object. Now fully concealed, only someone who walked right onto the dinghy would spot it.

She climbed over the rock and moved higher along a rock cliff. The turbulent seas below her crashed into the base of the cliff. The rock was fractured enough for good footing as her hands searched out the abundant hand holds. As she moved along the cliff, a cleft in the rock revealed a small cave. She crawled inside and dumped her load. *This will have to do until I'm rescued* she thought.

Kotone sat and tried to think where Jack would be. As she relaxed a bit, sleep came over her. The stress of the prison escape followed by the attack by Alberto took her strength away. She moved back into the cave with her belongings and sat against the rock wall. She was asleep in minutes.

When she awoke it was pouring rain outside. Her cave remained dry but Kotone moved toward the front of the cave to look out. Below her the waves crashed into the base of the cliff and spray flew up toward her. She moved back to her gear and found the flashlight. The sun was setting, and the dark night made her cave black. She found some crackers and ate a handful. Water from her jug kept her hydrated. She inventoried her food and figured she had something to eat for about five days. Water would last about the same time and then she'd have to rely on the creek water.

It was a fitful night as she kept thinking she heard voices coming along the cliff. But no one ever appeared at the mouth and she sat up most of the night watching. At daybreak she again ate and drink a little. She wanted a place to relieve herself but not where dogs could smell her. Kotone climbed down the cliff toward the ocean. Near where the waves were still crashing, she did her business hoping the waves would wash away the scent.

Climbing back up to her cave, she retrieved the knife. She decided to find a spot to observe the beach to see if anyone was tracking her. She had spotted a large boulder in the jumble of rocks she could crawl under for concealment. She slid on her belly into the tight space and was rewarded by a view of the entire beach. One melon size rock cut into her side and she moved it to the side. Now comfortable, she waited.

It was mid-morning when she saw movement off to her left. Her heart raced as a man with a gun came out of the valley and walked along the creek. Moving right past the hidden dinghy the man reached the beach, stopping to study the sand. He looked left and right and then looked up at the cliff Kotone was hidden in.

Kotone felt like the man was staring right at her and she froze so as to not give anything away. The man turned right and began walking down the beach right towards her. Panic grew as he drew nearer. She gripped the knife and scanned to see if any others followed. The man was patrolling alone, and she assumed he was seeking her.

Alberto must have finally regained consciousness and ran back to the fortress. Now people were looking for me to take me back to my cell she thought. But Kotone was just as determined never to be in that cell again. As she shifted to back out of her crevasse, her elbow caught the rock she had moved. A shot of pain ran up her arm and she dropped the knife. She turned to move the rock further and an idea came to her.

She shimmied out of her spot while pulling the rock with her. Figuring it weighed about fifteen pounds and was about the size of a human head, it required both hands to lift it. She moved forward, holding the rock against her stomach.

Kotone was on her knees holding the rock below her as she crawled up onto the lip of the cliff. The man continued to walk toward her position while scanning the area where he walked. She hung just below the top of the cliff, out of sight of the man. A large boulder on her right blocked her body as she peered around the edge to check the man's position. He was walking right up to where the sand stopped, and the cliff began. As he disappeared beneath the cliff, Kotone stood and carefully walked out toward the edge. The heavy rock hung at her waist in both hands.

When the man turned to return down the beach, Kotone jumped off the cliff, aiming the rock at the man's head. It hit like a watermelon dropped off a roof. A popping sound accompanied by a groan and the man crumpled onto the sand. Kotone landed on top of him as the rock rolled out of her hands. Blood oozed out the man's fractured skull as Kotone looked away.

Scanning for anyone else and seeing no one, Kotone went to work stripping the man of his equipment. When he was picked clean, Kotone grabbed his shoulders and jerked his body toward the surf. The waves came in, and as he floated she shoved the body out to sea and watched momentarily as the current took him under.

She gathered up her haul and climbed back up the cliff. She soon returned to her cave and inventoried what she had captured. Her prize was an AR rifle and a 9mm handgun. She knew how to use both weapons from her time living in Wyoming. Jack had taken her out shooting many times and she felt confident that she could defend herself. *At least for awhile,* she thought. *And I'll make them pay if they try to take me back to prison.*

She pulled the magazine out of the AR rifle and shook it for sand. Then she grabbed the bolt handle and pulled it back. A round flew out and she gathered it up and forced it into the top of the full magazine. Then using her flashlight, she inspected the semiautomatic rifle for sand. She blew out the few grains that had found their way into the breech when the man hit the sand.

She checked the bore and satisfied it was clean, clipped the magazine back in and released the bolt. The gun clacked as a round was pulled from the magazine into the chamber. It was ready for firing now. She switched the indicator to safe.

Then she did the same with the man's 9mm handgun. Satisfied no sand was in it, she hit the tab and the slide slammed home a round.

The tactical vest she had taken off the man held two more magazines for the rifle and two more for the 9 mm. A combat knife in a sheath was attached to the side of the vest. And in one pocket of the vest she found a radio. She turned it on and listened.

* * *

"Jack, Wake up. I think I hear something," Lamarcus said in a quiet voice.

Jack snapped out of his sleep and turned to his friend. "What?"

"I think I hear something behind us."

Both men raised slightly and turned their head side to side. Each was attempting to catch any noise emanating from the island they had crossed hours ago. They each turned to face each other and stopped. There was something.

"Monkeys." Lamarcus said.

"Why are the monkeys complaining?" But Jack knew the answer before he had even asked it. The monkeys protested anytime a human walked through their territory. And they would complain in a loud vocal way. That meant only one thing.

Humans were coming their way. And these humans were not going to be friendly.

Both men held their pose as they continued listening. The monkeys stopped their complaining but now there was a new noise. A much more dangerous noise.

"Shit, dogs." Jack said.

"They got dogs out tracking us?" Lamarcus asked.

Jack swiveled slightly to focus his ear for the new noise. It was just a faint yelping, but it was the unmistakable sound of dogs on the hunt.

"How did they get our scent? Dogs need something to get their initial scent from. We didn't leave anything back there," Jack said. The look Lamarcus gave him forced him to change it to a question. "Did we leave anything back there?"

"Jack, I figured since you came out the front door of that fortress that everyone would know we were here."

"Lamarcus, what did you leave behind?"

"I'm sorry Jack. I just didn't want to carry it across the island."

"Where's your piss bottle?" Jack asked. His anger showed.

"Back at the spot overlooking the fortress. When you were in such a rush to get moving I just sort of kicked it under some brush."

Jack looked at his friend. "And your poop bag?"

"Same place. You carrying yours?"

"I got my piss bottle. And I haven't pooped yet."

"Sorry Jack, I just . . ." Lamarcus said and was cut off by Jack.

"Well, we know those dogs are after you at least."

"What, you gonna leave me?" Lamarcus asked.

He had to think. The dogs would be upon them in maybe thirty minutes if they were lucky. *How many men are with those dogs?* Jack thought. *And we are being squeezed against six armed men in the valley below. Not a good place to be.*

He assumed that the men below didn't know dogs were hot on their trail. And with the smashed base radio, the men below wouldn't have gotten word of reinforcements coming. Jack had to act quick before they figured things out.

Picking up the requisitioned radio, Jack switched to broadcast. Lamarcus' eyes grew big at what was happening. Jack held up his finger to be quiet and depressed the button to speak.

"Hey assholes. Are you listening?"

A short delay before a voice came over the radio. "Who is this?"

"This is your worst nightmare," Jack said. "But I'm in a generous mood today."

The voice from the cabin came back over, "I don't know who the hell you are but bugger off or we will find you."

"Well hold on mate, you're probably wondering why you haven't heard from base back at the fortress?" Jack asked.

"What about the fortress?" the voice asked.

"They are sort of indisposed. So listen up, I'm only offering this once." Jack transmitted.

"Look mate, you are messing with people who don't take shit from anyone. At least anyone who lives very long."

"Listen shithead. Your friends at the fortress won't be joining you, ever." Jack lied slightly. "But we don't want to hurt you. We only came for the woman. Leave the valley and we won't kill you."

"Teton, is that you?" A woman's voice came over the radio.

Jack knew it was Kotone and somehow she had grabbed a radio. She was using a code name that he would recognize from their time living in Jackson, Wyoming to tip him off.

"Moose, is that you?" Jack knew Kotone would recognize the name of the town just outside Jackson near Jack's brother's house.

"Teton, I know where you landed on the island. I'm two hundred meters west of that spot."

273

"Hey bitch, you're dreaming if you think you're getting off this island, along with whoever came to help you." the voice came over the radio.

"Last chance. Just walk away and no one gets hurt," Jack said.

"Screw you, asshole," the voice said.

Down below on the terrace of the cabin things were busy. Jack and Lamarcus watched as they counted five men head off into the tropical rain forest.

"Jack, why'd you tip them off?" Lamarcus asked.

"Tried to get them to leave, but their loss. But we know where Kotone is now, so it worked."

"So, what's the plan?"

In the background the yelping of dogs grew stronger as they neared their position. They had to move and now with the five men ahead of them were out patrolling too. Jack assumed that the dinghy hadn't been discovered but he wasn't sure of that.

"Moose, you have eyes on our landing spot?"

"Affirmative. No activity there yet." Kotone said. "And Teton, I can cover you."

Lamarcus looked at his friend. That Kotone could cover them meant she was armed. That she had a radio meant she had taken it off the missing guard, number six.

Lamarcus looked at his friend and asked, "Is she really armed? And does she know how to shoot?"

"I taught her myself. Great shot. And if she took number six guy's radio, she must have taken his weapon also."

"But can she shoot to kill if we get in a tight spot?"

"I think we already know that answer. I doubt number six gave up his stuff willingly."

The two men quickly discussed their plan. They needed to move but they weren't sure where the remaining five would be. Since they heard that someone had landed on the island meant a boat. And if they knew Kotone had eyes on the spot, they would concentrate on the coast line.

Jack looked at the weather and judged that above the cloud cover the sun was setting. They had spent most of the day waiting on the top of the cliff for something to happen. Darkness could be their friend as they had night vision gear. Jack wondered if the other side had any. They would just have to risk it.

They checked their weapons followed by placing their monocular night vision gear on their head straps. They shoved their remaining gear in their backpacks and hefted them onto their backs. Jack led out with Lamarcus carrying the big sniper rifle.

They tracked along the top of the cliff until they reached the opening where a ravine cut through he rock. They had climbed out of the valley along the small animal trail. But Jack kept going as he avoided the normal route down. They would move closer to the ocean and hope the cliff gave way somewhere up ahead.

Fifteen minutes later a likely spot for them to drop down showed itself. The storm was still moving heavy cloud cover across the island, but the rain had stopped. A combination of the setting sun and the heavy clouds made twilight very dark. While not as dark as it would be in another half an hour, the low light offered just enough darkness that the night vision began to work.

Jack stopped at the top of the crevasse that led toward the creek. He handed Lamarcus his rifle and dropped his pack on the ground. From their years together in the Marine Corps, Lamarcus knew what to do. He dropped to the ground and swung his sniper rifle into position. He would provide top cover as Jack went down to reconnoiter below.

Jack pulled out his silenced Ruger as Lamarcus handed him his 9 mm. Jack stuffed the 9 mm into his vest and stepped lightly down the hill. It was steep enough that he had to dig the sides of his boots into the earth to keep from sliding, while his free hand grabbed at branches or roots to steady him. Keeping to one side he used the rock wall for as much cover as possible.

He swung away from the ocean at the base of the cliff and crouched as he walked. He stopped near a boulder pile to scan with his night vision. Down here the tropical tree cover made the valley even darker than above. As he moved his head back and forth looking for one of the guards, he caught the glow of someone laying partially concealed. The man was one hundred feet down and was guarding the toe of the slope where they would move toward the beach.

The man was positioned too low to protect the ravine Jack had just come down and Jack would make him pay for his mistake. Dropping to the ground, Jack crawled forward. He was approaching the man from his left rear quarter so unless he turned to check, he wouldn't see Jack's approach. And if he didn't have a night vision device, he wouldn't see him in the dark.

Jack got within twenty feet of his target and stopped. Holding very still, he lined up the front and back sights of his Ruger handgun. The built-in night sights on top of the gun enabled him to place his gun on target. He pulled the trigger slowly. Both hands felt the recoil and the small pop sound from the suppressor. The man's head slumped down.

A short crawl forward confirmed that the man was dead. Jack scanned the area for any other humans, and seeing none, called Lamarcus on the radio. Jack took up the 9 mm as he guarded his friend's descent down to their position.

Lamarcus dropped the pack and Jack swung it back on. He grabbed his AR rifle as Lamarcus held the sniper rifle. Both watched different sectors for unfriendlies. The dinghy lay a short distance downhill and to the left. Jack led off traversing the slope as he moved back to the base of the cliff. The cliff itself was dropping as it approached the sea, but it still allowed for protection from one half of their area unless anyone was on top looking down.

Anyone above looking down would need vision enhancement to see down into the dark forest now. The darkness was almost complete as they stopped where they would have to turn down to the beach.

They continued their scan of their area for any more guards, and seeing only clear forest moved out. The slope was gentle as they walked in a crouch with each of them watching to one side. They needed to work together to avoid any surprises.

They were soon just above the beach, the creek laying just ahead. Jack knew if Kotone was two hundred meters to the west, then that put her in among the rock cliffs that were just visible in the dark. They were more outlined by the white sea water crashing into the rocks and the dark skyline where the cliff rose out of the sea. She would not be able to see much to shoot at from there so Jack made a decision.

"Moose, still there?"

"Still here Teton."

"Move west for extraction if you can."

Jack wanted her out of any chance of being hit if they were about to get fired upon. Since she couldn't see much, she couldn't help them so better to have her away from the beach.

"Jack look," Lamarcus whispered. "Across the beach by the cliff."

A faint image of a human on the other end of the beach made its way to the night vision scope. While night vision had a limited range, the guard was just on the outside of their range with enough of a signature to announce his position.

Jack motioned that they would move to the dinghy. The two crawled the final two hundred feet to where the dingy was concealed. Seeing no other humans in their scopes, they made the boat ready to move.

"Do you want me to shoot him?" Lamarcus asked.

"No, that last guy didn't have any night vision. We'll assume they all don't. We should be invisible to that guy across the beach at least until we hit the surf and he sees us against the white foam. We'll move fast and hopefully he won't see us."

"I can shoot him."

"That will alert the rest to where we are. Let's take our chances."

Keeping their rifles out if they needed them, they swung the guns onto their backs. Each man grabbed a side of the rubber boat and dragged it toward the beach. Jack kept them in the trees as much as possible even though it meant a longer movement. Checking their line of sight to the guard on the opposite side, Jack concluded that the trees blocked them on the beach.

With a quiet command, both men ran fast across the beach, the dinghy between them. They flung the boat into the surf and as Jack climbed aboard and began pulling the starter cord, Lamarcus pushed the dinghy deeper. As the water reached his waist, the motor caught. Jack grabbed Lamarcus by his webbing and as he pulled him into the boat, he gunned the engine. The dinghy flew forward. Lamarcus grabbed at the thwart in the center of the boat as he slid himself in on his belly.

Jack hit an incoming wave and the motor revved. A shot followed by two more rang out but the man was firing blindly. Jack twisted the throttle and the dinghy leaped over the swells. Once out past the surf and far enough for even a shooter with night vision to miss, he pushed the handle and the dinghy turned west. Now paralleling the coast, as soon as he passed the end of the beach, he swung toward shore. Lamarcus was sitting in the bow now and scanning for human life.

"There," he yelled. Jack looked to shore and saw his goal. A figure was scrambling along the cliff toward the water. Jack slowed as he approached the spot where the glow of Kotone lie.

Jack could now make out her shape with his unaided eye and he pulled closer to the rocks. Kotone moved out onto a large boulder.

"Jump." Jack yelled.

The glow jumped feet first off the rock and disappeared under the water. Jack kept the dinghy moving so he had steerage as he kept the boat away from the rocks. While the seas had settled some, there were still large swells crashing into the rocks. He started to panic as Kotone had not surfaced and he and Lamarcus both searched the water.

Suddenly a yell to their right announced her surfacing and Jack twisted the throttle and spun the boat They were on her in seconds and Lamarcus grabbed her arm and pulled her over the side of the rubber tube. She flopped into the bottom and Jack gunned the outboard. He headed out to sea, suddenly remembering that he had to call their ride to come get them.

Chapter 22

The Grenadines

Misty Duran sat eating her dinner in the lee of the island. Anchored in a safe bay from the storm, she had ridden out things quietly. The other two sailboats continued to be her neighbors as each was content to sit and enjoy the safe harborage.

It had been two days now since she had dropped Jack and his friend off on Vluchteling. Jack had estimated that it would take him about that long to rescue his wife, so she wasn't surprised when her CB radio squawked to life.

"Albany, Tree here."

Since bad guys on Vluchteling could hear any CB broadcast, they had worked out call signs for each other. Misty was Albany for her and Jack's encounter in Albany, New York. Jack was Tree after his nickname for his dog that Misty had traveled with.

"Albany here, everything OK?" Misty transmitted.

"Sort of, but we need you right now. Mission accomplished. Will meet you south south west of our last location."

"Roger. Figure one hour."

"Make it faster if you can." Jack's voice pleaded.

Misty hit the switch that lowered the outboard motor into the water. She touched the electronic start and the engine fired right up. She shifted it into forward gear as she hit the mast lights. Now illuminated, the boat started to move forward slowly as she ran across the deck and onto the starboard hull. Laying on the bow, she snatched the anchor line and pulled up the slack.

Then moving back to the main deck, she gathered in the anchor line as the outboard moved the boat forward. Seeing the line start to go between the two hulls, she quickly wrapped the line around a cleat. The catamaran balked as the anchor fought its hold on the bottom. But with the line pulling straight up, the anchor lost its fight.

Misty grabbed the now loose line and pulled. Soon the metal chain was coming aboard followed by the anchor. She lifted the anchor aboard and dropped it in its place in the box on the deck. Leaving the line uncoiled on the deck, she ran back to the cockpit and swung the tiller to head to sea. She increased the engine and the big cat picked up speed. She switched on the running lights and left her mast lights on. They would help Jack spot her as she approached Vluchteling.

Once outside the bay, she steered the boat to starboard and placed the cat on a northerly heading. She decided to run on the engine, as she didn't want to raise the sails and deal with rigging out the boat. The distance was short, and she had enough fuel to easily make her pickup. And then she would have the ease of maneuvering once Jack spotted her. She knew she would not see Jack in the dinghy, and was relying on the CB to guide her in.

She made her way back forward and coiled and stowed the anchor line. It would be a mistake to leave an uncoiled line on deck. *Too much chance of it washing overboard where it could tangle with the propeller, stopping the boat. A sailboat had to be tidy for a reason* she thought. *Not a good time for any oversight.*

After about forty minutes she assumed that she would soon be visible to Jack. And right on time the CB squawked.

"Turn off your mast lights, we see you. Stay steady and we'll intercept."

"Roger." Misty replied. She flicked her mast lights off and continued steady. She knew her red and green running lights would be visible if not her white light on her stern. Misty scanned the ocean ahead for any sign of her pickup. She knew Jack had a flashlight and any small light carried a long way, even with the swells. The dinghy would be visible at the tops of each swell, so she watched for a light going on and off.

Off her starboard side she spotted a light. Then the light disappeared. Then returned. She adjusted her course to intercept. She slowed as she drew nearer and the light became more steadier. Before she knew it, the dinghy loomed into sight. Misty dropped the throttle down and shifted into neutral. The boat's momentum carried her up to the dinghy.

Lamarcus threw her a painter and she pulled them alongside. Jack helped a woman aboard before he threw his pack aboard. The woman collapsed on the main deck while Lamarcus climbed over the gunwale and stood up. Jack switched off the outboard and then moved under the lifeline onto the cat. Grabbing the painter, he pulled the bow of the dinghy up to where Lamarcus could grab one side. The two men lifted the rubber boat aboard, stowing it on the main deck.

"Thanks Misty. Let's get out of here."

"What heading Jack?"

"Due west," Jack ordered. He felt the Wharram move to the new course as he grabbed Lamarcus. "Let's get the sails up."

Lamarcus had learned his job in sail raising and moved to the sheet for the forward main sail. Jack shook out the sail and Lamarcus wrapped the line around a winch. His quick work had the forward sail set. Jack jumped onto the doghouse and took off the ties on the rear sail. Lamarcus repeated the maneuver and the rear sail was set.

Misty swung the two sails to opposite sides as she ran wing on wing. With the wind coming over their stern, each sail would catch the wind. That left the head sail useless and it remained in its roller furling.

Jack climbed into the cockpit and located the electrical panel. He switched off the running lights. Now totally dark, the catamaran risked being hit by any other ship in the area.

"Lamarcus, you're on cleaning duty while I provide watch."

Lamarcus knew he had weapon cleaning detail. Since they hadn't put their weapons in a water proof bag, the guns had been exposed to salt water. Each gun needed to be broken down, cleaned and oiled before any rusting damage occurred. Jack kept his night vision on while he checked for any signs of trouble near the boat. He would rely on other people's lights for ship avoidance.

Seeing that the ocean seemed clear around them, he walked back to where Kotone lay on the deck. Jack was concerned that she had injured herself in the jump off the boulder.

He knelt down and placed his hand under her head. "Kotone, are you OK?"

As she rolled her face toward him, Jack saw tears flowing down her cheeks. Worried, he began to run his other hand down her body, checking for injuries.

"What are you doing?" Kotone asked.

"I'm looking for injuries."

"I'm fine Jack." She sat up and turned to look at him. "Thank you for coming for me."

"Of course, always and forever." Jack said.

Kotone sat quietly and didn't offer anymore. With the outboard switched off and lifted on board, the only sound was the swoosh of water just below them where it moved between the hulls.

"Come and meet our rescuer." Jack helped her to stand and they walked around the doghouse into the cockpit. In the dull light of the compass, Misty saw the woman she had been cajoled into helping. Her beauty stood out, even in the low light.

"Misty, my wife, Kotone." Jack said.

The two women exchanged greetings. Kotone sat down next to Jack as he continued to scan the darkness for anything they needed to worry about.

After a few pleasant minutes between the three, Kotone noticed the berth just inside the doghouse. She made her excuses and crawled inside. She was soon asleep. Jack maintained his watch as Misty kept a westerly course. The steady wind moved the Wharram at a good rate of speed. With its twin hulls and light weight, a Wharram catamaran could run with the wind like no other boat.

As the first signs of daylight shown on the eastern horizon, Jack dropped into the port hull and found Lamarcus asleep on the dinette bench. The guns had been packed back into their waterproof bag and the cleaning gear sat on the dinette. Jack took off his monocular and laid it on the dinette table. He turned on the propane stove and heated water. Soon two cups of English Breakfast tea were in each hand as he climbed back into the cockpit. He handed one to Misty as he sat down.

"Still drinking tea, heh." Misty said.

"Yes, but I can make you coffee if you'd prefer."

"No tea is good."

"As soon as I'm finished we'll change heading and set a course for St. Croix." Jack said.

"Why the U.S. Virgin Islands?"

"Kotone can catch a flight there back to the mainland. We have some unfinished business."

"We do?"

* * *

As happened on their sail south from Miami, life on the boat quickly returned to normal. Once they were sure that no one would follow them from Vluchteling, the standard watch schedule took over. With four people on board, each person would have a three-hour watch followed by a nine-hour break. The boat had to have someone at the helm watching at all times. While the Wharram's autopilot could steer a course in anything but heavy weather, human eyes were needed to see dangers to the boat.

Misty, having been the most rested from her wait in the Grenadines took the first official watch at 6 a.m.. While she had been awake all night sailing, Jack and Lamarcus hadn't really slept for the past two days. They had racked out when the sun brought daylight and no visible threats in sight. Lamarcus had crashed as soon as the weapons had been cleaned with Jack following him soon after. Kotone still slept on the berth in the doghouse that was more for the solo sailor that had to rest but stay close to the cockpit.

About two hours into Misty's watch a head appeared from the doghouse. Kotone crawled out of the cave like space and stood up. She stretched and took in the fresh sea air.

"Feels good I bet?" Misty said.

"Yes, freedom. Wonderful feeling." Kotone said.

"Get some good sleep?"

"Yes. I was tired. The stress of the last couple of days. That, and sleeping in prison never was a real pleasant experience."

"I have some clothes down below. You might want to take a bath and change. Watch things while I go grab something. We're about the same size."

Kotone thanked Misty and sat while she went to the starboard hull and disappeared down the short ladder. With a small Bimini top over the cockpit, Kotone moved to a shaded spot on the opposite side of the cockpit. The tropical sun was already bearing down, and her skin was unprotected.

Misty reappeared from the hull and handed Kotone a shirt, shorts, and some under clothes. Kotone held up the bra being offered.

"Yeah, we can see how badly it fits," Misty said. "I'm afraid I'm less endowed than you."

"No, it will work. I haven't had a bra since I was arrested. Even one too small should be better." Kotone looked around. "I assume the shower is a bucket on the deck?"

"That's right, you've sailed before. The bucket is just inside the doghouse. It has a line on it for dipping in the ocean."

Kotone reached inside the doghouse and retrieved the five-gallon plastic bucket. All long-distance sailors got used to salt water baths as most boats didn't have enough freshwater on board. She dropped the bucket off the stern and held on tight. The bucket quickly filled, and with the speed of the cat, tried to pull her in with it. She pulled hard and brought the full pail on board.

She carried it in her left hand while in her right she carried the soap and shampoo Misty had offered her. Once in the middle of the forward deck, she stepped out of her clothes and threw them overboard. She wanted no reminder of her time on Vluchteling.

Now naked, she used the plastic ladle to scoop out some water and dump it over her head. The warm Caribbean water felt wonderful as she lathered up her hair. She ran the bar of soap over her body and then rinsed herself off. One final pour right from the big bucket and she placed it down on the deck.

She ran her hands over her body acting as a squeegee. The remaining water was wiped off with a small hand towel. She stepped back into the cockpit and pulled her panties on. The bikini style panties fit. She pulled on the loaner shorts and they were also a good fit. *Misty and I are about the same size down there* she thought. *But now for the test.*

Kotone slipped into the bra and placed the cups over each breast. The overflow of flesh was obvious. She tried to reach around to hook the clasp.

"Here, let me help." Misty said as she stood up. She grabbed the two ends and pulled slightly. "I'll hook it on the loosest clasp."

With three clasp settings, even on the largest one Kotone's breasts were squeezed against her chest. She looked down and adjusted the bra, so the extra flesh oozed out the top of the bra. After Kotone slipped on the V-necked shirt, the cleavage stood out.

"Well, that will have the boys' interest," Misty said.

Kotone smiled at the comment. *Yes, I'm married now* she thought. The island had interrupted their honeymoon.

"Thanks. I'll return them when we get to St. Croix and I can shop."

"I'd say keep them, but you do need a bigger size." Misty smiled as she said it. "The bra anyway. The rest fits you well."

The two women chatted for awhile about clothes and sailing. Kotone's hair dried in the warm breeze as they sailed north. After a few moments of silence between them, Misty changed the subject.

"If you don't mind me asking, how did you ever get Jack to marry you?"

Kotone looked at her and remembered that this woman had been in Jack's life after Kotone had left Jack the first time. She didn't know the full story but she knew enough that Jack and Lamarcus had gone to war with this woman. And now she was asking me how Jack and I got back together. *Is there something still between she and Jack?* Kotone thought.

"We had two false starts before," Kotone said. "We ran into each other at his son's wedding in Montana and it just took off from there."

Kotone wanted to know more about this woman. Jack had admitted that there was another woman he had been with since he and Kotone had first broken up. Kotone knew men sought out female companionship and were reluctant to be alone. And she knew this other woman was the one that had stepped into her spot after their time in Wyoming had ended.

"I know you and Jack were an item a while back. He didn't express any interest then?" Kotone asked.

"Heavens no. Jack rescued me when my sailboat sank, and he took me in. We had fun for a while, but he was drawn to the west, while the call of the Caribbean took me" Misty said.

"So you live on your boat year-round?"

"No, I have a home in the British Virgin Islands."

Kotone knew that Misty was wealthy from her trip to Hawaii to rescue her sister. Misty had put up the money, so they could complete their mission of ruining the lives of those that had kidnapped Kotone's sister. Jack had left out the details but Kotone knew that Misty had been very helpful.

"And anyone in your life. You are young and attractive and should have someone who is special to you." Kotone said.

"And rich. Money complicates everything. You never know when someone wants you versus wants your money. That was special about Jack. He never seemed to care about the money."

"So why not you and him?" Kotone asked.

"We are very different people. Too independent I'm afraid."

Is she telling me I'm dependent on Jack? Kotone thought. She's right in that Jack is always coming to my rescue. First in Kansas while riding my bicycle. Then in Hawaii finding my sister. And then pulling me off that island. Kotone grew quiet and Misty noticed the change.

"I didn't mean to imply anything, Kotone," Misty said. "Jack and I had fun together and then went our separate ways. We had too many differences to be a couple."

Kotone sat quietly as Misty explained things to her. It wasn't helping. Kotone stared back at the other woman and estimated that she was a couple years younger. Misty was a little shorter but had a good athletic figure. *She could afford that* Kotone thought. *And while Misty was smaller breasted, she certainly filled out her bathing suit well. All the attributes that would attract a man.*

"But since you asked, yes there is someone. Back on Virgin Gorda."

Kotone gave a blank stare at the statement. Misty elaborated.

"Virgin Gorda is the island in the British Virgin Islands where my home is. I moor my boat in the main harbor in Spanishtown."

Misty nodded she understood. "And he is a good man. I hope. You deserve the best."

"Thank you Kotone. Yes, he's a good man. He's from Sint Maarten. Thats on the Dutch half. We met when I did a sail down there from my home."

Kotone drew quiet at the mention of a Dutch island. She had just escaped from one of the Dutch islands and didn't like being reminded. Misty saw the reaction.

"Kotone, not all Dutch men are pigs like the one you ran into."

"I'm sorry. I'm sure he is good to you."

Lamarcus stepped out of the port hull from his forward berth. He walked back to the cockpit after a stop in the head. The Wharram Tiki 38 had one head in the starboard hull forward of Misty's cabin. As he sat down Kotone excused herself stating she was hungry. She went into the main salon in the port hull. Jack was asleep in the berth aft of the galley. When Kotone returned to the cockpit to eat her food Lamarcus was alone.

"Here Lamarcus, I hope you drink coffee." Kotone said.

Chapter 23

Loosdrecht, the Netherlands

While the British royalty had their Buckingham Palace and the French had Versailles, the Dutch royal family lived at Het Loo. Located southeast of Amsterdam, the palace consisted of a large red brick palace set among acres consisting of water features and nature. Unlike their European cousins, the Dutch royal family had their palace away from the tumult of the capital at the Hague.

And unlike Buckingham Palace, Het Loo was open to the public. At least the grounds were, as the royal family still lived in the palace. And unlike Versailles, the Dutch still had their Queen and had not chopped her head off. The Dutch royal family held a much more plebeian standing, if such a statement could be made.

The kings and queens of the Netherlands took their station in life much differently than the British crown. The Netherlands had since the 1500s seen a more leveling effect on the country. The Dutch had arrived on the world stage in the 1500s as the merchants for the world. Dutch traders spread around the world as the wealth in Holland grew, and it was the first place a middle class of citizens developed.

Up until then, there had been the aristocracy tied to the crown. Beneath the aristocrats were the serfs, or the poor. But the merchant class of Holland soon developed into a third class, a wealthy middle class of people. And the Dutch artists Vermeer and Rembrandt captured this evolving change in mankind.

Vermeer is famous for capturing people in their daily tasks: pouring milk, playing the piano. Common people painted doing their day to day activities with exquisite interplay of light made Vermeer one of the art world's greats. Along with Rembrandt, the Dutch masters painted the merchant class as their wealth allowed what previously had been only the privilege of the rich.

Rembrandt left us images of common people going about their lives. But he showed us the middle class of people, ones that could afford a painting of themselves. Throughout art history the rich and powerful had paintings done of themselves. But it was in Holland, where the not so rich but well off patronized the art world.

And while the Dutch soon fell behind in world power to the English, the attitude of the Dutch continued to support middle class development. More than in any other country in Europe, personal freedom from tyrannical governments was cherished and fought for. And the Dutch royal family understood this national drive for equality while still representing the Dutch people.

But there were still some who never took the Dutch spirit to heart. Some who still held the belief that a ruling class was mandatory for a well-ordered society. And in ruling, they would take their rightful rewards.

Emile Dupong was one such man. Young, rich, aristocratic, he came from a long line of Dutch royalty that continued to hold the belief that might is right. That the common man was not capable of ruling themselves. And that an elite was needed to keep society from breaking apart.

Many year before the prince had awarded the Dupong family with the island of Vluchteling. The Dupongs had held supreme power over the island ever since and only recently had opened it up to tourists. Before then, the small population lived and worked alongside the Black Tufted Marmosets. The island still had limited facilities for tourists and controlled the number of people who traveled to the island.

But each spring found Emile Dupong flying back to the Netherlands to enjoy the weather and flowers. Springtime in Holland was world famous for the tulip festivals, and Emile was determined to be home for the celebrations. The winters were spent having fun on Vluchteling, but spring and summer were the season to be in Europe. It was prime tourist time in Holland, and Emile enjoyed being the available playboy to all those young females visiting.

"Emile, bring your breakfast out here on the terrace. It's a beautiful morning."

"Coming mother," Emile said. He stepped through the double glass doors onto the tile terrace overlooking the lake. Loosdrecht was a small village to the south of Amsterdam. A half hour train ride from the station in nearby Hilversum would take one into the main train station in Amsterdam. Not that Emile ever rode the train anywhere. That was for the little people. His family had a chauffeur and many Mercedes cars to transport the family around.

"You have to admit, Emile, that springtime in Holland is the best."

"Yes mother. But I'm happy to leave for the winter. The Caribbean is wonderful while you sit in the snow here."

"But why do you put up with that old stone fort on Vluchteling? You could afford to build someplace nice there."

"But our family has been part of that fortress for three hundred years. It makes me feel so connected to Prince Charles."

"Suit yourself. You just won't catch me on that island again. Haven't been there in twenty years and don't plan on going there ever again."

"It's different now. You should go and see the changes, Mother," Emile said.

They sat on an Italian inlaid tile terrace, stone alabaster surrounding them. Behind them sat a three-story house of Italian design. Large and out of sorts with the nearby neighbor's red brick houses, the expansive grounds kept them out of sight. The ten-foot walls and stately trees surrounding the house added to their separation.

But on one side of the estate sat the lake that made Loosdrecht famous. Connected to the canals of Holland, the lake held large canal boats as well as sailboats of all sizes. Ocean cruisers sat at docks from where they had moved along the canals from the North Sea.

Emile sipped his coffee and planned his day. He would take the Porsche out for a drive and swing by De Hoge Velune National Park. The short forty miles would be nothing in the Porsche and he knew the park attracted single young females. They came for the bicycle trails and wildlife throughout the park. And with loaner bicycles all around the park, one just jumped on and rode, leaving it wherever one stopped.

The Kroller-Muller Museum in the park held van Gogh and other Dutch paintings and was the perfect place to take any prospective woman to impress her with his art knowledge. Then a spin in the Porsche to the nearby Het Loo for a Dutch history lesson followed by an evening in Amsterdam. All that was guaranteed to get what he wanted. And Emile Dupong was happy to take it from all those wanton women.

* * *

Two days of sailing brought them to St. Croix. After a brief stop they moved on to Saint Thomas across the channel. The two main islands of the U.S. Virgin Islands offered fine hotels. Jack checked himself and Kotone into one that overlooked the harbor where the Wharram was docked. Misty borrowed their shower and then returned to her boat leaving Jack and Kotone alone for the first time since her escape.

Lamarcus had boarded a flight back to Boston as soon as they docked, and he could get a seat. Work back at the Cambridge Police Department called. After an afternoon of shopping for clothes for Kotone, they returned to their hotel. Things had been left unsaid during their two-day trip north. Even any semblance of a honeymoon had been on hold.

"Jack, we haven't talked about the prison."

Jack took one of the comfy chairs by the sliding glass doors leading out to the balcony overlooking the harbor. Kotone sat on the bed with the pillows piled up for support. The light cloth curtain billowed in the breeze coming in through the open door.

"If you're ready."

"First I want you to know he never did anything." At Jack's quizzical look, she added. "Alberto."

"Who?" Jack asked. Alberto was an unknown to him. "Who is Alberto?"

"The guy who set me up, so he could rescue me. He expected plenty of favors for being my rescuer."

"Oh, you mean Emile Dupong. That's his real name."

"Well, he fed me some bullshit story that he was Alberto, long time fisherman of Vluchteling."

"No, he comes from an old aristocratic family in Europe that's owned the island for centuries. Nice set-up. Lock up single women on trumped up charges, psychologically torture them and then swoop in and rescue them. Word is he's been doing it for years."

"My God. And no one has gone to the authorities." Kotone said.

"Seems that once he's played his white knight role, he tires of them and moves on to another. The women are so glad to get off the island no one has ever filed a complaint. And who would they file it with. The family is part of the Dutch government, so where would you go?"

"But Jack, he tried."

Jack was silent as he looked at his wife. She was processing the demons that had been forced on her on the island.

"All he got off me was a knee in the balls and a frying pan whacked against his head."

Jack smiled. He loved this woman more every day. But he knew it was a good thing that he had arrived in time to get her out.

"He deserves more," Jack said. "It's good that you didn't wait around to see what would have happened next. Word is no woman had ever rejected him."

"But Jack, I killed a man on the island."

"Kotone, I know." She looked at Jack as to how he already knew. Jack added, "He didn't give up the radio because you asked nice."

"I crushed his head with a rock. Jumped off a cliff and his head just popped on impact."

Jack cringed slightly hearing how she had killed him. He knew it was her only option because if she had been captured her life would have been over.

"You did what you had to do, Kotone."

"He had his back to me. I could have let him live. He didn't know where I was."

"Stop. He worked for evil and he would have shown you no mercy. You were right to kill him."

"You think? You say that so naturally. That's one more person I've killed."

Jack knew of the two other deaths that Kotone talked of. Both self-defense as so determined by the legal system. This third one would never be taken to court, but Jack did recognize that for a woman three deaths on their conscience was not easy to reconcile.

He stood and walked to her, sitting on the edge of the bed. He took her in his arms as she began to cry. Soon she was sobbing, and he felt the wet tears hitting his bare arm. He just held her. The time went on and Kotone's crying slowed. She lifted her head and looked into Jack's eyes, an expression of gratefulness shown back at Jack.

Jack leaned down and kissed her mouth. He pulled her closer as she wrapped her arms around him. Kotone pulled them back onto the bed as she lied down, Jack beside her. His hand found her breast and cupped it gently. Her tongue found his mouth as they kissed deeply.

Coming up for air, Kotone said, "Jack, thank you for being in my life."

"Forever and always."

"Is it OK if we just hold each other tonight?"

Jack moved closer and rolled Kotone onto her side. He gripped her and pulled her tightly against his stomach. Now spooning, they fell asleep.

Chapter 24

Charlotte Amalie, Saint Thomas, U.S. Virgin Islands

The early morning trade winds caressed Jack and Kotone as they slept wrapped in each other's arms. The morning sun was infiltrating the light curtains as the room rose in temperature. Lying still with their clothes on from the night before, the couple began to stir.

Jack awoke laying on his back with Kotone snug in his arm pit. Her right leg was atop his stomach with her leg extended along his. Blinking his eyes open, he smelled Kotone's freshly washed hair from her bath the night before. He pulled the fragrance into his nostrils and luxuriated in the smell. He had been afraid that this would all be taken from him and he just wanted to let it linger.

As he stared at the ceiling remembering the other times they had been in such a similar position, Kotone stirred. She moved her leg and her knee dragged across his groin. The sensation brought his body to attention. He reached around and ran his fingers along her right arm. She moaned slightly in her sleep. A twitch made his desire grow as Kotone moved slightly. The movement released her right breast against his chest as he felt the flesh flatten through the cloth.

Jack slid down the bed carefully as Kotone rolled onto her back. His thumbs caught the top of her shorts as he moved and they slipped down revealing her nakedness. Moving to the side, Jack raised Kotone's legs and spread them slightly. Her sleep continued. His mouth found its mark as she began to moan. Jack continued massaging her with his tongue as she spread her legs wider. Soon her body was moving to his rhythm as a hand came down to guide his head.

Jack knew she was awake but wanted to slumber while he brought her to a pinnacle. Kotone thrashed in the bed and then grabbed Jack. She pulled him on top of her as her hand guided him inside her. Now wide awake, she took over as the two finally enjoyed their honeymoon.

The morning had turned to afternoon when a knock at the door finally stirred them out of bed. Jack threw on his Big Dog shorts as Kotone disappeared into the bathroom. Jack opened the door to a smiling Misty.

"Didn't want to disturb you before noon. But did you guys want to do lunch together?"

"Yeah, I'm starved. And I'm sure Kotone is also."

"Meet me downstairs then," Misty said.

Fifteen minutes, two quick showers and they arrived in the lobby. Kotone had gone to the local police the day before just after their arrival. She had no papers or passport so when Homeland Security arrived on the dock, she was technically not admitted to the U.S.. She would have to have new IDs issued and air expressed to her before she could fly. Her sister in California had been contacted to help track down what they needed. Until they arrived, she was stateless.

Jack had been told it would take about a week to get the required identification. The story that her bag had washed overboard in the storm was taken at face value. Finding a restaurant near the hotel, they grabbed a table near the water. The umbrella offered relief from the sun.

"Since you two are stuck here until your new IDs show up, I'm going to head home," Misty said.

"Oh, is it close by?" Kotone asked.

"Virgin Gorda is just 30 nautical miles that way," Misty said as she pointed across the island toward the British Virgin Islands. When they sailed between St. Croix and Saint Thomas the day before, she had pointed out Sir Francis Drake Channel separating the Virgin Island group, half American and half British. "Takes me about four hours if the trades keep up."

"I'll email you when we are ready to continue, Misty." Jack said. Kotone looked at him. This was news to her.

"Are we all sailing somewhere else?" Kotone asked. "We haven't talked about it, but I'm sort of ready to get home. As soon as I can fly, can we go home Jack?"

Misty looked at Jack with the expression that announced that some things had not been said to Kotone that the other two knew. Jack saw that Kotone suddenly knew that something else was going to happen.

"Jack, what is it? What's going to happen?" Kotone asked.

"I'm sorry I haven't brought it up before. It was just that you were still dealing with getting off the island."

Misty sat quietly as the two others looked at each other sternly. Jack knew Kotone needed answers, but this wasn't the time or place.

"Kotone, let's have a nice lunch and then send Misty off. We can talk about it later today."

The silent treatment Jack received for his answer kept things icy during lunch. The three walked down to Misty's catamaran and as Misty started the engine, Jack and Kotone worked the docking lines. Misty pulled away from the dock as Jack placed his arm around Kotone and held her tight. Kotone offered no comment except to wave and wish Misty safe voyage.

The two walked to the end of the promenade that lined the harbor. Now far from any prying ears, Jack sat Kotone on the concrete wall holding a mass of flowers. The stern look he received made him apprehensive about bringing up what he was about to bring up.

"Kotone," Jack started. "I'm putting you on a plane to Missoula and your sister's as soon as you can fly."

"And you will be where?" Kotone asked.

"I'll be finishing the business that Emile Dupong started on Vluchteling."

"And by finishing the business, you mean what?"

"You don't want to know," Jack said. He gave her a look that meant that she was not to ask what he was up to. With their history together, he hoped she would accept the answer.

"Jack, I don't know. We have to stop this, what we end up doing."

"And what is it we end up doing?" Jack asked.

"You know. People dying. Usually because of me. It needs to stop."

"It will. Just as soon as I get back."

"I'm not sure it will. Life just keeps coming at us. Why can't we be like other people?"

"Kotone, I didn't ask this Dupong character to screw with our life. But I can sure keep him from messing with us again," Jack said.

"But Jack. We will never be on their terrible island again. I'm sorry I ever wanted to see Black Tufted Marmosets in the first place. Can't we just go home?"

"It's not your fault you wanted to go to his island and have a pleasant vacation. He started this war. I aim to finish it."

"Where are you going then?" Kotone asked.

"I'm going gunkholing for awhile." Jack said.

"Gunkholing. What the hell is that?" Kotone asked.

"Gunkholing is slow cruising on a sailboat though a scenic area, in this case the British Virgin Islands." Jack said.

Kotone looked on with a questionable look.

"Kotone, Misty and I will just be having a sailboat trip and nothing more."

"So, you're going to go back to Vluchteling and finish the job?" Kotone asked.

"Not exactly," Jack said.

"How not exactly? If not Vluchteling, where?"

Chapter 24

Mid-Atlantic Ocean

The Wharram catamaran hissed through the water headed east. Kotone had received her new identification and Jack had put her on a plane to Miami. There she would transfer for a flight to Missoula and a pick-up by her sister. Jack caught a short hop to the small airport on Virgin Gorda. He found a room for rent and called Misty. They arranged to meet the next day, buy supplies, and set sail that evening.

The first four days had been spent heading north. They needed to pick up the winds that would carry them to Europe. Once they reached the correct latitude, they swung their heading toward Gibraltar. It was over 4,000 nautical miles to their destination as the crow flew. With the detour north for favorable winds, it was even a longer journey.

But with a catamaran that was easily capable of maintaining a twelve-knot speed, Jack assumed they would reach their destination in three weeks. While racing cats were capable of 30 knot speeds, the Tiki 38's a2 knots was double what Jack had experienced sailing monohulls.

Now with only two on board, the watch schedule was four hours on, four hours off.

Misty and Jack spent most of their time in their berth catching up on sleep. A quick meal between watches was about all the time they spent together. Now in mid-ocean, Jack carried his waterproof bag onto the deck. He gave Misty ear protectors as he pulled a pair on himself. Unstrapping the bag, he pulled out the Barrett sniper rifle that Lamarcus had carried on the island. They had never been required to use it. Now Jack wanted to get familiar with it.

Jack had extensive training in marksmanship shooting in the Marine Corps and he had kept his skills fresh over the years since. But he had never fired a Barrett and wanted to get used to the recoil off the .338 Lapua round. He unclipped the bi-pod legs and set the rifle on top of the doghouse.

Pulling a magazine out of the bag, he clicked in four rounds. He shoved the magazine into the bottom of the gun. With the bolt open, he could see the top round ready to be chambered. He then grabbed a plastic bag and placed some of the boat's garbage inside. He wound the plastic together and tied it in a not, leaving enough air in the bag to create a balloon like object. Throwing the bag over the stern, it quickly floated away from the fast-moving cat.

Jack asked Misty to luff the sails and the cat slowed to a crawl. Misty moved out of the cockpit, so she was behind Jack who now took a prone position atop the doghouse. He shoved the bolt forward. The bag continued its float away as Jack took a look through the Leopold scope. Jack referenced the Barrett Optical Ranging System or BORS. This aided the shooter in determining the correct setting for the scope in order to hit a target.

Once he was dialed in, Jack relaxed as the trash bag moved further astern. With low swells, he maintained continuous vision with the target. When the trash bag was about 200 meters astern, Jack squeezed the trigger. The gun exploded as it sent the 300-grain bullet streaking toward the target with over 4,800-foot pounds of force.

The water erupted and it took a minute for Jack to see the trash bag was gone. He repeated the motion several times with each trash bag meeting a similar fate. He turned to Misty and nodded that they could pull the sail in and get moving again. He disappeared with the rifle down into the main salon. An hour later he returned to the cockpit.

"All clean and stowed." Jack said.

"Jack, I haven't asked. I know better. But how are you going to take a shot with that beast and not be heard or seen."

"My problem to figure out. If I don't show up after a week, just turn around and head home."

"I know we have history together and I understand what makes you tick. But do you really need to do this? You are risking a lot. Why not just go live your life with your wife?"

"Misty, you have always been there for me. And you don't know how much I appreciate it." Jack said.

"You did save my life, you do remember."

"I was saving your dog's life actually. You just happened to be nearby." Jack said as he teased her on their experience together.

"And Jackie thanks you for that."

"Where is Jackie by the way. Figured she'd be sailing with you."

"I left her at home with a friend. She's getting old and doesn't get around like she used to."

"My old dog too. When he got shot in Maryland, sure slowed him down. But I got a new version in London."

"So, take your bride and go be happy with your old and new dogs Jack. Don't do whatever you are planning."

"Thanks Misty. But duty calls. I'll take your advice on the sail back to America," Jack said.

But first they had to complete their sail east. The Wharram soon entered the Straits of Gibraltar but they didn't stop. Another five days found them off the west coast of Italy. The Tyrrhenian Sea shimmered in the morning light as Jack stepped out into the cockpit. He had gotten cell service that morning and placed a follow-up to the email he had sent before leaving the Virgin Islands. Things were about to change, and Jack checked the chart as to their position. He had given the coordinates to Misty the previous week. By noon they were approaching their destination. At least Jack's destination.

"OK, there is Capri," Jack said as he scanned the horizon through the binoculars. "Just make for the southwest corner of the island."

"You know I've been to Italy before, but it was with my husband."

"I'm sorry I can't accompany you into port but I'm entering the country a little less obtrusively. Sort of like illegal aliens."

"And don't tell me what you have planned please. I want to sit in Sorrento Harbor and relax a little bit."

"And don't forget to try the British Pub on the main street. Good food and reasonable prices." Jack offered. He had been to Italy with his brother when he and Ed had spent time in Sorrento.

"And why on Earth would I eat in an English Pub when I'm in Italy?"

"Oh, you are one of those then. I forgot you have all the money in the world. In that case the wood fired pizza place in the center piazza is good. Just a short walk up from the harbor."

"OK Mr. Gastronomic, I think I can find my own eating establishments just fine. And I plan on staying in a hotel while I'm here. And maybe renting a car to drive the Amalfi Coast."

"Great experience. My brother has money like you so he rented a Ferrari and we each drove the Amalfi. He drove one way and I drove the return trip rather than drive around on the Autoroute."

As they continued to discuss travel plans the Isle of Capri grew bigger. Soon the cliffs of the south end of the island towered over the sailboat. Misty changed course so the boat would move up the west side of the island. Once Jack met his contact, she would swing east and sail the short distance to the mainland. Sorrento lay a short way along the peninsula on the north side.

Tourist boats passed them by as they made their way around the isle. A couple private motorboats moved past taking in the sights. One power boat swung toward them as Misty kept her course steady. The wooden power boat came up from the rear and pulled alongside the cat. Jack recognized the pilot and had his bag ready. A quick exchange and the motorboat was away, now carrying two people. Misty kept her course set as the motorboat disappeared around the headland on the west coast of the island.

"Good to see you Jack," the woman pilot said.

"Valentina, thanks for the pick-up on short notice."

"I assumed that it was important."

Jack was sitting in the seat next to where Valentina stood steering the motorboat. He looked at the other motorboats carrying tourists as they made their way around the corner of the island. Up ahead was a large gathering of water craft.

"The Blue Grotto," Valentina said as she pointed to the cliff. A set of stairs led down to a large gathering of small rowboats. Off shore, larger boats disgorged tourists two by two into the smaller craft. As Jack watched, the rowboats would disappear into the cliff through a very low cave. The tourists had to lay in the bottom of the boat while the waterman rowing grabbed a cable, dropped down and pulled himself into the chamber. Valentina motored on by heading for Marina Grande.

"Never been. Didn't stop long enough in Sorrento when I was here to take the trip to Capri." Jack said.

The motor noise made talking difficult as both were speaking loudly. Jack studied the woman at the helm. She wore extra clothing for the cool spring weather, but something was different about her. When they last had been together, they had been naked in a hot tub overlooking the Teton Mountain range in Jackson, Wyoming.

In spite of the clothes, Jack remembered the bronze body underneath the clothes. The curly bouncy hair and skin tone gave away Valentina's heritage. Half Italian and half Somalian, she was the result of Italy's resurgent empire. Italian Somaliland in Africa had been an Italian colony up until the end of World War II. That Valentina's father had lingered there after the war was attributed to his proficiency in both English and Somali. As a native Italian, he had worked in the Italian Embassy, and married a local woman. Valentina had been born after they had returned to Italy when life in Africa became dangerous.

But Jack marveled at the resulting beauty that the mixed races produced. When he first had met her Jack had described her as Halle Berry's younger sister. The two truly could have been sisters.

"You should see Capri. Everyone should before they die." Valentina said.

"I've seen it. I watched *It Started in Naples* with Sophia Loren and Clark Cable."

Valentina turned to give Jack a dirty look. "What does that have to do with anything?"

"It was filmed mostly on Capri. I've been inside the Blue Grotto and I've been to Anacapri and the cable car. And I've sat in the main piazza in the center. So, I've seen it all already," Jack said. He waited for the Italian's temper to explode.

"You Americans, you think you know a place because you saw a movie. Let me tell you, Jack Wesley . . ."

"Hold on Valentina," Jack interrupted, holding up his hand. "Just kidding you. I would love to see Capri, but maybe next time. This is a business trip."

"Well, if you are here in Europe for what I think you are, then you should know on the other corner of Capri is Villa Jovis. It was one of Tiberius' villa that he used to come and stay in on the island. Back about 30 A.D."

"I've seen lots of Roman ruins when I was here with my brother."

"But you should know Villa Jovis has a special history. Tiberius would invite people he wanted to get rid of here for a little vacation. Then he would throw them off the cliff next to the villa," Valentina said. She pointed at the high peak on the far horizon.

Jack shuddered at the thought. But he could relate to the appeal of removing your enemies in a sudden emphatic method.

"I'd use the same technique this trip, but don't think I can get my target to travel to Capri."

"So tell me who we are gong after?" Valentina asked.

Jack told her the entire story of getting back with Kotone and them deciding to get married. The excitement of a Caribbean honeymoon that turned into a nightmare was related with a few of the more gruesome details left out. When he was done they were approaching the main harbor where a ferry to the mainland waited.

"And I have to ask, what was the body count?"

Jack knew Valentina well from an episode in London they had been involved with. The body count on that one had been high compared to Vluchteling. Even so, he was reluctant to admit to much.

"Only two dead."

"And I assume one to go," Valentina said.

Jack didn't reply. He didn't have to. She was an intelligent perceptive woman. Jack wouldn't need to enter Italy by motorboat with no Customs check if it was legitimate business he was involved in. Valentina worked for the Italian equivalent of the CIA, called the SISDE. They had met when she had hid on his canal boat in Southern France to escape the clutches of the Russian mob.

Valentina maneuvered the motorboat up to the dock where a local man was ready to tie them off. Jack grabbed the rear painter and stepped onto the dock to tie them off. Once secure, Valentina switched off the engine. She handed the keys to the local and signed a paper he had on a clip board. She received a receipt. Jack had his waterproof bag slung over his shoulder waiting for the final transaction. Completed, they both moved off along the stone break water toward the pier for the ferry.

Valentina pointed at one of the row houses lining the street which ran along the breakwater. Stone steps led up to a door on the second story.

"Sophia Loren lived there." Valentina said.

Jack stopped momentarily and gawked at the building. It looked familiar.

"Your movie. That's the house they had Loren and her brother living in for the movie."

"So, you've seen the movie?" Jack asked.

"Of course. Any movie filmed in Italy. Even if it's an American movie."

"Well half American, Sophia Loren was Italian," Jack said. Valentina smiled at the reference and pulled Jack forward. They made their way to the ferry and walked onto the ship.

Valentina produced two tickets she had purchased on the way over.

The ferry soon moved away from the pier and turned to head toward Sorrento. The two found seats on the port side so they could enjoy a view of the Bay of Naples. They were on the shady side of the ship and Jack found a wind breaker to pull on from his backpack.

Entering Sorrento Harbor, the ferry tied up and lowered the exit gates. A crowd of tourists made their way to the waiting buses and taxis to ride up to the center of town. Valentina led them toward the parking lot carved into the base of a cliff. Sorrento sat atop a long cliff and one narrow road twisted through the ravine leading up from the harbor.

Valentina stopped outside a Mercedes van and opened the side door. She slid the door back and then walked around to the driver's side. Jack lifted his waterproof bag into the van and slid the door shut. He climbed into the passenger seat and buckled up. The diesel engine soon clattered to life and Valentina shifted into gear. The white van climbed slowly up the hill and turned just before the main piazza. Traffic was bad in the tourist town and the Italian driver wound her way east along the peninsula. At each small town the traffic backed up and the two would sit waiting for the clog to move.

Finally, they reached the Autoroute and Valentina wound up the Mercedes as they headed for Naples. Sticking to the right lane most of the time, Valentina drove through Naples staying on the expressway. Once north of Naples the traffic eased up.

"Monte Cassino," Valentina said as she pointed at the abbey high on a hill across the valley.

Jack had seen the abbey on his visit to Italy with his brother. He knew about the U.S. Air Force flattening the medieval abbey in World War II and the controversy it still created. The German defenders had not occupied the abbey but instead sat on the surrounding hill. But once it was rubble, the German's occupied the bombed out abbey and extracted considerable losses by the Allies in capturing the place.

"Are you going to beat me up about America destroying that place?" Jack asked.

"Then you know the history?"

"Of course. Many places were destroyed but we didn't start it."

Valentina said nothing in response. Jack knew her family had suffered through the war. The two sat quietly until they approached Rome. It was decided a rest stop was necessary and Valentina pulled into the Autoroute service area. They stepped into the restaurant and Jack grabbed a tray. He soon had half a chicken and some vegetables. Valentina made her selection and they found a table to sit at.

"It's an 18-hour drive so do you want to stop part way and get a hotel? I threw a pad in the back if you want to take turns driving straight through."

Jack's mouth was full of chicken and he chewed his food. It was the best baked chicken he'd ever eaten.

"You know, this is the best chicken. And in a road side restaurant like this. Amazing.

"Thank you Jack. Yes, Italians know how to cook. And I didn't want to stop at McDonalds."

"No argument from me." Jack said. He studied the woman sitting across from him. She looked different than the last time he had seen her, but he couldn't put a finger on what was different. "I think we need our rest, so let's get a hotel."

Jack noticed a look of relief from Valentina. *So, she definitely wanted to stop* he thought.

"We will hit Switzerland and the Alps about sunset, so I suggest we stop there. We can drive through the Alps in the morning."

They finished their meal and were back on the road skirting around Rome. Again, the traffic built until they were on their way to Orvieto north of Rome. It was the same each time they approached one of the big cities of Italy. Bologna and then Milan slowed them down briefly but soon they were back to moving at cruising speed.

At the Swiss border Valentina stopped at Customs to buy a vehicle permit. Any car driving in Switzerland had to have a permit sticker. She pulled off the Autoroute and found a small hotel. Jack grabbed his two bags and followed Valentina into the lobby. She spoke to the clerk in Italian and paid with her credit card.

Jack was relieved when the clerk handed over two keys. They had not talked about sleeping arrangements and with them being intimate a short time ago, Jack wasn't sure what would happen. He was married now and wanted to be a good husband. He had never been a philanderer on his first wife even through the bad times before his divorce. And being still in his honeymoon period, he sure wasn't about to start now.

"Let's meet in an hour for dinner in the lobby," Valentina said as she handed Jack his key.

Jack agreed and stepped to his adjoining room next door. He opened the door and walked into a clean efficient Swiss hotel room. He placed his waterproof bag on the desk and dropped his backpack on the bed. He showered and put on fresh clothes. He laid down on the bed to await the remaining hour. He thought he heard a whirring sound and stood up to look out the window.

The window was open slightly and the sound seemed to be coming in from outside. He looked out and saw nothing but pasture and mountains in the near distance. The highway was on the opposite side of the hotel so the traffic noise was absent. He leaned out the window and saw that Valentina's window was also open slightly. The noise he heard seemed to be coming from her room.

He closed the window and grabbed a jacket for the evening air. Sitting in the lobby, Jack looked up as the elevator door opened. Valentina stepped out. Her clothes had been changed but they were the same type of baggy outfit she had worn earlier. She held a coat for the walk to the nearby restaurant.

Jack stood up and offered to help her with her coat. She passed it to Jack and he held it up. She slid in one arm after the other and then turned around as she clasped the belt around her middle. *She's gained weight* Jack thought. *Its in her face too. She is heavier than she was in Wyoming.*

Knowing that mentioning a woman's weight was a big no no, Jack kept tight lipped. They walked the short distance to a restaurant where they ordered their food. Jack caught himself staring at Valentina's face and estimating how much weight she had gained. It was difficult to tell by the clothes she wore so Jack just let it go. They chatted about day to day things as they ate. Soon they were back in their rooms with the commitment to an early start the next day. As Jack crawled into bed, he heard the same whirring sound he had heard earlier.

Valentina continued driving in the morning. With Jack an illegal alien in Europe it would not be good for him to be stopped by the police. The odds were small that their white van would attract much attention, but the mission was too important to compromise. So, Jack sat back as a passenger keeping the driver entertained. With the normal food and fuel stops, they were approaching Hilversum by the end of daylight.

"So, are we setting up in Hilversum like we discussed?"

"You have the GPS set on that hotel we saw online. We can check it out but it seems out of the way," Jack said.

They had wanted a nondescript lower end hotel near Loosdrecht to base out of. Hilversum was a large city with a variety of hotels available. They picked one located on the west side, so they were about five miles from their target. Pulling up outside, the hotel fit their needs. It sat right on a rural highway with a canal across the street. A-mix of commercial buildings were nearby so a white van would not be out of the ordinary.

Deciding it would do, they walked into the lobby which was also the bar for a restaurant. Valentina paid again and received two keys. The proprietor motioned them toward the upstairs where the rooms were located. Jack opened the door and found a ladder instead of stairs.

Knowing that life in Europe was sometimes different than the U.S., he grabbed the rope handrail and climbed up the ladder. It was not easy with his two bags slung on his back. Once upstairs, the hall and room layout resembled a typical hotel. They found their rooms and agreed to meet for dinner.

Jack opened the door and stopped. The room held a double bed and about two extra feet on only two sides. He stepped in and placed his water proof bag in the small space at the foot of the bed. The backpack landed on the bed as he looked for the ensuite bathroom. A narrow glass door separated the bathroom from the room and when he opened it he was amazed. A toilet, shower, and small sink had all been shoe horned into the space.

Jack stepped in to do his business and realized he couldn't turn to sit down. He stepped out into the main room, turned around and backed into the bathroom. He had heard about bathrooms so small that you needed to step outside to turn around, but this was his first experience with one.

The sun was setting by the time they returned to their van. Jack suggested they reconnoiter their target and Valentina pulled out a map she had downloaded off her computer. Jack studied it and gave directions to where they could observe discreetly. Valentina swung the van the short distance to Loosdrecht.

Loosdrecht was a small community sitting on a large lake. The lake was connected by canal to the main canal that took boats from Amsterdam to the Rhine River south of them. The town consisted of pleasure craft and canal boats tied up at various marinas. The odd restaurant and boat chandelier sat along the road as they drove through. A park began, and Jack motioned for Valentina to pull in.

The parking lot held a boat ramp and Valentina parked the van near the ramp. No other cars were in the parking lot. No other people were nearby, as it was dinner time for the locals and the wind was cool off the North Sea.

Jack pulled his binoculars out of his backpack and scanned across the lake. He checked the map Valentina had made and scanned closer. He found the large Italian house sitting in a green area of trees. He zoomed in and searched for details, spotting the outdoor furniture on the veranda with the alabaster balustrades around the edge.

"You see what you need?" Valentina asked.

"Seems to be the spot right across the lake."

"I'd estimate it to be four hundred meters."

Jack looked at her and then reached down and found his range finder. He aimed it at the house and a number popped up on the screen.

"Four hundred thirty to be more exact. Good guess though."

"Can you make the shot?" Valentina asked.

She doesn't even bat an eye that I'm here to shoot someone he thought. *And if it goes badly, she's just as involved as me. Her Italian government position won't help her out of this if I screw up.*

"I can drive over here solo so if something goes wrong you aren't here."

"Sure Jack. And they'll never tie the van to me with credit cards in my name for fuel and hotels. Besides, you need a spotter outside to make sure there is no one nearby when you shoot."

She was right. She had provided a hole on the rear door big enough for a sniper to lie prone in the van and shoot through. The noise inside the van would be hell even with a suppressor on. But the noise would be contained partially and anyone hearing it would have a hard time placing the origin. Unless they were close. So he did need someone outside looking out for him.

"And you don't have a problem with me taking out a darling of the European set?"

"When you sent me the email to meet me I did my research at headquarters. There is a file on this guy with complaints from women that he's assaulted in Europe. Just never enough evidence to get past the 'he said she said' stage. So, no, no problem for me that he departs this world."

Jack shook his head at Valentina's attitude. He loved her cool calculating approach to life. He knew it came from her undercover work searching out bad guys. She had been in plenty of tight spots over her career and Jack cared enough for her that he wished she would start thinking of a new career.

"When are you going to get out of the spy business?"

"Where did that come from Jack?"

"I care about you. And eventually being around bad guys is going to catch up with you."

"Are you saying I should be home raising kids?" Valentina asked.

"Nothing wrong with raising kids. Loved every minute of it when I did it. But you know what I mean. You've done your share of bad guy hunting. Let someone younger do it."

"Are you saying I'm getting old?"

Jack knew this wasn't going the way he wanted it to. He turned from his binoculars and saw Valentina smiling at him. He smiled back.

"No, you are definitely not getting too old," Jack offered quickly. "I'm the old guy around here."

"Married old guy at that."

"Maybe you should try it also." Jack said. He was struggling to get his thoughts out. Things were treading into deep water between them.

"Marrying an old guy?" Valentina asked. "You're already taken."

What did she mean by that? Jack thought. *Shit, this is getting out of hand. I need to change the subject.* Before he could speak, Valentina spoke up.

"I've already put in my papers, Jack. Next month will be my last."

"Leaving the agency. That's great news. What will you do?"

"Take some time off to start, then see where life takes me." Valentina said.

"Well then, let's do our job here and get you back to Rome safe and sound.

The next day was rainy so the two stayed in their rooms except for meal breaks to local establishments. Jack checked the television for a weather report and got what he was waiting for. The following day would push out the cold front bringing in a higher temperatures. It portended a warm day, the kind of day a good Dutch aristocrat would enjoy on their veranda. Plans were made for an early start to set-up at the boat ramp. And as it was a work day they assumed that there would be no other users when they got there.

They were wrong. Packed up and checked out of the hotel, Valentina wheeled the Mercedes van into the park. As they pulled through the parking lot they spied a local launching his boat into the lake. Valentina kept driving and pulled back out on the rural road. She found a cafe nearby and pulled in. Both of them stepped up to the counter and took hot drinks.

Chapter 25

Loosdrecht, the Netherlands

Emile Dupong sat in the sunshine sipping his coffee. He let the early morning sun warm him as he put yesterday's inclement weather behind him. And not only had the weather been depressing, but his lack of hooking up the day before had ruined his mood.

But he knew today would be different. The forecast called for a warm spring day and, after the previous day he knew that his opportunities for finding females to cavort with were markedly improved. He had learned that rainy weather tended to dampen any fun even if he had found someone. It was as if the lower barometric pressure such lows caused also affected people's attitude. The higher temperatures moving in would change all that.

As he waited for his breakfast to be served by the help, he laid out his day. He decided that today he would skip the Porsche and move up to the McClaren F1. Nothing screamed testosterone like a super car. The women would fall all over themselves to be in it, and the one who owned it would reap the rewards.

A skiff motored toward the estate from the south, two fishermen in it. Emile glanced at them and then scanned the rest of the lake. All else was quiet as the dockyards and marina awoke to a new day. Yes, life was good he thought. It would be his last thought on Earth.

His chest suddenly exploded as his heart was torn apart by a 300-grain bullet tearing through his torso. Hitting with over 4,800 feet/pounds of pressure, his body slammed against the back of his chair as his head snapped forward from the impact. The arms of the chair kept him upright as he slumped forward, his head resting where his chest had been.

Inside the home, a loud crack followed by tinkling glass caused his mother to turn at the disturbance. Seeing glass fly across the floor, she called for Phillip the butler.

"Phillip, something just hit one of the terrace windows and broke it."

"Coming ma'am," Phillip replied as he entered the room with a tray covered with plates. Breakfast covered the tray as he carried it out toward the terrace. "Oh, I see Master Dupong already on the terrace."

Mrs. Dupong stood looking at the shattered window and the broken glass on the floor. "Put that tray down, Philip, and get a broom to clean this up before someone steps in it."

Phillip did as he was instructed and placed the tray on a convenient sideboard. He disappeared into the kitchen to find a broom for sweeping. As he opened the kitchen door he froze at the scream behind him.

"Oh my God, no," Mrs. Dupong bellowed.

Phillip turned to what was causing the commotion and saw Emile slumped in his chair. The pool of blood collecting under the chair on the imported Italian tile told all.

* * *

Valentina needed no instructions to climb into the van and drive away. The sound of the .338 Lapua rifle firing had made the announcement itself. While Jack was prone inside the back of the van, the incrediblly loud noise caused by the powder overwhelmed the suppressor and the walls of the van. While the big velocity bullet was impossible to totally suppress due to the sonic wave cracked by its flight, anyone around the lake would have a difficult time placing the origin of the sound.

Moving the metallic sign back over the open hole in the right rear door of the van, she walked briskly to the driver's door and opened it. She climbed in and started the diesel. The clatter of the engine seemed to scream over the landscape as she shifted it into gear. She pulled away from the boat-ramp and turned left heading toward Hilversum. After a short drive in traffic they reached the Autoroute that would take them back south.

As she turned onto the onramp to the expressway, Jack appeared and climbed into the passenger seat. He strapped on his seatbelt and leaned back.

"Finished?" Valentina asked.

"We'll have to wait for the news to be sure, but a Lupus hitting center mass doesn't offer much chance at survival."

"But are you sure? If he survives he may be able to put things together with what happened on the island. He has Kotone's name and that means he has your name."

"He's dead. You are familiar with the standard NATO rifle, the M-16? Well the bullet I just hit him with has three times the destructive power as an M-16 round. He's dead." Jack said.

Valentina drove in silence the rest of the way across the Netherlands and most of Germany. It was only as they approached the Swiss border that the two spoke again.

"I'm thinking we should press on and get back into Italy before we stop." Valentina said.

"If you let me drive, we can do it all in one push," Jack offered.

Both were anxious to be out of the van. It was the biggest identifier they had to them being anywhere near the shooting. The sooner they could ditch the van the sooner it was not the risk it presented now.

"OK, you climb in back and get some sleep. You can take over when we hit Italy."

Jack unclipped his seatbelt and swung around between the two seats. He laid down on the mattress and rolled onto his back. He wasn't sleepy, but he knew he had to keep Valentina happy. He would rest and think about what had just happened and what it meant. As he contemplated the sail back across the Atlantic and the flight to Missoula, he dreamed of starting a life with Kotone.

The van swayed at the high-speed turns as Valentina drove the Autoroute through the Alps. The day grew late as they reached the southern Swiss border where Valentina saw the a highway rest area and pulled over. The two grabbed dinner after which Jack climbed into the driver's seat. He had spent two weeks driving in Italy and knew that Italian drivers were crazy.

But he had a Mercedes van now versus a Ferrari on his last trip and the experience was profoundly different. As his companion took a rest on the mattress, Jack was content with moving along with the other trucks. The only time he swung into the passing lane was to move around the slow movers. Keeping steady at the posted speed limit, every time he entered the left lane he seemed to immediately collect three cars moving fast. They would be inches from his bumper flashing their lights until he moved back into the right lane.

Then they would flash past always inches form his side. And he was amazed that even when he was in the right lane, the drivers would pass straddling the divider strips just missing his side. And always in packs of threes.

Having been instructed to wake her when they approached Orvieto, Jack called to Valentina. She quickly was at his ear as she stood behind him.

"You know what to do with the van?"

"Yes. And the rifle." Jack said.

"Good, take the Orvieto exit and drop me at the train station."

"Valentina, I don't know how to thank you."

"Just get back to the States without tripping up Wesley. Until you are out of the country, I won't be sleeping very well."

They had worked out his exit and he knew she was anxious to get home. The express train from Orvieto would deposit her at the main station in Rome where she could catch the Metro to where she lived. It was quicker than driving the van into Rome. And Jack did not relish the idea of driving out of Rome by himself. He had seen Rome traffic as a tourist in a taxi and wanted no part of it.

After a quick goodbye, Jack swung back onto the Autoroute and followed the signs that took him around Rome. He took the exit marked Naples and settled into the three-hour drive. The nighttime traffic was light as he made his way south. Again, the threesomes whooshed by and kept him firmly gripping the steering wheel. Valentina had programed in the route on the GPS unit on the dashboard and Jack glanced regularly at the display.

Soon it indicated an exit and Jack downshifted as he took the exit. Turning right, he followed the arrow on the GPS as it took him to the center of Naples. He knew Naples had a reputation and he hoped he could get through the city without incident. Its reputation was the reason he was driving into the city though.

Long the crime capital of Italy, the van would be left near the train station with the keys in it. Valentina explained that the van would be in the Middle East within a week where it would be sold. The GPS announced in English that Jack had arrived and he saw the train station he needed.

The Circumvesuviana train started at Porta Nolana and Jack pulled into a side street nearby. He switched off the engine and swung into the back. He slipped his backpack on and swung his waterproof bag over his shoulder. He opened the side door and stepped into the nighttime air. Making sure he had left the keys in the ignition, he slammed the sliding door shut.

Walking into Porta Nolana, he saw the reader board that announced the next train to Sorrento. He purchased a ticket with cash and walked to the waiting area to sit down. He studied the other waiting passengers and concluded that some were station thieves. Naples was infamous for tourist rip offs and he kept his back to the wall and his eyes wide open. He had slipped his wallet into his inside jacket pocket where his unused passport sat.

Without incident, he boarded the train headed to Sorrento. He relaxed some until the train pulled into the main Naples station where more tourists climbed aboard. Soon they were rattling along headed out on the Sorrento Peninsula. Jack estimated that the roughly hour train ride would leave him in Sorrento just before eleven. He had just made the last train, and while it would be late he figured he could find the Wharram. He would let Misty have one more night in her hotel before he called her.

Chapter 26

Sorrento, Italy

Leaving Italy was much easier than entering the country. Jack had called Misty after what he anticipated would be her breakfast time to announce he was ready to leave. He had spent the night in the doghouse berth where the pleasant spring night air made sleeping easy. But he was anxious to leave and return to his new life. He had been away three weeks now with no word from Kotone.

He just assumed that she had reached Missoula and her sister had picked her up. Visioning her sitting in Montana drinking coffee with her sister kept him secure. She was safe, and he would soon be with her to make their life together.

Jack saw Misty walking down the access road that led from the town center to the harbor. Misty's wide catamaran sat on the outside of the dock rather than in one of the designated slips. She carried an Italian coffee in one hand and her roller bag in the other. The cobble stones rattled the roller bag as she more carried it than rolled it.

"Good morning," Jack said as she approached.

"So, the world safe for you now?" Misty asked.

"As safe as I can make it. Do we need to go shopping?" he asked. They would need at least two weeks of food and water to make the return trip to the British Virgin Islands.

"No, I skipped renting a car and did all the shopping. It's all stowed away. So if you're ready we can leave."

Jack jumped off the boat and stood ready at the dock lines, thus announcing his readiness. Misty placed her coffee in a holder and lowered the outboard into the water. Starting the outboard, she motioned Jack to let the stern line go first. Shifting into forward, Jack raced ahead to let the bow line go, stepping onto the boat as it pulled away.

Misty increased speed as soon as they cleared the breakwater while Jack stationed himself by the forward sail. He took off the sail cover and threw it in the forward hatch. He stepped back and released the rear sail, the cover following the first.

"Ready," Jack said.

"Let's motor out a bit. Not much wind here close to shore."

From Sorrento to the tip of the peninsular was about three miles, the high cliffs blocking much of the wind. As they came around the last headland the Isle of Capri lay across the channel. Misty turned the boat and set a course between Capri and the mainland. Still the wind was missing.

Jack felt she wanted to be away from Italian custody as much as he did and knew the outboard was their only option. Passing Massa Lubrense on their left, the summer homes spilled down the embarkment where a small harbor lay. As soon as they were clear of Capri, Misty headed out into the Tyrrhenian Sea. Jack wasn't sure what separated the Tyrrhenian Sea from the Mediterranean Sea, but he just wished one of them would provide some wind.

The telltales on the rigging soon announced a slight breeze. Now far off land, Jack raised both main sails and ran the roller reefing, so the head sail pulled them forward. Misty raised the outboard and lashed it down for the journey ahead. Sitting down in the cockpit, it was decidedly quiet between the two boat partners.

* * *

The silence continued for the first week of their journey. It was only after two days of sailing past the Straits of Gibraltar that something out of the ordinary happened. Up until then, each had taken their watches in turn with few words between them.

But before Jack was due on the helm, he stepped into the cockpit with his waterproof bag. He unclasped the straps holding the material and unrolled the opening. He pulled out the Barrett sniper rifle and placed it in his lap. He unscrewed the Leopold scope and placed it on a towel by his side.

"More target practice?" Misty asked.

"Not with this bad boy." Jack said. He picked up the rifle and threw it overboard. Then he reached into the bag again and pulled out his Ruger with the suppressor on it. That one went overboard following the rifle. Pulling out his Smith and Wesson AR-15, he held it in his lap.

"Do you need a rifle? I can't fly back to the states with this, so if you want it it's yours." Jack said.

Misty hesitated and then asked. "I take it the other two guns are wanted in a crime?"

"Depends on your definition of a crime. I'd say the two on their way to the bottom were used in self-defense but that would be hard to explain to any authorities."

"And this one wasn't used?"

"No, unless Lamarcus got them from someplace he shouldn't have."

"In that case, no, I'll pass."

Jack pitched the AR-15 overboard but not before removing the red dot scope on it. Scopes didn't leave traces of themselves when they were used like a gun. Any bullet fired from a gun could be traced back to a specific gun. At least in theory. Other factors affected the suitability of any bullet being matched to a gun. But enough chances existed that Jack wanted nothing to do with two of the guns that had killed someone.

Pulling out the final 9 mm Glock handgun, Jack held it up to say it was up for grabs. Misty shook her head no and it went over the stern into the water. Ammunition went after the guns and then the bag itself. He wanted nothing left that might contain powder residue on it although he was too cheap to trash two good scopes.

"So, Jack, we haven't spoken much of what the last month and half has meant." Misty said.

"What do you mean? You helped me rescue Kotone and deal with the bad guys. And I'll always appreciate your help."

"As I've said before, you saved my life and I will always owe you for that."

"Well, consider us square now." Jack said.

"But Jack, what about your future? You are married now. Does Kotone want kids? Have you guys talked about your life together?" Misty asked.

Jack sat quietly and didn't answer his friend. They had been through a lot together and the latest adventure added to their closeness. That she was asking such pointed questions made him think about where his life was going.

Ever since his retirement from the police department, Jack had lived for one adventure after another. And it seemed that each adventure brought danger to him and someone close to him. It had been an interesting three years. *Has it only been three years? he thought.*

"Misty, you have been a good friend. Always there when I called. But I miss the closeness of one special person in my life. Kotone has been that person. Even when I was with you after she left me, she was always just a thought away. That we are finally married and can live our life together is wonderful to me."

"Well, I do hope it works out for you two." Misty said.

"And from the sounds of it, you seem to have found someone special."

"I hope so, Jack."

"And what about you? Are you planning to have kids?" Jack asked.

The look he received sent a shiver down his back. Misty looked away at the horizon as if scanning for an approaching ship. Jack saw her eyes tear up and knew something was there in response to his question. He let it sit.

The two sat together in silence as the big catamaran made headway toward North America. The subject passed as they never again talked of children and their future plans. The boat routine took back over as they stood their watches and slept in their bunks.

Two weeks later the Tiki swung along the north end of Virgin Gorda island, sailing close into shore, Jack dove off the boat and swam toward shore. He needed to be absent for Misty's arrival from Europe. Her passport would show an Italian visa and now she needed to be checked into the British Virgin Islands. Jack had a British Virgin Islands visa but no other, so he couldn't be aboard a boat just retuning from Europe.

Misty had told him how to make his way from the beach to Spanish Town where she would be tied up at her slip. She would be gone, staying back in her island house. Jack would grab his gear in the doghouse and make his way to a hotel. There he would make arrangements to leave. The two were done with each other as Jack headed to his new life.

Jack booked a flight the next day that would take him to San Juan, Puerto Rico and a transfer to a flight to Miami. A three hour wait, and he would be on his way to Denver. An easy connection there would finally get him on a flight to Missoula.

Jack called his son Carl in Denver to arrange to meet him when he landed. Jack wasn't crazy about flying, tolerating the experience to get where he wanted to be. But the four flights only increased his anxiety the closer he came to his goal.

Chapter 27

Missoula, Montana

The time zone changes as Jack traveled west helped him arrive in Missoula at a reasonable hour. As Jack gathered his bags a familiar voice caught his attention. Turning around, Jack spotted his son Carl walking up to him. Father and son hugged each other.

"Welcome back Dad," Carl said. "Hell, of a honeymoon."

"You can say that again, but where's Kotone? I thought she'd be here picking me up too."

Carl ignored his dad and bent down to grab the bags.

"Come on Dad, Stacey has dinner waiting. I bet you're starving."

Jack shrugged off the non-answer and followed his son out of the airport. They walked across the parking lot and Carl opened up his car's trunk. Throwing in Jack's pack, he slammed the lid.

They each climbed in the Honda and Carl pushed the sedan into gear. They were soon on the road leading into Missoula and Carl's house.

Jack recognized his Toyota Tundra sitting against the curb as they pulled into the driveway of Carl and Stacey's home.

"The Tundra do OK while I was gone?" Jack asked.

"Yes, I've been driving it once a week to keep the gas fresh for you."

Carl opened the driver's door while releasing the trunk lid. He circled around and grabbed Jack's bag. Without waiting, he headed to the front door and opened it. Jack scrambled to catch up. Once inside, Jack closed the front door and heard Stacey call to them. She walked into the front room from the kitchen wiping her hands on a towel.

"Hi Jack, good to have you back safe," Stacey said.

Jack gave Stacey a hug and felt her enlarged belly poke him. He patted her baby bump that had grown in the time he had been away.

"Good to be back. You are getting big," Jack said.

Jack knew they were dancing around the elephant in the room. Or lack of one as it were.

"I was expecting Kotone to be here. Where is she?"

Carl and Stacey both looked at each other and said nothing. Then Jack realized J.J. wasn't running around making noise. He was obviously somewhere else.

Stacey spoke first. "Jack, sit down. Can I get you a beer or something?"

"No, I'm fine. But an answer as to why my wife isn't here, please. Is she at home with Komatsu?"

Jack and Kotone hadn't really talked about where they were going to live once their honeymoon was over. Events sort of got in the way. But with Kotone and her sister living here in Missoula, Jack had figured they would settle somewhere close by. He liked Missoula, and with family there now, they both would want to stay close by.

Stacey and Carl took a seat together on their couch and sat close enough to hold each other's hands. Jack sat across the living room in an easy chair. He leaned forward expecting an answer.

"Dad, I'm afraid to tell you, but Kotone is gone. Komatsu too. The school year finished last week, and they announced to us that they were leaving."

"What? You mean they moved? Where? How?" Jack started to panic. The woman he loved had left.

"They didn't tell us where they were going," Stacey said. "I'm so sorry, Jack."

Jack sat stunned. She had done it again to him. Left him with no explanation.

"Dad, she did confide in Stacey," Carl said, "She said that she couldn't handle the deaths that seemed to attract themselves to her when she was with you. She said she had tried to tell you that in the Virgin Islands."

"So, nothing. No letter?"

They both shook their head that Kotone had not left them a letter to give Jack.

"Jack, you're welcome to stay here tonight. J.J. is with a friend tonight. You've had a long day getting here," Stacey said.

The offer of hospitality startled him. He looked at his son and daughter-in-law and knew he had to get away. He needed no reminder of what he had just lost.

"Thanks Stacey, but I need to get going." Jack said.

"Where will you go Jack, back to Wyoming?"

"No, I think I need a change," Jack said.

The End

Acknowledgements

First I would thank Timothy Johns and Jessica Schmidt, my tireless editors. Though they work hard to make sure my writing is presentable, place no blame on them for the final product. That all rests with me.

My proof readers offer valuable feedback at different phases as my draft is put together. Dick Martin, Jeanne Crownover, Larry Stoddard, Tiffany Martin, Barbara Foster, and John Briggs have all kept me from straying too far off on tangents.

Finding Morwenna Rakestraw to do the cover layout was a relief.

Mitch Press of World Book has offered his wisdom from his family's years in the book business. While not all encouraging, his guidance as publishing transforms in the digital age has been invaluable.

Dear Reader,

Thank you for your selection of reading material. I hope this book measured up to your expectations. The most critical part for a new author is getting the word out to other readers.

I would appreciate your help in spreading the word. There are three important things you can do. You need to understand the importance of the first one to my becoming a successful writer. If you do anything, go to Amazon.com and write a review.

1.	Go to Amazon.com and leave a review
2.	Tell a friend about this book
3.	Tell you your social network about this book.

Positive reviews made in various places will help readers find me.

Again, thanks for your support.

W.B. Martin

Read an excerpt of the exciting new Jack Wesley
adventure from W.B. Martin:

Pleasure Smiles

#8 in the Jack Wesley Thriller Series

Chapter 1

Boston, Massachusetts

The fall leaves of New England were at their peak as Boston sat under perfect weather. A continuing dry spell only enhanced the brilliant leaf color. The dryness almost made the yellows too bright to look at without sunglasses.

The reds and oranges bust in color from the dry summer end. Fall had just arrived but the days continued to be warm followed by cold nights. An old fashioned Indian Summer had been pronounced by the local television news pundits and the populace seemed to be out in force to enjoy every minute.

After the winter that had hit Massachusetts hard, no one was looking forward to any repeat. The entire East Coast had suffered under relentless cold weather and snow as the 'polar vortex' had announced itself numerous times.

Old timers in New England guffawed at the young and their labels for everything. Polar vortex was a new one that didn't sit well with them. They knew a good nor'easter came every winter and sometimes more then once. In the old days, snow would accumulate in inches per hour as a nor'easter blew mounds of snow onto the land as the storm came in off the Gulf of Maine. Nothing new to those folks.

Jack Wesley stared out the shop's windows at the color displayed across the street. Boston Common lay before him and the sight was none he had ever seen. Raised in the Pacific Northwest, nice Fall colors there amounted to a few small vine maple tress high in the mountains that turned bright red. The tress around his home town would turn a tepid yellow and sometimes orange to be almost immediately pounded to the ground by the side ways rain that showed up about the same time. The color display was typically dull and brief only to be followed with local flooding as all the fallen leaves proceeded to clog all the catch basins.

No, this was something else, he thought. *When I'm done today I need to rent a car and drive out of the city. I'm sure the countryside around Boston is spectacular.*

"Good afternoon Mr. Wesley," a customer said. "Its an honor to have you here today. Can you sign my book?"

Jack looked up at a teenager holding his book. This was a new experience and he still hadn't gotten used to being a celebrity. *Not that one book makes a celebrity,* he thought. But his numbers were moving up the sales chart that his agent emailed him each week. And now with the German edition out last month, things could get interesting.

"Thank you," Jack said. "Who should I dedicate it to?" This part made him nervous. Even after years of writing police reports, getting people's names spelled right made him nervous.

"Could you make it out to Brad?" Came the answer. "He's my boyfriend. He really wanted to be here today to meet you. He's a huge fan."

Brad, thank god. I can handle that, Jack thought. In the three weeks of his first ever book tour he had heard some beauties. And he was amazed at how often Mackalah showed up. He actually was remembering how that one went.

Jack took his pen and inscribed the inside title page on the hard cover book as instructed. He added a little personal note to Brad, closed it and handed it back to the young woman. She immediately opened and read the inscription.

"He'll love that, thank you."

"No, thank you for purchasing my book. And tell Brad I'll expect to hear from him on my website." The price of the limited amount of fame Jack was experiencing was that he now had numerous emails to answer on a daily basis. *I'm not sure how the big authors handled this part of celebrity,* he thought. *At some point they must hire staff to do it.*

With all the social media sites he kept up with since his book was picked up by a major publisher, his time for living was slowly disappearing. With a blog to write each week, he didn't see how authors had time to write their books.

And Jack was determined to move along on his second book. He had no intention of being a one book wonder. Each winter had been dedicated to writing and his second book was progressing. He was just amazed at how much editing and rewriting the publisher had required before his first book came out.

But summers were reserved for adventures. Jack would have to figure out what would happen to all his book promotional duties when the nice weather returned. But till then, he had books to sell and signings to attend. Jack was distracted as he thought of all the things the publisher had scheduled for him.

"Please sir, could you sign my book?" The voice was of an old cranky man. Jack looked up to the big white grin staring out from a large black face.

"Lamarcus, you old war dog," Jack said. "I thought I might see you."

"Still have time for us little people, Mr. Celebrity?" Lamarcus teased.

"Hey, knock it off. This fame stuff isn't all its cracked up to be," Jack said. "And I'm not even on the Times best seller list. I can only imagine."

"Yeah, fame, big money, fast cars and large breasted woman," Lamarcus offered. "Those are all hard to take."

Jack looked around and luckily no one else was in ear shot of his Marine Corp buddy's comments. He had noticed the the folks that ran the book store here on Beacon Street were a little snooty. *The big tit comment wouldn't have down well with them, even if spoken by a minority type*, Jack thought.

Decor had its limits, and Sergeant Lewis, as he would always know him, was a bit rough around the edges. Not that he couldn't shine it on when he had to. His making captain on the City of Cambridge Police Department across the Charles River being evidence of that.

"So, what brings you in, if I have to ask."

"To buy a book and get it signed by my famous writer friend," Lamarcus said.

"You didn't have to buy one, you know that."

"Well, I didn't want to steal the book from the store. Besides, you probably need the money, knowing you," Lamarcus said.

Jack took Lamarcus's book and wrote a long dedication in the front when he saw another customer walk up behind his friend. Handing it back, Jack asked. "Can we get together after this? I'm done in an hour."

"There's a Irish pub to the left and up the hill. Just past the Statehouse on the right," Lamarcus said. "I'll meet you there in an hour."

Jack finished with his signing duties and thanked the shop proprietor. Picking up his bag, he slung it over his shoulder and shoved it onto his back. As he opened the door to leave, the cool early evening wind coming in off Boston Harbor made him turn up his collar. *Boy, it drops in temperature fast when the sun goes down,* he thought.

Walking into the pub, he saw Lamarcus waving from a booth on the side. The Celtic music blared and the afternoon crowd of Statehouse workers mixed it up. The twenty-somethings that worked the political end of the Bay State looked to be maneuvering for companionship. Jack slid in across from Lamarcus and dropped his bag on the seat.

"Kind of noisy, don't you think," Jack almost yelled across to his friend.

"But so much to look at, don't you think?"

Jack scanned the crowd more closely and noticed that the female to male ratio was decidedly in favor of the males. In favor that they had more to choose from as the women out numbered the men. Many of the young woman were decidedly good looking and appeared loose enough from alcohol to be easy marks.

Turning to his friend, Jack commented, "Yeah, but even us old war horses would have a hard time finding love here. Too young and too liberal for the likes of us."

"Speak for yourself, you Wyoming redneck," Lamarcus said. "I for one, know how to entice the finer sex into just that."

"So retirement has freed up your time I see."

Lamarcus's attitude changed at the mention of his retirement. Jack knew his friend had risen up through the ranks, finally obtaining his cherished caption posting. He had earned it largely on Jack's help in cracking a case of a school shooter. Tipped off of an impending attack on a Massachusetts grade school, Lamarcus just happened to be there at the right time to stop the attack. Hailed a hero by the media and his superiors, Lamarcus was soon promoted to captain.

But a change in the political winds in city government had brought a less then reputable mayor to power. When corruption charges were leveled, Lamarcus was expected to blunt the State Police investigation. When he failed to pursue a cover-up the charges with the enthusiasm thought necessary by the police commissioner, he was offered retirement or a demotion. Lamarcus had taken retirement.

"Sorry politics caught up with you my friend," Jack offered.

"I guess it was bound to happen," Lamarcus said. "The Marine Corp oath I took wouldn't have it go any other way."

Jack lifted his wine glass and proposed a toast. Lamarcus raised his beer mug and held it aloft.

"To all enemies, foreign and domestic," Jack toasted.

"To all enemies," Lamarcus retorted.

A period of silence followed as the two comrades in arms reflected on the enemies they had fought over the years. And the comrades in arms that they had lost in those struggles.

After a few more rounds and much conversation, they were fully caught up with each other's lives. The crowd slowly drifted off to other locations for other activities as the two warriors talked.

Chapter 2

"Jack, I need your help," Lamarcus finally said.

"You've got it. What's up?"

"It's my uncle. You remember. My Dad's younger brother."

"Sure, fought in Korea with the 1st Marine Division. Survived Chosin. The Chosin Few they call themselves. How could I forget," Jack said. "Ooorah."

"Ooorah," Lamarcus added. "I think he's in trouble."

"What kind?"

"He's missing. His wife hasn't heard from him in over six months," Lamarcus said. "And two months after he left, he changed where his pension and Social Security check. got deposited."

"Why did he leave? And didn't she have a say in where his checks went?" Jack asked.

"They've been legally separated for a couple years now," Lamarcus said. "He was too cheap to move out totally so he was living in their basement. They have a house out in Mattapan. Been living there since I was a little kid."

"So he up and bolted and no one knows where?" Jack asked.

"Well, sort of. She got letters postmarked from Las Vegas about once a month up until the time when he changed deposits. Then nothing.. So we know he was alive and living in Nevada. But since then, no news."

"Any other family members in touch with your uncle? Did you ask them?"

"I'm the only one left. Besides my aunt," Lamarcus said.

"Did you check with the VA? Those checks have to have a live body to receive them."

"They confirm that his VA checks still are sent out each month. Social Security won't release any information other then he would appear to be still alive. The check is deposited electronically in a bank account in Nevada. That is all they offer. Same with his pension."

"So how much are we talking? Does your aunt know how much he gets each month?" Jack asked.

"She got half his pension and half his SSI. But even at that, he's taking home about three thousand a month."

"What do you have in mind then?"

"I want to head out to Vegas and see what I can track down," Lamarcus said.

"Have you considered that maybe your uncle doesn't want to be found. He had a reason he left." Jack said.

"And knowing my aunt, I would have left years ago. I always enjoyed my time with my uncle," Lamarcus said. "After my Dad left the family, he was my male role model for me. He's why I joined the Corps. But his wife was never a happy person. They couldn't have kids and I think she took it out on everyone. My uncle put up with a lot while he was there."

"Then be careful what you go looking for. You sure don't want to lead your aunt to him, from the sounds of it."

"I need to know," Lamarcus said. His voice cracked as he spoke by the emotion it brought up. "I need to know if he's OK."

"Then lets go make sure," Jack offered. "My only problem is I have a book signing tour set for Germany. My book has just been released over there and their expecting me next week. Any chance you can get started in Las Vegas and I catch up to you there. If you need any immediate help, I can break off the tour. But it sounds like routine police work to me."

"I guess you're right. I sure don't want you messing up your tour on account of some old timer hiding out in Vegas," Lamarcus said.

Jack looked at him sharply and tried to determine if what he had just said was sarcasm or not.

"Look Lamarcus, we go way back. You come first over any book tour," Jack said. "If you need me now, I'm there for you. Just spit it out."

"Relax Jack," Lamarcus said, "I'm just messin' with you. Just making sure it all hasn't gone to your head."

The two friends laughed at each other as they finished their drinks and paid their tab. Pulling on his jacket for the cold he knew awaited, Jack walked with Lamarcus to the door.

"Where you staying?" Lamarcus asked.

"The Lenox House on Exeter near Copley Square."

"Well, if your taking the 'T', we better hurry. Some stop running at midnight."

Jack checked his watch and realized how long they had been visiting. The cold bit into them as they walked briskly down Park Street toward the Park Street Station. The MBTA subway would get him back out to his hotel in no time, if they got in before the last train.

"Where are you headed, Cambridge?" Jack said. He wasn't sure if Lamarcus had kept his house in the city that had retired him. With his divorce a few years back, Jack knew that Lamarcus was known to step out with the ladies. Where he took them back to, Jack had no clue.

"I'm out in Newton now. Expensive, but the rich divorcee rate is sky high out there. So, its the good old Green Line for me too," Lamarcus said.

They reached the Park Street subway station just before Jack thought his ears and nose would break off. The cold was biting and it was a huge contrast from the warm sunny days he had experienced in walking to the book shop.

Paying the fare, they descended the steps and followed the Green Line signs for outbound. Other riders scrambled through the labyrinth of pedestrian tunnels as they sought out other lines. The Red Line took people north to Cambridge or south towards Braintree. The green line headed west from Park Street station and forked into multiple lines.

Since Jack was going just a short distance, he could take any one of the Green Line trains. Since the line split into multiple routes after Copley, Lamarcus could only take the Riverside train unless he wanted to walk a long way on the other rend. Luckily, a Riverside bound train pulled in and they climbed on board together.

Not a true subway line but a street car, Jack had to step up into the car, Lamarcus right behind him. As Jack turned to find a seat, he realized that they had picked the wrong train. He moved a short distance but did not sit down.

Jack glanced as Lamarcus came around him looking for a seat. His friend stopped and stood next to him as they stared at the back of the train.

"Shit." was all Lamarcus got out.

"Hey, you need to stop right now," Jack bellowed.

The five teenagers that had been beating some unfortunate rider stopped and turned at the intrusion. The five thugs were minorities and their victim wasn't. *Great, just what I need*, Jack thought.

"Who you yelling at?" One of the teens challenged. His glare matched his partners threatening poise.

"You shit head. Let the guy up now," Jack commanded.

He glanced and Lamarcus stood with his best cop threaten mode. But they weren't cops anymore. At least Lamarcus wasn't a cop. Jack carried a badge and gun, courtesy of the Teton County, Wyoming Sheriff.

Even after his thirty years of police work, this appointment was more an honorary thing that his politically connected brother had worked out. Jack was a real deputy sheriff in official terms, but from past experience with East Coast law enforcement, knew that fact carried less then full weight.

Because of trouble he had had in New York state and the subsequent pissing match between Wyoming and New York, he was reluctant to identify himself. And even more reluctant to draw his weapon which was safely tucked in his small of the back holster.

"Watch your mouth or I'll rip it out of your head, honkey." Came the answer.

The foot holding down their victim prevented him from getting off the train's floor. The teen holding him down pushed his fist into his opposite palm in deviance.

Lamarcus finally spoke, "You boys need to simmer down and let that boy up now."

"Look Uncle Tom. Just cause you hanging out with whitey there don't make you something special." the leader said. "Now, you two go crawl away and we won't hurt you."

"Not going to happen," Jack said. His hand lifted his jacket in the back and waited close to his weapon.

Four of the teens started to move forward. The fifth kicked the down teen and stood guard over him, preventing his escape. Jack and Lamarcus moved apart so they had more room for what was coming.

Because of the closeness of the train's empty seats, only two teens could approach them at a time. The first two lunged, one being met with a baton that suddenly appeared in Lamarcus's hand. The metal rod shape weapon struck one teen across the neck and he fell in pain, screaming.

Jack met the other teen with a high booted kick to the chest, sending him crashing back into the other two charging teens. They stumbled for a minute, then regrouped. At the change in dynamics and with two of their cohorts on the floor, they each drew a weapon.

A knife appeared in the hand of the teen in front of Lamarcus. The baton immediately swung with a blow on his wrist as the knife flew across the train. Grabbing his now broken wrist, he stood as Lamarcus applied the baton to side of his knee, dropping him hard onto he floor.

But the fourth thug pulled a gun. A small caliber semi-auto, it held seven shots that could kill or maim. As he raised the weapon to fire, Jack grabbed the thug's gun hand and forced it down. The gun went off with an echoing blast. With Jack's other hand, he smashed the perpetrator in the side of the head. The teen staggered and attempted to raise his gun again.

Lamarcus ended the struggle with a baton across the back of his legs. Dropping the gun as he fell, he clutched his knees in agony. Jack took the gun, ejected the magazine onto the floor and cleared the round in the chamber. He slipped it into his coat pocket.

The fifth and final teen quickly took his foot off the down teen and offered to help him up.

"Hey man, we was just funnin' with you." He held the injured youth steady and pretended to brush off any dirt from the floor. "We do this all the time, don't we."

The victim broke free and walked behind Jack. Everyone staggered as the train pulled into the Copley Square Station. The train driver ran off the train and soon two uniformed transit police ran onto the train. Their guns drawn, they motioned everyone to place hands on the side of the car and spread their legs.

Jack and Lamarcus joined the teen thug and the victim in complying. *No time to identify myself,* Jack thought. *Things will get sorted out in a minute.*

With one cop holding his gun on everyone, the other started searching each person. Feeling Lamarcus's sleeve, he reached in and retrieved a now compact baton from where Lamarcus had returned it. The officer threw it toward his buddy.

After the victim, the cop searched Jack. He hit the small handgun in Jack's pocket first. The cop retrieved the gun and after making sure it was empty, threw it on the floor away form everyone.

"You're in trouble carrying a gun in this state. I don't suppose you have a permit for that, do you?" The cop asked.

"No I don't. I have something better," Jack answered.

"What's that?"

"Can I lift the front of my jacket up?" Jack asked.

"No, you just stand right there grabbing the wall."

The cop reached around and felt along the front of Jack's coat. Feeling hard metal, he reached up under the fabric and retrieved Jack's sheriff badge.

"What's this?" the cop asked. "Deputy Sheriff, Teton County. Where the hell is that?"

"Wyoming," Jack answered.

"Well, you're a long way from home, cowboy," the officer still holding the gun finally said. "That don't carry much weight in this here town."

"Well, be careful on my back for what my sheriff asks me to carry with his badge," Jack said.

The cop conducting the search moved to Jack's back and located his Glock 9mm. He pulled it from its holster and held it up for his buddy to see.

"That my friend is worth twenty years in this state," the second cop said.

The first cop finished his searches of all eight people as his partner called for back-up. With Lamarcus and Jack in handcuffs, they were lead away first while the new crew took over the teens.

"Nice welcome for your out of town guest, Lewis," Jack said.

"It will get straightened out once we get to the station. Should be someone I know there," Lamarcus said. "Thirty years of policing in Cambridge should help."

Lamarcus was partially right. They ran into someone Lamarcus knew almost right away. It took another three hours before the right people were

376

contacted that got Lamarcus freed and his baton returned.

Meanwhile Jack sat in lock-up waiting. A desk sergeant finally showed up and opened the cell door.

"Wesley, let's go."

Jack stood and headed in the direction the sergeant indicated. A police lieutenant was waiting in his office as Jack was shown in. A chair was offered as the lieutenant continued reading a paper he held. The sergeant returned to his duties.

"Mr. Wesley, you seem to have stepped in it," the lieutenant said. "We've checked your credentials and they are legit. We get a lot of people in here with some flim flam ID from some two bit law enforcement office somewhere out west. All so they can carry in our state."

"So I'm free to go after you return my weapon and badge," Jack offered.

"Not so fast Deputy Wesley. As I said, you credentials check out, but we still have a problem. You had a small semi-auto in your pocket we took off you. We're running ballistics on it but it matches the description of a gun used in a drive by shooting over in East Boston one hour before we picked you up."

"And the fact I took it off the perpetrator instead of letting him keep it adds nothing to the story," Jack said.

"The teen said he'd never seen that gun before."

"And they hand out gold shields to idiots in this city," Jack said, his irritation growing. "Did you think he'd say, 'sure-man, that was my gun and I just pumped off a few shots at some home-boy for the fun of it'."

"Simmer down cowboy, or you'll find your ass in my jail."

Just as Jack was about to add insult to injury in the case of the dimwitted lieutenant, Lamarcus walked in with a uniformed officer. Jack could tell by the captain's rank on his shoulder that Lamarcus had moved up the food chain of the Boston Police Department.

"That will be all lieutenant. If you'll excuse us," the captain said. He waited for his red faced officer to leave the room, the door closing with extra force. "Now Deputy Wesley, a word before you go. Captain Lewis has personally vouched for you and informs me that you did thirty years in Oregon as a police detective. He also has informed me that you are leaving my jurisdiction forthwith. Make that so and think twice before returning. You may not have your friend to cover your ass next time."

"And my Teton County issued equipment . . ." Jack started to ask.

"Will be returned to you at the front desk," the captain stood up and without acknowledging either, walked out the door.

"Well, thanks I guess," Jack said as they walked to the desk sergeant. Putting his Glock back in his holster and clipping his badge on his belt, he asked. "I suppose I have to walk back to my hotel now?